From the Midway

From the Midway

Unfolding Stories of
Redemption and Belonging

5/20/20

Chris,
Here's to all our stories unfolding
with authenticity, courage & grace.
All good wishes,
Leaf

LEAF SELIGMAN

BAUHAN PUBLISHING
PETERBOROUGH, NEW HAMPSHIRE
2019

Revised edition, March 2020

©2019 Leaf Seligman
All Rights Reserved

To contact Leaf, go to her website, **www.leafseligman.com**

Book design by Sarah Bauhan.
Cover design by Henry James.
Cover photograph "Peeking Under the Circus Tent."
Used by permission of the Wisconsin Historical Society.

BAUHAN
PUBLISHINGLLC
PO BOX 117 PETERBOROUGH NEW HAMPSHIRE 03458
603-567-4430
WWW.BAUHANPUBLISHING.COM
Follow us on Facebook and Twitter – @bauhanpub

Printed in the United States of America

For Robin

CONTENTS

CAST OF CHARACTERS

Kimball's Traveling Emporium – Jack Reynolds, Manager
Beasleys' Traveling Amusements – Earl Beasley Sr., Founder

The Brothers:
Earl Beasley, Jr.
Stan Beasley
Tom Beasley

Sisters:
Alma Jean Cole
Emma Beasley

Hammer Toe – Ernie Morton

Flipper Boy – Sebastian

Tiny Laveaux – World's Smallest Woman

Sven Anders – Sword Swallower

Lizard Man – Julian Henry, son of Alice and Colin

Bettina – Bearded Lady, daughter of Della and Clem, sister of June
and Arnold

Miss Beulah Divine—World's Largest Woman – Ida Mae Appleby

Leroy Haines – Giant

Lisabelle – Dancing Girl

Stony – Jim Edward Cartwright

The Geek – Jimmy Williams

Orvis Leominster – carousel operator

Cheever and Ewell – carnival workers primarily responsible for looking
after the oddities

Greta Gottleib, daughter of Ernst and Esther Gottleib, protégé of
Constance Hunnewell

THE BEASLEYS

After years of selling patent medicines, Earl Beasley stumbled on the perfect curative: he began peddling oddities. Customers suffering from tired backs and rashes, ringworm, itchy feet, even goiters or gnarled knuckles could forget their troubles as they gazed upon the less fortunate. Beasleys' Traveling Amusements opened its first season in 1910 at the county fair in Tupelo, Mississippi. In the first two years, it traveled to twenty-six counties in six southern states. The lines for the rides and agricultural exhibits remained steady, but the midway always drew the biggest crowd. People munched popcorn and peanuts, licking their salty fingers as they pressed toward the talker advertising a look at nature's greatest oddities. Outside the tent, the Strong Man warmed them up with his astounding feats, but the real treasures unfolded inside. Nothing improved the customers' dispositions better than viewing creatures more tortured or ugly than themselves.

Before Earl began hawking distractions, he scoured deep woods and depressed hollows, dispensing tonics, lotions, and other remedies to farmers who couldn't reach or afford doctors. He might have continued in that business were it not for a Yankee journalist named Samuel Hopkins Adams, who wrote an exposé in 1906 of fraudulent claims and hazardous ingredients in patent medicines. By 1910, some of Earl's customers grew suspicious, so he hatched a plan.

A meticulous businessman, he had kept records of every customer over the years. He called on Miss Constance Picklesimer, whose unusually petite stature he'd been unable to cure, and three years later he offered her a job as the world's smallest woman. At a stocky three-foot-two she wasn't, but Earl banked on customers who didn't know otherwise. He gathered six former customers and then hired a line of dancing girls, a talker, and three machinists who could operate and repair rides.

By 1912, when Earl's three sons took over the operation, acquiring human attractions gained an evangelical fervor. His youngest son, Tom, only twenty in 1912, first heard the Lord when he was seven. Earl, a lapsed Methodist who considered himself a man of science, administered tea from a gypsy woman to stop Tom's unintelligible spew of prayers, but the boy refused to recant. By the time he was sixteen, he had taken Jesus as his savior. There was nothing Big Earl could do. He waited for him to join the ministry, filling tents with Pentecostal followers, who looked to Earl like oddities themselves the way they shook and fell and spoke in tongues. But the pull of the family business emerged stronger. Filial piety, Tom called it. Told Big Earl the Bible demanded it. So when a fracture appeared in a gear, or someone's prize bull got sick after the first night on display, Tom huddled together in prayer with his brothers, the white workers, and the dancing girls. Sure enough, the bull got better, and Randy, the lead crewman, would inspect the gear the next morning and swear the fracture was gone.

His son's miracles spooked him, but Big Earl did nothing to intervene. To his surprise, when the first revivalists found their way to the fairgrounds, wagging their fingers at sins of the flesh, Big Earl stepped out, drawing himself up to his full six feet, four inches, and spoke like Moses, tablets in hand. "Lord done blessed this show with His own mighty hands. He's given us a way to uplift the lowest, most tortured of the species. He's called upon my family to give dignity to those born without, and He's instructed me to gather the modern-day Eves, the temptresses among us who threaten the sanctity of your homes, and confine them to more artistic endeavors."

When he was done speechifying, even the most devout rattled, "Amen, brother," and filed out.

Earl Beasley had no idea where the words had come from, though years of selling had gilded his tongue. "The Lord," Tom told him, "works in mysterious ways." The light in his son's eyes unnerved him like the ghost stories his father used to tell. He watched the boy closely. Tom had a head for figures as well as psalms; he relished counting money as much as his brothers did, tithing his thanks to the Lord.

While his sons managed the daily operations, Big Earl prided himself on his ability to convince attractions to leave their families and join him on the circuit. He hired the finest sign painter he could find to embellish their distinctions and deformities, as he liked to call them. He loved to stroll along the midway, watching patrons study the larger-than-life panels that formed a wall. Children would exclaim as parents yanked them away. Women would dab their faces with handkerchiefs, and men would spit tobacco juice and shake their heads. Wallets or coins would appear as the men sent their wives and children to peruse the pies and jams in the agricultural hall while they heated themselves in the froth of dancing girls and then cooled off viewing a lady dwarf and corroded-skinned man.

Big Earl decided early on that the best way to maintain order in the company was through separation, with just enough visibility to allow each employee to register that someone else had it worse. At the top of the fortune heap were the dancing girls and the Strong Man, who garnered audiences for their talents and pleasing looks. The white workers came next: men who operated rides, ran game booths, sold concessions, and the sideshow talker, a loud-mouthed fellow with a grape jelly stain on his forehead who could happily distinguish himself because he stood *outside* the tent filled with oddities, drawing people in. The handful of colored men who pounded stakes, erected tents, lifted the heaviest equipment, mucked stalls, and dug latrines had only to glimpse the parade of human attractions they tended—the man with lizard skin, the midget, the bearded lady, the world's fattest woman, the boy with fins instead of limbs. The punchlines of nature's cruelest jokes drew solace from their meager paychecks and the respect Big Earl accorded them. He made it clear to all the rest of the crew that the oddities, as he called them, were to be treated like rarefied ugly insects that pollinated flowers. Without them, they would not prosper. No one was to call them freaks.

Earl's sons followed his orders, but among themselves, they began to envision their own entertainment empire, filled with oddities the envy of every circus and traveling dime museum.

"We got to find the ones that's truly pathetic," Stan, the middle son, said. He always wore a collar and cuffs on his shirt. Figured himself the best looking of the three. "Barnum and some of the others elevate their oddities. Call 'em princes and 'General,' stuff like that. But who's going to believe some sorry fellow with warts descended from a king?" He smiled, smoothing the strands of hair that threatened to fall forward from his widow's peak.

"I don't see much point in pretending the fat lady's a queen, but we have to tell them rubes she's the fattest lady ever lived. Otherwise, they won't part with their nickel to see something that unappealing," said Earl Jr., dark like his father and just as tall. "We got to get us a talker and a ballyhoo."

"What kind of nonsense word is that?" Tom asked.

Stan answered, "Little brother, I can see you ain't been doing your reading. The Bible ain't the only thing worth looking at. I've read a lot of other shows have one of the oddities outside, with the talker, to lure folks in."

"No sir," said Tom, baby-faced but shrewd, "We are not putting a sample outside. That's why we got signs. We emphasize their distinctions in full color, and that, brothers, will be enough. Otherwise, you're going to have this freak fighting with that one over who gets to sit out front."

"Don't call them freaks. They're our bread and butter, boy." Earl Jr. smiled his thin-lipped, toothy grin.

"More like roast beef." Brother Stan winked. "I'd say the fat lady's worth more than her weight in cow."

"Now listen here," Tom continued. "We're not displaying them together on the stage. I don't care what the other shows do. This here's Beasleys' Traveling Amusements, and we're different. God Himself has shone His countenance upon us, and our freaks, rather our treasures from God, will each get their own special booth. With curtains that automatically open and close. That way, the performers know they're one of a kind, and the audience, if they look too long at one attraction, might miss the next. Then they'll have to pay to see it all again."

Stan shook his head, thumb and forefinger cocked across his chin, marveling at his baby brother. "All that tent-stomping hasn't emptied your head yet. You got a mind for money."

"The more we make, the more I give the Lord. His percentage comes first. Sweet Jesus in his everlasting kindness will offer us the most twisted, pitiful of the fold. But yea, those who do so abuse his fallen, will suffer unto themselves."

"What the hay are you quoting?" Earl Jr. said, face squeezed tight like he'd bitten a sour apple and swallowed the worm.

"Earl," said Stan, "Brother Tom has got the spirit. You ought to know that by now. Got that fancy language, that golden tongue so he can preach to the heathens about the glories of the Lord."

"Be careful who you blaspheme, boys," Tom chided.

Earl raised his hands. "Nothing wrong with faith, little brother. I got plenty of that. What you say in the revival tent is your business, but in carnival land, you got to speak plain. None of that Bible verse or brimstone, you understand? Folks come here to get away from their troubles, not to get an earful of church."

"We all know the Lord needs His day, Tom. That's why we're closed on Sundays," Stan said.

"That's right, and every Sabbath, I'm going to see to it you and Earl pray."

Together, the brothers kept Beasleys' Traveling Amusements running smoothly, turning a profit year after year. Their two sisters in Memphis also helped out. Emma, the eldest sibling, made costumes and acclimated new acts. She'd married back when Big Earl still sold patent medicines, but within six months her scoundrel of a husband disappeared. After that, she devoted herself to the family business, reminding her sister there were three kinds of men: the ones you could hire to transport a load, the ones who deserved to be tied to the train track, and kin. That was it.

Alma Jean, two years older than Tom, boasted fiery auburn hair, soft as the coat on Big Earl's Irish setter, and green eyes set to turn a man's world on end. A quiet, studious girl with a penchant for reading, Alma dreamed of attending college, but Big Earl considered it a waste of his hard-earned money. Snake oil stood a better chance of enhancing her already sufficient charms. He finally consented to send her to finishing school if she promised to work for the family business to pay off his investment.

In 1914, she did him one better, marrying a Memphis lawyer by the name of Samuel Cole. Every year Alma Jean and Sam hosted a formal ball where guests were invited to invest in Beasleys' Traveling Amusement Corporation. A subtle solicitation occurred in the smoking parlor with the after-dinner brandy. While Alma Jean entertained the ladies by playing the piano, Sam's most prosperous clients and business associates were given a chance to invest in something slightly tawdry, but financially sound.

The Beasley brothers prospered by touring back roads and mountains in search of oddities. They advertised for men who possessed unusual strength, and there was always a fellow desperate enough to be the Geek. The challenge came in finding the oddities that got tucked away. Every few weeks, Stan and Earl Jr. strode into a small-town general store, dressed flashily enough to signal they had money, but plainly enough not to arouse suspicion. Chewing on a sour pickle or a stick of jerky, they explained how God had a reason for making the unfortunate souls whose bodies kept them housed in a temple of difference. The lame, the deformed, the unbearably fat. Even those born healthy but later rendered unrecognizable through some hideous accident. They all had a purpose.

Outside of Guntersville, Alabama, in search of a man they'd heard about with elastic hair, the brothers got invited to Sunday dinner. Zebediah Rosewell pulled Earl aside and asked if either one of them was married.

"No sir, I'm afraid we've got our hands full running the family business. But I bet a man good as you has a handful of lovely daughters."

"Just two between my seven sons. Pretty girls, though." Zebediah grinned.

On the other side of the room, Stan charmed Zebediah's wife.

"Why just on the way over, Mr. Rosewell told me you bake the best pies in Marshall County. Now tell me how a man finds himself a woman whose talents are as fine as her looks?" Pearly May Rosewell put her fingers to her lips, too shy to smile in front of a man wearing such a fancy suit and oxford shoes. Over the head of the blushing woman, Stan winked at Earl. If either brother'd had a mind to marry, the Rosewells would have offered their daughters up.

But all three Beasley brothers preferred life on the road to settling down. While Stan and Earl Jr. partook in comforts of the flesh, Tom sought tabernacles. Occasionally, he would sneak off and testify in some hardscrabble sanctuary or revival tent. And whenever a brother needed a wife to make a delicate call, Alma Jean stepped in. When Stan went to retrieve Flipper Boy from a New Orleans hospital, he took her along. Together, they presented the perfect Christian couple ready to adopt the small boy who flapped his fan-shaped limbs.

Stan borrowed his brother-in-law Samuel's name, even though the likelihood of the nuns realizing they'd given a child to the South's largest carnival seemed slimmer than a sideways dime. Once Stan and Alma Jean brought little Sebastian back, they turned him over to Emma, who raised him for three years until he was five—old enough to go on display. Emma could raise anything. Big Earl teased that she could coax peaches from a dogwood tree. Her attitude with children was kind yet firm, as if each word, gesture, and lesson were a stitch pulled confidently through cloth. By the time Flipper Boy was three and a half, he could name the southern states and count as high as the fingers and toes he didn't have. She had Tom build him a canvas swing that held him securely in place. He would swing for hours, singing nursery rhymes and practicing words while she sewed.

In 1917, the Beasleys enjoyed a bumper crop of acquisitions. Stan found Leroy Haines, a gentle giant eight feet tall, in Talladega, Alabama. Stan paid a visit to the school for the deaf and blind, where he found a child almost as amazing as Helen Keller, but the girl's parents refused to let her leave school. Only momentarily disappointed, Stan picked up a tip about Leroy. The only problem with the trip was that he was too tall to fold into the cab of the truck, so he had to ride on the bed of it wrapped in a pair of blankets Emma had sewn together to cover a prize hog.

The giant provided problems only insofar as Ewell and Cheever, the colored men who tended the oddities, had less than a day to build him a suitable bed in the trailer he filled by himself. Ewell and Cheever modified the door for Leroy just as they had for the fat lady, but inside, Leroy still stooped.

The Beasleys prided themselves that a human attraction never quit. They boasted to their investors how they treated their special charges as considerately as Noah had cared for the animals on his ark. The colored cooks made a full Sunday dinner each week but the amenities ended there. The Beasleys maximized their profits by providing just enough to keep their exhibits from leaving. Every oddity had a costume, but the Beasleys provided no extra clothes. Those had to be bought, and wages were low—twenty dollars a month—just enough for them to feel like workers. Otherwise there would be no loyalty to play upon. Every November when the circuit closed till the next season, Big Earl gave every performer three silver dollars for each year of service, so those who wanted to could travel home.

The ones without family wintered on the property adjacent to the Beasley homestead, their trailers tucked discreetly out of view in the back field, only a couple hundred yards from the family graveyard, where Big Earl's wife, Edna Louise, had been laid to rest in 1903. Emma looked after the ones who couldn't care for themselves, and every Thanksgiving and Christmas, she hosted a holiday dinner in the house. Big Earl and the boys went to Alma Jean and Sam's, but they sprung for the dinner and begrudgingly consented to let the attractions dine in the house. At first, Earl Jr. protested. "They'll root through the closets and pocket the silverware," he warned.

"Look, Earl," Emma countered that first year, "Flipper Boy can't get to a closet and Tiny can't even reach the silver chest. Besides, you make them feel special, trusted even, and you can dangle that over them forever." Finally, he relented. Her brother's attitude infuriated her. After all, she'd been tending the oddities for years, measuring them for costumes, raising the child performers until they were old enough to join the show, and caring for them in crisis. The year Leroy Haines's mother died, the brothers packed him off to see Emma, who rode with him to Talladega, offering him thumb-sized sandwiches and minted tea to feed his grief. Earl Jr. cursed his sister's kindness and gave Leroy two days off.

Over the years, Brother Earl took credit for acquiring the most popular oddities, even when it required precious little work. Sitting at the walnut desk that belonged to his mother's father, Earl lifted the cigar out of the humidor and ceremoniously sniffed its sweet scent, running it under the tip of his nose. Eyes shut, he inhaled slowly, then exhaled a long slow ribbon of breath. Alma Jean stood in the doorway of the room Earl had claimed for his office in the family house, and waited for her brother's reverie to end. She had no idea how a man could linger over an unlit cigar, but waited just the same. Alma Jean believed in the value of pleasure, her long soaks in a hot bath filled with luxurious oils. Her brother opened his eyes like a man emerging from a cave.

"Sorry to disturb you," Alma Jean said, "but there's a fellow here says he wants to work for you."

"Where is he and what's he do?"

"He's in the library looking at Granddaddy's saber."

"You didn't let him take it down from the mantle, did you?"

"I wouldn't worry about that. He has no arms. He claims he can hammer nails with his toes."

"Hmm. He a good-looking man?"

"He's got a fairly sweet face."

"One the ladies could love?"

"Well, one they could stand to look at. Why?"

"Because we need a draw for the ladies. They're not much interested in deformed women. Some snigger at seeing another one so tiny or fat, but on the whole, the sideshow appeals to men. That's got to change and a nice-looking fellow normal except for his arms could be what wins the ladies." Earl set down the cigar. "Send him in."

She returned with a sandy-haired fellow, five-foot-ten, dressed in clean overalls and a chambray shirt. Earl extended his hand out of habit and then joked, "I'd shake your foot, sir, but no telling where that shoe has been."

The man smiled. "Name's Ernie Morton and I got an act for you." He slid the canvas rucksack off his back and slipped off his specially made shoes. "Mind if I sit?"

"Not at all."

"On the floor?"

"Go right ahead." Earl stepped back and watched as Ernie peeled his socks off with his big toes. With his teeth, he gripped the rucksack and shook the contents out: four half-inch-thick boards the size of a child's slate, four one-by-four blocks, a tiny thatched roof, a couple dozen nails and a hammer. First, he grabbed one of the boards between his toes and propped it against the one-by-four. Then he gripped a nail with his left foot and lifted the hammer with his right. He brought his foot down sharply, driving the nail into the wood. Swift clean strokes and deft maneuvering. Within four minutes, Earl stared down at an assembled doll house. Ernie stretched his toes.

"That's quite a trick," Earl said, passing Ernie a cigar.

Ernie smiled, took the cigar with his left toes and inserted it in his mouth. "Thank you," he said, the words dodging the stogie wedged between his cheek and top teeth.

"You lose your arms in an accident or were you born that way?" Earl lit his own cigar.

"I come this way. Can I ask you a question?"

"Go ahead." Earl puffed, lost in his own pleasure.

"If you was to hire me, would I get a stage name?"

Earl had shut his eyes again so he could focus on the cigar's flavor. He let Ernie's words drift to the floor and then he answered. "I don't reckon Ernie Morton would be much of a draw. How about The Amazing Hammer Toe?"

"As long as folks don't think I got malformed feet. I'm proud of my feet, you know. They're perfectly formed. Did you notice?" He lifted his left foot up in the air. "Look at that. Perfect descending order. No middle toe that sticks out, no calluses, no corns. I keep 'em clean and neat. Lots of powder and softening cream. Like I said, the ladies like 'em."

"It don't bother women you got no arms?"

"Some it do, but mostly they feel sorry." That was all Earl Jr. needed to hear.

"All right then, I'll just need you to sign a contract." Earl stepped behind his desk and pulled a piece of paper from the drawer. He grabbed a pen and his lighter from the blotter and then leaned over to light Ernie's cigar. Without prompting, Ernie removed the pen from Earl's hand and waited for him to set the contract on the floor.

"You get three months off every winter, all your meals, board, and twenty dollars a month. No entanglements with other performers and no showing up drunk when you have to perform. What you do on travel days is your own business."

"Hmm." The smoke from Ernie's cigar billowed, his head erupting through the small cloud.

"What's the problem?" Earl asked.

Ernie slipped the cigar out of his mouth with his toes. "I've heard good things about your show, which is why I came to see you, but Jack Reynolds over at Kimball's Traveling Emporium offered me thirty a month, plus tips."

"What's a man need with thirty when he gets room and board?"

"Traveling money, Mr. Beasley. You said yourself I'll have three months off. I like to go places, buy nice things. Just because God didn't give me arms don't mean He gave me shabby taste." Ernie brought the cigar back to his lips and puffed. "Truth be told, women like expensive things." He winked at Earl.

"I run the best show in the South."

"Exactly, sir. That's why I figured you'd pay well, turning a profit like you do."

If Earl hired him and kept him happy, Ernie's loyalty could galvanize the others, but on the other side of risk, he could stir up the pot.

"It's not cheap to run a business, especially one on the road. I got people and equipment to move, to say nothing of financing trips to find folks like you. Not everybody walks through my front door. But I'll tell you something, not one oddity has ever left to join another show."

"Surely you remember the $30,000 Nutt?"

"I'm a Beasley, not a Barnum."

"Something to think about, isn't it, a dwarf making thirty thousand dollars in three years?"

Earl passed Ernie an ashtray. "I'll give you thirty a month and five percent of the draw."

Ernie flicked his ashes. "And that was fifty years ago."

"Mr. Morton, this here's Memphis. My circuit's the South, small towns, farm counties, people with dimes, not dollars, in their pockets. You want to ride on up to New York City and join the circus, go right ahead. What I run is a first-rate show. We treat our people right. Not a malcontent in the bunch and that's the way I intend to keep it, and if that doesn't suit you, I'm sure my lovely sister Alma will see you to the door."

Earl watched Ernie push the pen across the paper, careful to loop the *o* in Morton and cross his *t*. "Where'd you learn to write like that?" Earl asked.

"Practice. Years of practice. Feet are a lot more maneuverable than we imagine. These toes have made women beg for more." He took another puff and blew out three perfect rings.

Earl grinned. He could hear Tom thanking Jesus for the profits he'd just signed.

As successful as Earl Jr. was recruiting performers, he sent Stan on the thorny calls. Stan signed Flipper Boy, the Bearded Lady, and the Geek. When a smaller carnival threatened to set up in Biloxi the week before the Beasleys were scheduled to come, Earl Jr. dispatched Stan to settle matters. Without so much as a threat of violence, Stan suggested the other company switch their operations further west or east. "You have folks coming to our show after they been to yours, they're gonna tell their relatives in the next county which show to see. Word gets out folks can see a whole array of attractions like we got, not to mention all kinds of other amusements, they're apt to pass up on your assortment of draught horses and dolled-up farm girls, whereas you take that show down the tip of Florida or over to the miners in West Virginia and they'll turn up in droves. Best not to tempt a poor man with two kinds of pie."

The competition moved to Florida, where years later, Stan passed through, hoping to hire a Seminole named Indian Jim. When he paid a visit to the other operation, he found men wrestling alligators in front of howling crowds. Best to let each region draw on its own resources. Beasley Brothers would stay away from gator wrestling as long as the competition kept out of the South, away from the oddities he and Brother Earl prided themselves on collecting.

The traveling museums and circus sideshows that ventured into their territory lured a few customers away, but the Beasleys never suffered a shortage of the curious or discontent. The South produced an unending supply of backs bent, hands roughened, and dreams diminished by poor crops or unscrupulous landowners. After the balm of glory promised by the Hereafter began to fade, the weary carried their tired souls out of the revival tents and into the ones that dotted the Beasley landscape, drinking in relief—sweet and momentary as late afternoon rain.

ORIGINS OF FLIPPER BOY

The nuns at the hospital in New Orleans knew they could not raise him, but they could not let him die either, so they allowed a couple named Cole to adopt the boy with flippered limbs. The pair told of a sign from God to find a stray lamb separated from the fold, so the nuns released the child they had named Sebastian, crossing themselves and mouthing a grateful prayer.

From the moment Stan and Alma Jean brought the boy to Memphis, he took to water, tiny fins splashing in the bath. Emma told him his uncles would build him a throne. She called him "Little Prince" and said he had come from Poseidon, god of the sea. When he turned five, she pronounced him ready, and true to her promise, the Beasleys built him a platform with gold ribbons and his own curtain that opened and closed. He had to sit shoulder-deep in a glass tank of blue water for hours at a time. Emma told him it was the way his true daddy, the water god Poseidon, would find him, so each day, one of the colored workers lifted him into his tank, where he sat until his lips turned blue as the water. His tiny nipples tightened and his skin wrinkled, but Earl and Stan made sure Ewell and Cheever fed him cotton candy and popcorn whenever he asked.

Flipper Boy always garnered the most *oohs* and *aahs*. Since he was so young, Emma insisted they shorten his display time, which worked to the Beasleys' advantage since the supply never quite met the demand. The line for the Oddities of Nature Pavilion snaked around ropes set up outside the tent. As Flipper Boy came and went, he studied his rendering—one he did not fully recognize—and mouthed the words, "Son of Poseidon, God of the Sea."

At night, in the dry warmth of his bed positioned next to Tiny's, the dwarf woman who looked after him once he joined the show, Flipper

Boy pulled his fins in close, wondering if his father had fins, too.

Neither the Beasleys nor the nuns knew the truth of his origin. Not even his mother, Nadine, knew what she had birthed. The midwife never let her look at the bundle she carried out. When Nadine Paris discovered she was pregnant, she nibbled pretzels and nursed a bottle of beer. Between her line of work and the way she and Pierre Lambert went at it every Friday night, it didn't surprise her one bit. She accepted Pierre's proposal and moved from Miss Ethel's bordello in the French Quarter to the tiny fisherman's shanty he lived in on the bayou.

They met at Miss Ethel's, though Pierre never engaged in carnal acts there. Nadine was in the kitchen helping arrange a tray of hors d'oeuvres the day Pierre knocked on the back door with his bucket of shrimp. Nadine worked in the kitchen before she was old enough to service the men, and still wandered back there whenever she could. When the young man with the shock of coal-black hair and the fishy-smelling apron asked her out, she laughed aloud. A second generation prostitute being courted by an Acadian Catholic shrimper. He watched the water run from her eyes. She wiped away the tears and nodded. He bought her dinner the following Monday and waited a month to kiss her. He was the first man she'd met who ate supper at Miss Ethel's and refused anything else. She agreed to marry him two days after the old sailor with the missing teeth and the raspberry colored cheeks rocked into her harder than the pounding surf.

When Pierre insisted she relinquish her trade, Nadine begged him to let her work in the kitchen at Miss Ethel's. He said there'd be no way to explain to his family why his wife worked in a brothel, so he took her home to live in his shack. Four generations of fishermen, he told her proudly as he carried her through the door, but she had grown used to the fineries of the bordello with its heavy drapes and imported tapestries. His cabin held no potted palms or leopard skins, no curios or oil paintings, just a small crucifix and a water-stained photograph of his father standing on a boat.

Though Pierre expected her to lie beneath him only on Fridays, and Saturdays if she liked, she missed the company of other women and Miss

Ethel's pantry stocked with delectable treats. The constant smell of fish made her stomach so queasy she barely noticed the first waves of nausea. A second month without bleeding passed. She caught a ride on one of the boats that traveled the canal and returned for an afternoon to Miss Ethel's, where she sat in the kitchen licking salt from the pretzels and sipping beer.

In the months than ensued, boredom plagued Nadine. She plotted bringing the baby back to Miss Ethel's to live. But under the watchful eye of Pierre's mother and sisters, escaping would be difficult. Throughout the pregnancy, her mother-in-law sewed little dresses and nattered at her in Cajun. Mornings, after Pierre left for the day, Nadine lay in the bed, yearning for her friends, almost nostalgic for the sweet smell of her best customers, with their tailored suits and clean fingernails.

She managed to visit the French Quarter just once in her sixth month, while Pierre's relatives attended mass. As soon as she returned to Miss Ethel's, she heard the unmistakable voice of the old sailor, singing sea shanties as he opened the door.

"Girlie!" he exclaimed, rough hands leaping out to greet her. "Where you been all this time? I come back two months ago and you was gone. Miss Ethel said you retired."

"I'm having a baby." She drew her fingers across the rise of her belly.

"Whose?" he asked, his big hand cupped around the side of her face.

"My husband's, I suppose. I got married. Or maybe yours." She kissed his hand and then released it. "You were my last customer before I met up with him."

"Where is he?"

"Fishing, shrimping. Makes his living from the sea like you."

"Kissed by Poseidon, are you, the way you fancy men of the sea?"

"Must be. Why else would it be my lot in life to end up smelling of fish?"

"You back working?"

"No, silly man. I just snuck over to see the girls. I got to get home. Good to see you, though." She let him embrace her, unaware he'd bedded her mother at Lulu White's Mahogany Hill long before he requested her.

∾

When her labor started, Pierre fetched the midwife, Madame Bontemps, who'd been delivering babies for forty years. As a girl, she could read the wind's direction or the height of the river to tell what kind of birth it would be. The day she set out for Pierre's cabin, the sun rose too fast, as if it were rolling clear out of the sky, the wind blowing like an old man anxious to set foot in the grave.

Madame Bontemps pried Nadine's legs apart, wriggling her finger inside to gauge the width of the opening. The child would slide out smooth as a mackerel making its way to sea, a freak of nature not meant to walk the earth.

Nadine shrieked twice. The midwife pulled. One slippery shoulder popped out and then another. No arms or legs. Only fins. She severed the cord, dropped the afterbirth in a bucket and carried the swaddled infant into the hall.

"A babe of the water," she told Pierre. She pulled the blanket back to reveal a fin. "Got the same for feet."

Pierre bit hard into his lip. His mother insisted the baby belonged to God.

"Give it to the nuns, then," he sputtered, "but Nadine must never know."

∾

"Mama Tiny, you think I'll ever get old?" Flipper Boy asked as she changed him.

"What makes you ask that? You ain't but six."

"I want to see my daddy, Poseidon, but I don't know where's the sea."

"Ocean's all around the borders, but it's a big country. I don't think the Beasleys travel that far."

"Will you take me?"

"Maybe someday, if I get money to hire a car."

She fastened the cloth around his bottom and then worked his fins in her hand.

"That tickle?" she asked.

"No. Who's your daddy?"

"Old moonshiner named Bill."

"What's that?"

"Makes mountain liquor. Stuff you ain't old enough to drink."

Her hands on his fins sent shivers up his spine. He glanced up at the mural of the ocean with its whitecaps and cresting swells. Tiny had the signpainter fill the ceiling with sea.

Flipper Boy wriggled to let her know he wanted to sit up. She climbed on the bed, her own short legs on either side of his hips, hoisted him, and then propped him against the headboard. "There, now you can see the rest of the world."

"I like the ocean better. Promise you'll take me there?"

"I'll try." She scooched down beside him, her shoulder brushing his upper fin.

Immersed in the water, strapped in his seat, Flipper Boy watched the eyes of the people lined up to see him. His second week in the tank, he watched the face of a boy his age crinkle, the eyes narrowing, the nose flattening, the mouth turning sour as the wail climbed the back of the boy's throat. The cries pierced the tent like giant scissors, leaving a hole wide enough for both boys to fall through. Flipper looked at the boy's mother, hoping she would comfort him or carry him out, but she just stood there saying, "Don't worry, sugar, it won't happen to you."

At night, he lay in between the sheets on his bed, eyes closed, dreaming of the ocean, fins pulling him effortlessly to his father's throne.

The day Ewell got distracted and forgot to secure the safety straps, the curtain shut and was about to re-open when Flipper Boy sneezed so hard he lurched forward, slipping off his seat. His fins flapped uselessly. The light above turned into thick ribbons hovering overhead. He opened his mouth to holler. Water rushed in.

The curtain closed, leaving him alone underwater. Holding his breath, he flapped furiously with his fins until the curtain re-opened.

On the other side of the glass, a new set of people stared. The sign out front depicted him as half boy, half seal. Would anyone realize he wasn't supposed to be fully submerged? The water grew darker. Suddenly, he heard the thwunk of a hand entering the water—an arm reaching around his torso, yanking him out.

A clot of onlookers watched. The man looked around for someone who would thank him kindly for his trouble and take the boy off his hands. The water soaked the man's sleeves and dripped onto his shoes. "Jesus, boy, are you taking a piss or what? Where's the manager? Somebody take this freak off my hands."

No one had called him that before. The sound stung the way it did when Ewell told him he didn't care who his daddy was, his shit still stank. He hated wearing diapers, but Tiny couldn't be bothered in the middle of the night to set him on the slop pot, and no one would carry him to a latrine if he needed to go after breakfast. During the shows, he had to hold his bowels, even his pee. The faintest hint of yellow escaping from his costume would ruin the show.

With no sign of Ewell or Cheever, there was nothing to do but ask the stranger to set him back in the water. The man hoisted him into the tank and lowered him onto the scoop of seat. "The belt," Flipper Boy instructed. "You have to fasten the belt."

The man rolled up his sleeves and reached in to find the strip of webbing that lashed him to the chair. When the curtain re-opened, the crowd had thinned, disappointed no doubt that the son of Poseidon the sea god couldn't really swim.

That night, Tiny tried to cheer him by singing an extra-long lullaby, but he still felt soggy with humiliation as she sang. When she turned off the lamp in the trailer, he begged Poseidon to carry him far away. When he awoke the next morning, still below the painted sea, he prayed for real fins that could save him from drowning beneath watery skies.

LIZARD MAN

The first sign that he was different came as a baby, when Julian Henry's mother could not cure his unrelenting rash, but that he didn't notice until later. Initially, he remembered wondering what was in her cup: the mysterious substance looked like dirt. He kept pointing his two-year-old finger, a lazy way to express his curiosity, but his mother, Alice, took it as a sign. She had not been particularly religious before her son's birth. A quiet Presbyterian. But after the first year of trying ointments and remedies, with no relief for her baby's scaly skin, she began wondering if she had been cursed. The doctor in town diagnosed him. Ichthyosis. Unsightly, not contagious, no known cure. Alice's sister mentioned the biblical precedent of skin lesions signaling spiritual impurity, though Alice preferred to dwell on Jesus, who healed the lepers, thus suggesting that Julian, because of his suffering, had a special in with the Lord. That set the stage for the miraculous discovery that he had been sent as an emissary to deliver God's word on earth.

"Sacrifice," she heard him whisper as she peered at the grounds in her cup. "Give up your worldly pleasure that you might better serve your Lord." She gazed at Julian, his arm raised, and realized what she had given birth to after all. She had not been punished; no, she had been divinely chosen. Jesus knew she would understand Julian's powers, whereas others, like Julian's father, with his repulsion to the boy's skin, would completely miss his special gifts. But God knew Alice Henry would see beyond the surface to look deep within her child's soul. She passed the test of faith. He sent her sister to fool her, tempt her to turn from her own son, but she alone stood with him, casting no aspersions, never surrendering to doubt.

As she poured the coffee down the drain, her voice crested along the words *Mine eyes have seen the glory of the coming of the Lord.* Julian toddled behind her, finally mustering the energy to say, "What's in your cup, Mama?" but in her reverie, Alice did not hear.

When she first sewed wings made of white felt to his romper, Julian felt special. His mother spent an entire day fitting him, positioning the wings, and brushing his hair. When his father arrived home that night, eyeing the outfit, the words fell sharply, the edges scraping Julian even if the meaning landed as a dull thud. "You can dress him any way you please, but he's still going to have that hideous skin."

His mother shrieked and brought her hand to her mouth. "How dare you speak that way in front of him? Colin, you're awful. He is a child of the Lord." She didn't dare tell him of Julian's powers. Her husband scoffed at religion more times than not, a sign of his own impure heart, no doubt. He claimed his revulsion came from memories of his aunt with psoriasis. The vision of her arm, drooping with skin, the flakes sifting into his oatmeal bowl, lost in the mush before he could scoop them out, still haunted him. How he, of all people, could have fathered a son whose scales never faded convinced Colin Henry that God was either a cruel bastard or a fake.

Young Julian sensed his father's disgust. When he ran toward him, Colin turned away. Suddenly, he had to fetch a tool or check something outside, but he never invited Julian to come. Alice, aware of her husband's discomfort, tried all the more to assure Julian that he alone inherited God's special gift. She filled the hours of her husband's absence with Bible study. Every morning she read to Julian. Sitting in his mother's lap being cuddled was alluring enough, but when he began to listen to the curves in his mother's voice, the stories unfolded.

By the time he was four, Julian remembered most of the characters she'd introduced him to, and Alice began teaching him to read. She printed one word on a card and pointed to its corresponding object: a chair, a bowl, her dress. Julian matched the sounds with the pictures and then progressed to assigning the proper configuration of letters to the characters she drew. Abraham. The name made him giggle, but Alice used her strongest voice as she sketched the patriarch. "Abraham trusted the Lord the way I trust you. God spoke directly to him, just like God speaks to you." Her tone softened as she spoke.

"Abraham," he repeated, "the father of Isaac." The lessons became more arduous. The more he absorbed, the more convinced Alice was of his powers, but she decided to debut them at a church other than her own just in case they were met with skepticism. Shortly after Julian turned four, she dressed him in his angel outfit and took him to a revival meeting at a Pentecostal church on the edge of town. Greeted by the congregants upon their arrival, Alice was quick to tell of her son's prophetic gifts. The women clumped at the door peered at the small boy with wings on his back, their gaze moving across the patchy face. Julian watched their eyes travel, the horror tugging at their faces. Someone shrieked.

"Only one so tormented in the flesh," his mother told them, "could be so divine in the soul." Taking their cue from her, the women's vision changed. They knelt in front of him, drawing the pastor's attention.

"What have we here?" he asked.

"My son is an emissary of the Lord. He's been sent to remind us of the purity of heart. Those like his father look away, but folks who know the Lord and welcome the spirit of Jesus can see into my son's soul. And he can see into ours. Lord speaks right to him, Pastor."

"How can you be sure?"

"Oh, I've waited, asked God for a sign. Julian took to the Bible like a crow to bread, hungering for the words his Heavenly Father wrought."

"Come here, son." The pastor reached out his arm. Julian, who had never been welcomed into his father's arms, could scarcely believe any man beckoned him. He inched toward the stranger whose face seemed longer than any he'd seen. Julian noticed the yellowed teeth and the tiny pits in the pastor's skin, the starchiness of his breath.

"And what does God tell you, son?"

Suddenly the man seemed larger than life. His mother beamed behind him. Julian closed his eyes and wished for words. None came, so he opened them. The long-faced man still filled his view. "That lady in the green dress, she's been having trouble. The Lord wants her to know he loves her in spite of sin."

"Sister Cooper, what's this boy talking about?" The pastor looked alarmed.

The woman peered so hard at Julian he wanted to cry. "How'd you know? I've been feuding with my sister, Reverend. Done spoke about her behind her back."

"Hallelujah. The child is blessed." A large woman, whose blue dress rippled as she spoke, knelt down and hugged him. Julian caught sight of his mother, hands clasped across her bosom.

"Yes, Lord," she said, eyes cast upward. "You have blessed my son."

After that, Alice took Julian to her church, where the pastor encouraged her to share the wealth of God's bounty by taking Julian around. By the time he turned five and could recite verses with little prompting, they had visited a dozen church meetings and two revivals. At the market, when townspeople recognized him, he cringed while she smiled with self-satisfaction.

In his outfit, he always drew attention. People staring frightened him, but as they drew near, his mother would whisper, "Listen to Jesus. He'll tell you what to say." Her breath warm in his ear, the crowd gathering expectantly, he began studying their faces. Sometimes older boys or drifters would hurl suspicion or even contempt.

"Take the little bastard home," a man hollered near the courthouse.

"Shut up, you old drunk," a woman responded, though the man did not look even as old as his father.

His mother never asked if he wanted to wear the costume or ride the streetcar downtown. She simply began each day with Bible verses and a story and then told him that, like their savior, Jesus, he had his own crown of thorns. He liked the words he learned from the Bible, their weight on his tongue, and he liked the pennies and nickels women pressed into his palm as they bent over, their eyes burning holes into his. But on the days he saw other children, he wondered what their lives were like. What did ordinary boys do with their mothers all day?

At night, after they had returned home, before his father left for work at ten, Julian would sit patiently at the table, waiting for his father to ask him about his day. He spent as little time around the boy as possible, printing newspapers far into the night, sleeping deep into the day. Unlike his wife, he found nothing symbolic or spiritual about his son. The scales simply reminded him of his aunt and her perpetually flaking skin.

Julian knew better than to reach for his father, who would nod to him as if hoisting some reluctant load. His earliest memories were of his father's hands large on his torso, holding him at bay. Julian wondered how his father's embrace would feel. Would he hug harder than his mother did? How would the calloused fingers feel? Because of his skin, he preferred the currency of pressure, squeezes, firm grips, bear hugs, to the caresses and light touch his mother usually offered him.

No matter how many conversations he overheard where his mother urged his father to hug him, to lift him onto his shoulders or carry him to bed, his father refused. If Julian approached him fully clothed, his father might allow him to sit on his lap, balanced precariously on his knee, but the few times Julian tried to snuggle, to let his weight fall into his father's belly and chest, his father quickly shifted him and held him upright. After a while, Julian simply skirted his father's chair.

In the morning, on the way to the kitchen, where his mother conducted their daily Bible study, Julian paused by the door to his parents' bedroom, listening to his father breathe. He found the raspy sound somehow reassuring. Ear pressed to the door, he imagined slipping under the covers, tucking himself between his father's arms.

As he got older, the lessons got harder. There were no pictures for though or thou or begot. He grew restless, longing for other activities. He wondered what other children did.

"They go to school," his mother explained.

"What's that?"

"It's a place where ordinary children go to learn their numbers and words."

"How come I can't go there, too?"

"Because you are special, not like any other little boy. You alone have been chosen as a messenger of God."

He couldn't quite imagine a school, but he wished for the chance to go just the same.

His father didn't raise the subject of school with him, but one evening before his father left for work, he handed Julian the paper and asked him to read. Julian tried. He had learned to sound out words, though the ones in the newspaper felt different. He had no pictures to go along with them.

"I want you to practice reading this every day, you understand. There's more to read than just the Bible. If your mother's going to keep you home, then you need to read everything you can so the world doesn't pass you by. If there's a word you don't know, you ask. Understand?"

What Julian understood was a way to reach his father. Every afternoon while his mother straightened the house or prepared for dinner, Julian scoured the newspaper, circling unfamiliar words with a red pen his father had brought home from work. Then, when his father got up, Julian presented the list of words. Slowly, a world blossomed before him—of inventions and revolutions, uprisings and strikes. A world so far removed it was hard to believe, harder than the one laid out two thousand years before. But what mattered most in those moments of discovery was the steady breathing of his father by his side, the way his father's hands moved through the air, and sometimes, inadvertently, landed on his shoulder.

Alice noticed her husband's interest, worried it would distract Julian from the message of Jesus. The more Julian read the newspaper, the more he wanted his father to take him where other boys went: ball games, parades, county fairs. Finally, one Sunday, after Julian had returned from church with his mother, he asked his father if they could go to a baseball game. He watched his father, waiting for his answer, aching for an outing suitable for a boy without scales or wings.

The next Saturday, before they went to see a local team play, his father handed him a cap and insisted he dress warmly. Julian sat perspiring in his long-sleeved shirt and trousers, noticing the boys in their short pants, the men with their shirt sleeves rolled up. Though he felt foolish sweating into his clothes, he relished the hour next to his father in the bleachers. It was the first time he had seen his father outside of the house, cheering, hollering, waving like other men. It wasn't until half-way through the third inning, when Julian whispered to his father that he had to pee, that a boy behind them pointed and said, "Look at him, Daddy. He's got funny skin."

Julian had heard comments before, but his father, who had taken him nowhere, retreated from the words. "Come on," he said, ushering him away. His mother would have said, *Mind your manners, sonny. My boy is blessed by the Lord,* but all his father could do was escort him from the bleachers.

After he'd relieved himself, he inhaled the smell of peanuts, listening for the sound of the ball flying from the bat. His father asked, "Have you got a feel for the game?"

Julian nodded.

"All right then." His father's hand rested on his shoulder as he led him out. "There'll be others."

But there were not.

Though it spared him having to face his father's embarrassment, he longed for an outing without his mother, where no one praised his powers or noticed his skin. When she took him out, she gloated, deepening the pain of his father's shame even more.

In the afternoon, his father still read with him, but the world shrank. All the stories his father had printed disappeared, the letters growing so small Julian could barely read them. The events on those pages existed somewhere else, in a place he could not find, where neither parent could take him. The walls of his house grew tighter. The aisles of churches grew so narrow he could hardly move. He begged Jesus to free him, to part the waters like God had done for Moses, and let him escape. In the bathtub, he submerged his head, holding his breath for as long as he could, until his reflexes sent him upward gobbling for air.

He began to notice what other children were doing when he and his mother went into town. Children trying on shoes, or buying candies, their hands clutching pennies they offered an adult they could barely see behind the counter. Brothers and sisters restless in their Sunday clothes, and older boys running full steam toward the trolley, coat tails flying in their own self-created breeze. And there he stood, on the corner of Park and Monroe, draped in white flannel with small wings attached, his mother laying claim to the miracle she created.

At night, he began to dream of running away, peeling off the angel suit and chasing after the big boys, embarrassed in his underdrawers, but running so fast no one could tell. He would hop on the streetcar and beg the boys to take him away. As he lay there imagining his escape, his mother slipped in, sat next to him on the edge of his bed, reassuring him it was better to be paid attention to for one's virtues rather than one's flaws. God in His infinite wisdom had found a way to bless him, and she had been keen enough to recognize it. But as she kissed his brow, he furrowed it, anxious to have her leave. As soon as she rose and pulled the door behind her, the emptiness expanded like a balloon, enlarging until it popped, and that's when he realized without her, he would feel like the only person on earth.

The morning Julian turned seven, he woke to his mother's touch, her hand grazing his forehead, then nudging his shoulder. "Wake up, sleepyhead. I've got a surprise for you," she cooed. Sleep still crowded his head as he squeezed his eyelids against the light and then opened them. The sunlight framed his mother, her eyes dancing, arms extended. "Come, let's see what the birthday boy got."

A new toy? Maybe a bike he could ride far away, into the Wild West, where he could disappear into the hills, leaving all the grief-stricken ladies on street corners who waited for his heavenly pronouncements. The hallway grew shorter with each step. "Look in the kitchen," his mother instructed. As he neared it, he could hear scratching. In the corner by the stove sat a large box with a blue ribbon wrapped around it. The scratching intensified. Julian rushed over. At last, an animal, something to rescue him. When he opened the box, out popped a black cocker Spaniel puppy, its nose prodding Julian's fingers, its soft tongue licking his face. Julian ran his lips across the silky ears of the dog, the softness sending water to his eyes. The dog's tongue traveled across his face and hands as they each lapped up sensations new to them. He named the dog Jesse as he carried the water bowl from the sink, walking slowly so as not to spill, setting it beside the food his mother placed on the floor. Julian stroked the dog's back as it drank the water and sniffed the food. The rest of the day, he did not let Jesse out of his sight. With no other children to come celebrate, the pup alone denoted the changing year, tail wagging wildly, a trail of pee rolling off the paper, puddling on the floor. That night, Jesse curled next to Julian on the bed. Though the waters had not parted, for the first time in his life, Julian thanked Jesus anyway.

The second time came four years later, when Jack Reynolds paid a call. Jesse jumped on his gabardine trousers, leaving dusty paw prints as the tall, sandy-haired man shooed him away. When the man introduced himself as the manager of Kimball's Traveling Emporium, Julian watched his mother's face tighten like a sphincter unwilling to let anything pass. She had seen the sideshow at the circus once as a child and stood resolute that her son would not become a traveling oddity. Jack Reynolds did his best to explain they would provide a bigger and better format to showcase her son's powers. Why confine his audience to one town when he could join their circuit and visit thirty towns a year? No doubt the Lord had sent him to do justice to such a miraculous child. It would be downright selfish to keep the boy at home when thousands could be touched by his grace, and how could a God-loving woman such as herself not answer the Lord's call when her son had been doing it for years? Julian listened to the first person he ever heard out-talk his mother, wondering if Jesus had finally sent someone who might rescue him.

The only problem Jack Reynolds faced after he convinced Alice to let Julian join up was keeping her home. She wanted to come along as Julian's manager, to assure that he was not billed as a child with unusual skin. He was to be presented as a messenger from God, an earthly angel. Jack promised he would personally oversee Julian's act. While she was welcome to attend the show free of charge at any time, Jack Reynolds explained that parents were not allowed to chaperone their children. He assured her they would provide companionship and

Christian supervision. As Reynolds talked, Julian watched his father, hand wrapped around his chin, listening. As soon as Reynolds paused to breathe, his father spoke up, offering no opposition to his son seeing more of the world than churches and revival tents, but he expected his wife to stay home.

She brooded. "If he's part of some spectacle full of others, he's apt to be overlooked. We're not talking a simple talent like dancing or singing. Julian here might be the only person alive known to communicate directly with the Lord."

She rubbed her hands on the side of her apron as Julian stood behind her and watched, praying the man would think of the right words to say.

"Ma'am, I can assure you that every man, woman, and child that encounters your boy will know they have seen an angel of God. We'll make postcards for folks to purchase so they can commemorate the very moment they laid eyes on a child so blessed as yours. No doubt Mr. Henry will be printing up some stories about the show in the newspaper. I can guarantee you, folks'll know you sent them this special little messenger of the Lord."

His mother told Jack Reynolds to wait right there while she spoke to Julian and his father in the other room.

"You want to do this, son?" his father asked, leaning in close. "Because if you do, it might be a real good idea, getting out and seeing things."

After waiting his whole life for Jesus to actually speak to him, Julian Henry accepted the call. "Yes, Papa, I'd like to go." Instantly, his mother's eyes watered. "I'll be fine, Mama. Remember, my wings are the arms of Jesus carrying me." She sniffled and hugged him so tight he felt submerged in the tub.

She packed a bag with the latest of his angel suits, pajamas, and two sets of ordinary clothes. As she wiped a washcloth over his face and around the soft cartilage of his ears it occurred to him that no one had mentioned whether he could bring Jesse. Julian pushed his mother's hand away and ran back into the parlor where Jack Reynolds sat with his father discussing the printing press. "The dog, sir, I have to bring the dog. Otherwise I won't go."

"Why son," his father interjected, "I'm sure Mr. Reynolds here can't be concerned with the whereabouts of your dog."

"I'm afraid the road is no place for a pup. You'll get to see other animals, though."

Julian stood firm, hoping Jesus was listening. "I'm sorry, sir, but I need my dog." Much as he wanted to escape his life, he couldn't bear the thought of leaving Jesse behind. He could just see his mother, hunched over her sewing machine, making the dog his own tiny wings.

Jack Reynolds ran his tongue over his front teeth and made a sucking sound. He breathed out his consternation, and then said, "Don't you think your dog would be happier at home?"

Julian rattled his head so hard that the man consented. "But only on a trial basis. If it don't work out, we're gonna have to send him back, you understand, son?"

"Yes, sir," Julian answered, convinced for the first time in his life that God had come to save him.

His mother cried as Jack Reynolds walked him to the door. "Dear Lord, look after my boy," she whimpered. She mouthed Bible verses as Julian led Jesse on his leash, Mr. Reynolds carrying the dog's box and Julian's bag. When they reached Reynolds's car, his father said, "I love you," and patted his head.

He arrived at the Emporium and quickly learned the talker would tell folks about his amazing powers, and for an extra dime, they could speak to him directly and receive a personal message from God. Neither Jack Reynolds nor the owner, Charles Kimball, cared how Julian derived the message each paying customer needed to hear. "You're on speaking terms with Jesus, so just ask him," Jack suggested the morning of his first show. He stood on a stage with a man wrapped with serpents, which gave Julian the willies. He decided anyone that familiar with snakes might just be in cahoots with the Devil, so he asked Mr. Reynolds if he could stand at the far end of the stage next to the pair of children with sloped faces and pointy heads.

His first night, he leaned over his cot and stroked Jesse's silky fur, the

weight of aloneness settling in his chest. The two pointy-headed children and a girl with no arms shared the trailer. As they drifted off to
sleep, Paco and Arroyo nattered, their words just sounds that swelled
and crested into wriggling rhythms that reminded Julian of birds. Lisa,
the armless girl, snored as he lay in the dark petting Jesse, half frightened
and half relieved. He had never slept near strangers nor been around so
many people who did not stare. He thought of asking Lisa to play marbles until he caught the thought in midair. Suddenly, he felt silly lying
there among other children so obviously deformed that they did not
have to pretend to be anything other than the oddities they were.

He minded his manners and surveyed the other performers the first
few days, searching for someone he could play with, or even talk to,
but no one expressed much interest. The others spoke to him, usually to inquire where he was from, but like Lisa, who demonstrated
great dexterity with her feet, playing on her miniature piano, they
declined to shoot marbles. The pointy-heads swallowed two of his
marbles before Lisa warned him to keep the shiny balls out of Paco
and Arroyo's sight.

At night, he lay awake, thinking of questions he could ask the men
who surrounded him. All the news his father had told him came tum-
bling into his head. He knew about the women who wanted to vote and
the Triangle Shirtwaist Factory fire and all the deaths from pellagra even
before the Traveling Emporium canceled their tour of South Carolina
the year so many people died there. In the dark, with his hand resting on
Jesse's ribcage as it rose and fell, Julian practiced questions he could ask.
Lisa's snoring became a purr as the questions swirled in his head. He slid
into sleep, dreaming of the Muscle Man hoisting him onto his massive
shoulders, hands gripped tight around Julian's ankles, the meaty fingers
clutching with no notice of the patchy scales beneath.

At breakfast, he circled around the questions hovering in his head.
He spotted Freddy, stripped of his knives, dressed only in his balloony
pants and a white undershirt, hands flying wildly as he shared a story
with Alex, the fire-eater. Julian waited there on the bench, saving room
for Freddy to join him. Eggs growing cold, Julian followed Freddy's

trail over to the chow line. So intent on tracing Freddy's movement, Julian failed to notice Toby, the human pincushion, approaching from behind, his spidery leg looping over the bench.

"How's it going, kid?" he asked as he set down his tray.

No, wait! Julian wanted to scream, *Not you. That seat's for Freddy, a man with a skill, not some pathetic lout who makes a living piercing himself.* But it was too late. Toby's words fell like droppings on Julian's plate. Freddy looked over, indicating toward Julian with his head. From Freddy's look, Julian could tell he had become the fodder of conversation.

When Freddy and Alex passed in front of him to sit at another table, he pulled in his head.

"Hey, Turtle Boy, great story. Oughta draw in those tent stompers like crazy now that we got a little angel in the show."

Julian tried hard to read the inflection, his eyes straining against the angle of his dropped head. It wasn't revulsion he heard, just insignificance: a good ruse, the butt of a joke, nothing more. Julian pushed against the human pincushion and yanked his tray.

"You gonna eat those grits?" Toby asked him.

"No, and neither are you," he said, lifting the plate from the tray, letting the contents slide onto the ground.

He could feel the tears welling, his eyes burning, a knot rising in his throat. He had not realized how accustomed he had grown to the looks from ladies who had congregated around him back home, sucking in their breath like pity caught on a nail. His mother's stories about him had spread like mint, overtaking the last seedlings of truth as the women began to cluck and pray. He had tried to hear God, searching frantically for the Lord's will in those women's eyes as their disbelief transformed into faith, but he had never heard the messages. And now it seemed no one heard him.

He sprinted back to the trailer, his breath hammering his chest, fists clenched, arms moving like pawls. He burst through the door, half expecting to find Paco and Arroyo or Lisa still there, but no voices called out. He stood, caught in the grip of his own fear, clenching his fists so that his fingernails pressed into his palms. The words *Who am I?* crawled across his brain. Slow as a dirge, he lifted one foot, then the other, until he stood before the mirror on the wall. He studied the face as if he were inspecting an unfamiliar insect, noticing the shape of his eyebrows; the angle of his nose, slightly upturned; the breadth of his lips, which reminded him of a slice of pear, a sliver of smoothness amidst the otherwise scaled terrain. For a moment, he looked past the scales, but then just as quickly they returned to his view. He shut one eyelid at a time so he could see whether the crescent above his eye crackled the way the rest of him did. He turned his head as if the slightest movement might be his last. Nothing but the still heat of morning. He edged his way to the door and latched it before returning to the mirror. The shades drawn against the heat, he pulled off his undershirt and unfastened his shorts, letting them fall. Slipping his thumbs between his skin and the waistband of his underpants, he peeled them off, absorbing the sight of his own flesh dangling there. He twisted around to inspect the scales on his rear end, roughly the same shape and size as the keys on the typewriter in Mr. Kimball's office, but without purpose. No crisp letters to correspond with his keys. Only the false whisperings of Jesus.

If only his mother had asked him what he really heard. He remembered when he was five, the lady at the corner of Brighton and Elm who had asked him whether her no-good scoundrel of a husband would be back. The sound of the word *scoundrel* tickled him, though he had no idea what it meant, so he had shut his eyes and tried to imagine it. Pictures of tall waves came to him. "No, ma'am," he'd answered, "he's out to sea." Her eyes had filled up with tears so quickly he added, "But Jesus will heal your heart," so she hugged him anyway. His mother had no way of feeling the terror he felt inside.

He pulled up his underpants and shorts, notching his belt extra tight. Arms poking through the sleeves of his shirt, he popped his head through and growled, "Ain't nothing but a boy with ugly-ass skin, and don't none of them fellows want to know you. That bony man in Decatur's the only one knelt down to give you a hug. You better hope that poor man's little girl didn't die." He watched his own lips separate around the vowels punched with all the venom he could muster. Jesse barked in the corner. "Shut up," Julian barked back. He grabbed the dog's collar. Jesse began licking him.

"What you licking me for? You just do it 'cause you don't know any better. Damn fool. You and my mama." He dragged the dog across the floor. "Out you go. Get you some air."

On his twelfth birthday, Julian looked over the line of people approaching him. At the back of the tent, he thought he saw someone wave. He blinked to focus. The upraised palm remained in view. He followed the length of the arm to the shoulder, where the chest and neck got lost behind a tall man with a hat. But the hand stayed there. The woman directly in front of him yanked his robe.

"Hey, sonny, when is the Messiah going to come?"

He quoted Revelations and watched her file past. He looked for the hand again, but it was gone. He found the tall man with the hat, but could not see beyond. In front of him, a thin, bespectacled man with greasy hair spoke. "And behold, the Lord passed by, and a great and strong wind rent the mountains, and broke into pieces the rocks before the Lord . . ."

Julian smiled as he answered, "but the Lord was not in the wind; and after the wind an earthquake; but the Lord was not in the earthquake; and after the earthquake a fire; but the Lord was not in the fire; and after the fire a still small voice."

"I just love that part, don't you?" The man grinned, his short teeth snippets of joy. Once in a while, a viewer sought only a little biblical banter, which came as a great relief.

Suddenly, the tall man had shifted to the side and Julian saw his mother.

"Hi, Mama," he whispered, wondering if she would expect him to deliver a message to her from Jesus. Had she come for that?

"Praise God," she shouted as she approached.

"I got a break at three. I can talk to you then," he said, quietly as he could. She stepped to the side and let another woman speak to him. He wished she wouldn't watch him, but there was no way he could get her to leave. By the time his break rolled around, she'd watched him offer verses to three women and a man carrying his small son. The talker told the patrons to exit quickly as the show would be closing for fifteen minutes, so Julian instructed her to wait for him behind the stage.

He hoped none of the other performers had noticed her.

"Why didn't you tell me how vulgar it is?" she asked as soon as he stepped into earshot. "Those poor slope-faced children and the armless girl up there with a snake charmer and the contortionist. Hardly a fitting location for a messenger of God."

"Depends on how you look at it." Jerry, the talker for the show, had caught her comment as he passed by. "Can you think of any place more in need of His message?" Jerry smiled and kept moving.

"That's one way to look at it." She stroked Julian's face. "I miss you something terrible. They treat you all right?"

"Yes, ma'am, they treat me fine. You come alone?"

"Your father brought me, but he didn't come in. Doesn't do well in crowds." She reached in her handbag and pulled out a large envelope. "He wanted you to have this, though. For your birthday."

The envelope didn't fit in his trouser pocket, so he set it on the shelf next to the extra postcards featuring all the performers. "I'll look at it later."

"I'm sorry I didn't bring you a cake. I have something else." She pulled a tissue-paper-wrapped packet from her bag. He peeled the paper away from a tiny gold cross.

"I can't believe I never thought to give you one before. Pretty, isn't it? Fourteen carat gold."

Not a slingshot, not a jackknife, not even a baseball glove. Julian snatched his next breath.

"Let me fasten it on you." She reached around his neck, the thin chain sliding into the crevices between scales.

"Doesn't that look nice?" Her smile expectant as ever.

"I got to get ready to go back."

"So soon? It's hardly been five minutes. How's Jesse? I still can't believe they let him stay."

"He's fine. Pointy-heads love him."

"Sign says they're ancient Aztecs."

"I have my doubts."

"Doesn't matter anyway. Jesus loves them just the same." Her eyes welled with tears. "I wish you'd come back home. It's not the same without you."

He looked past his mother, in the direction of the tent that housed the girlie show. His father was probably waiting there. "I got to go."

"You think that talker man would introduce me? Let them see who discovered your gift in the first place?"

"Now, Mama, you don't want it to sound like you're taking the credit for the miracle."

She appeared stung. "Of course not." She took his face in her hands and kissed him. "Jesus ever mention what's in store, for us, I mean?"

Lips tight, brow furrowed, scales rising like frost heaves, he whispered, "Sacrifice," then watched her face tighten. "He just keeps whispering 'sacrifice.'"

That night, he opened the envelope and pulled out what looked like a page from the newspaper. The headline read: *World's Best Son Thrills Thousands!* Below, an article extolled miraculous acts of prognostication. He folded the paper in half, then into quarters, then eighths, and tucked it in his drawer, where it stayed until the following week in Decatur, when a haggard-looking man filed in front of him, tears running from his eyes. The man knelt before him, his thin hands and bony wrists tied like a knot wishing itself into a bow.

"They said she'd heal. Got better before she got worse. All I want to know is, did she find her way to Jesus?"

His dark eyes stones set deep in place, deeper than the night he'd squeezed Julian so hard he'd bent his wing.

"Yes, sir. For the righteous have entered the Kingdom of Heaven and in the Lord's house they dwell."

He kept his eyes shut until he felt the man's grip around his ankles loosen. When he opened his eyes, he watched a trail of teary snot drip onto his shoes. Without thinking, he lay his hand on the man's thinning hair. That night, when Julian returned to his trailer, he set fire to the envelope, watching it crackle on the ground, writhing like some pathetic figure, bright orange in the blue-black air.

From that point on, when he wasn't on stage at the Emporium, he picked pockets and devised schemes to trip little children or frighten their parents so no one would ever mistake him as an instrument of God. The gap between his stage persona and his other self widened, as if the earth had split beneath him. Within months, he became utterly mean-spirited and bitter as unsweetened chocolate, his head permanently tucked between his shoulders. His pranks became so vicious that Lisa told the owner. The water over the door and the honey in bed annoyed her, but the loud bangs and snakes in the drawer frightened her, and were it not for Jesse, she feared Julian would light the trailer on fire some night just to see how quickly she and the pointy-headed brothers could get out.

Jack Reynolds leaned on the boy, trying to get at why he had turned sour quicker than cream left in the sun.

"I don't want to play no savior."

"You don't. Angels ain't saviors. Don't you know the difference, boy?"

"I'm not an angel, either. Why can't I be a two-legged lizard?" He kicked the dirt, sending a tiny cloud of fury across the earth.

"Look here, son, your mama told me that ever since you was little, you delivered messages from God. Now that is a bigger draw than alligator skin, and the combination makes it sweeter. Little leper-looking boy speaks God's truth. Quotes them verses like he's clean. Gives hope to other distorted critters. No sir, son, we ain't about to yank one of our most popular acts."

"Shit," Julian sputtered.

"You can raise all the hell you want when you ain't working but it won't convince me to change your act. You understand? I hired you, boy, and this is a business. You pull too much and you won't get hired anywhere else. Talk travels and showmen got the biggest ears. Now go on and get ready and keep that dog of yours from crapping near the trailers or I'll ship his ass out of here." Reynolds gave him a fiery look.

Julian cursed him, wishing, for the first time since he'd left, that he were back home.

❧

He saw her coming, thighs rubbing like a cricket, knees slightly bowed, bracelets jangling on her wrists, dark hair bobbing like she owned the road. He sat on the step of his trailer, cigarette poised in his lips, watching as she traveled toward him, her eyes darting every which way until they landed on him like great splats of rain.

"Well, what have we got here?" She looked him over, squinching her eyes and raising her eyebrows simultaneously.

"What are you staring at, Shorty? Ain't you ever been to a ten-in-one show?" He felt like spitting just to keep her from encroaching, but his mouth rattled dry.

"They hire you for your poison tongue?"

"I reckon they would if they hired you on account of your personality."

"Not bad," she said, looking right at him. "I always appreciate a quick wit. I suppose you figured it out already, but I'm Tiny. Welcome to Beasley World."

He sat, unmoved by her introduction. She exuded none of the frantic need of the women who used to cluster around him, nor did she possess the unassuming charm of Jack Reynold's wife, Erma, back at Kimball's Traveling Emporium.

"Thanks," he muttered.

"You got those scales on your pecker?"

"What's it to you?" If he'd had a tail, he would have flicked it by now.

"Just making conversation, that's all."

"Not hired to talk. That's why I came here."

"Suit yourself then, Lizard." She winked, then strutted off.

The name stuck. A handful of other shows had performers with alligator skin, so Earl Beasley liked the variation of "Lizard Man." He had the signpainter draw a great green and brown-flecked tail coming out of Julian's green satin shorts, and an elongated snout in lieu of a nose.

"What'd you paint me like that for?" Julian asked, shocked at the image unfurled on the midway.

Stan Beasley snorted. "To draw folks in. You ever work a sideshow before?"

"Six years with Kimball's Traveling Emporium. Didn't your brother tell you that?"

"Well, what kind of sign did you have there?"

"I was an angel, supposed to receive messages from the Lord."

"Didn't want to do that here?"

"No, sir. I signed an agreement with you folks. I don't do nothing but get stared at on account of my scaly-ass skin. I'll be out of here tonight if anyone tries something different." Julian popped up his head and clenched his fists. "Personally, I don't cotton to the picture."

"Flipper Boy sits in a pool all day like he's part seal, so of course we're gonna draw you with a tail. Don't be stupid on us, Lizard. After all them years in the business, you know same as I do, it's all in the presentation." Stan backed away as if he'd stepped in dog shit. "Besides," he continued, half smirking, "everybody's prettier on the sign."

At least at Beasleys' he got his own trailer, but with Jesse dying that last summer at Kimball's, the nocturnal emptiness circled like flame licking stone. He almost asked if he could bunk in with the Strong Man or Anders, the sword swallower, but he couldn't bear the thought that either would reject him, so he endured the long nights alone, watching the others form attachments or set off to visit the whores in town.

The only comfort came during the fraternity of waking hours. Here, the other performers no longer viewed him as a child, so they offered cigarettes and liquor. Tattoo Man invited him to play cards. Lizard detected no distinction between those whose appearance earned them a living and those who depended on an unusual skill. And while the company prohibition of relations among workers curtailed blatant activity, he sensed some members of the troupe maintained liaisons all along.

His only visit to a brothel, accompanying Tattoo and Anders, proved disastrous. The seven women sitting in the parlor snickered when he arrived, three of them jumping up to surround Anders with his tall, Swedish good looks. A small brunette woman sidled up to Tattoo, who was almost fifty, but no one approached him. The madam flicked her head at a homely blonde with a mole above her right eye. Finally, the woman advanced, her sigh audible. Maybe she was new to the trade, he told himself, as he stood there, waiting for her to touch him, to lead him by the hand as the other women had done with his companions. Her eyes burned hot as white coals.

"Follow me," she said, her hands tight at her side.

Once inside the tiny room with its bed shoved against the wall, she quickly closed the door.

"This some sort of initiation ritual?" she asked.

"For who?" he said, arms dangling, groin aching at the possibility of touch other than his own.

"Me, for Godsake. Is this what Miss Martha does to all the new ones, call you in here? If we can do you, we can do anything type-of-deal?"

He sniffed her perfume. Sweet like tea with too much sugar and no mint.

"What's the matter, you don't talk?" she asked, still standing as far away as the room permitted.

"I been talking all my life. I'm ready to rest now."

"How much money you got?"

"Twenty-seven dollars."

"I'll give you that much back if you let me alone. Please, mister. I'm real new to this."

"You ain't much to look at either, not like them other girls."

"I could talk to you real dirty or maybe you could lie under a sheet and I could touch you through that."

"You're worse than my father, pathetic drip of piss he was."

"You did this kind of thing with him?" The color drained from her face.

"I'm not a monster, you little twat. Just not blessed with any more looks than you." He grabbed the door handle, the heat rising in his ears.

The door banged open as he exploded into the hall, his stride swallowing the floor until he got out, pushing past the madam, who tried to intercept him at the front door. "To hell with you and your ugly-ass whores," he spat as he reached the threshold. "I'm going to buy me a drink."

He realized he'd have to come back to meet up with Tattoo and Anders, but he wandered around for the better part of an hour first, the minutes ticking, his member drooping, the whore's disgust bitter as bad moonshine on his tongue.

Lizard stood at the edge of the agricultural exhibit hall, the *baa*s emanating from the other side. Bass *baa*s and alto bleats, so many in rapid succession he wondered what was going on. It was early, barely six, the sky bruised by the distant threat of rain. He scanned the building, raising his eyelids as if to chase the sleep still lingering there. In the far-right corner, a corral of sheep huddled, baying at no one in particular as he moved along the outskirts until he could see their faces, coal eyes set in black muzzles and white, following his movements as he neared. The rams penned in isolation across the room shifted, shooting their rat-a-tat bleats at him. Lizard stood his ground, edging closer to a ewe, her wool pressing against the side of the pen. Nostrils flaring, she sniffed as he extended his hand. Slow as ice melting, Lizard unfurled his fingers and waited as she sniffed, her breath humid against his skin. Caught momentarily in the delicate grip of her mouth, the damp heat, the gentle bite of her teeth, her tongue traveling the shank of his thumb, tingles rose across the nape of his neck. Her jaw loosened and she began to lick his palm. Sensations the color of peach flesh rippled through him, orange-gold filling him like summer rain. She cocked her head as he scritched her wool, his fingers massaging her skin as they gravitated toward her rump. He bent over the rail and dropped his head so he could feel her wool brush his cheeks. He slid his hand around the slope of her belly to the warm teats. The expansion and contraction of her breath traveled up his arm, into his chest, until his own breathing matched hers. For a moment, time evaporated into that one stream of breath, short then long.

That night, Lizard squatted by the fire, its flames biting the night sky. Tattoo and the Strong Man stood near him, roasting wieners on a stick. Lizard lifted the bottle of gin next to him and took a sip.

"You sure you don't want a wiener?" Tattoo asked.

"Yeah, I'm sure." He nursed the gin and lit a cigarette instead.

"You get teased when you were a boy?" the Strong Man, a fellow by the name of Tommy, asked.

"What kind of question is that?" Lizard demanded, his thighs beginning to burn.

"Just curious. I don't really see where skin like that would be of much interest to people. But I figured younguns would be apt to say something unkind."

He felt the warmth of his early morning encounter flicker, then get swallowed into the center of the flame.

"You ever hear of Isaac?" he said, his gaze trained on the fire. "His daddy Abraham was prepared to sacrifice him to show his devotion to God. Dragged that boy up a mountain and drew his knife. The Lord let Abraham slay a ram instead."

He didn't see Tommy roll his eyes at Tattoo. He just held an empty stick over the fire and let it drop, its shape mutating at the whim of flame. "It's in Genesis, Chapter Twenty-two. An angel appeared, called out to Abraham. Isaac's heart must have been pounding by this time. Bible never tells how he felt."

"How's that tie in to you?" Tattoo asked.

"Imagine being lashed down like that by your own father." Lizard drew on his cigarette.

"You better eat something, Lizard. That gin's gone straight to your head." Tommy held out a roasted wiener impaled on a stick.

Lizard stepped back, his heel wobbling as he shifted his weight. He shut his eyes and pictured the agricultural hall. The smell of the flock returned. "I reckon there's a little bit of God lurking in every sheep."

"You sure you don't want something to eat?" Tommy waved the wiener.

"I told you I'm not hungry."

"Maybe you better get some sleep." Tattoo smiled, the line of his lips hazy through the flame.

Lizard flicked the butt of cigarette into the fire and drained the last bit of gin. He felt a dribble slide down his chin over the lump in his throat.

"Night, fellows," he mumbled as he staggered away, aching for the sound of God's voice, willing to settle for the touch of a kindhearted whore. He fell across the bed in his darkened trailer, mumbling for long gone Jesse, the sound of his own voice breaking, the scent of the ewe lingering pale yellow in his hand.

TINY LAVEAUX

Tiny Laveaux was the only performer in the oddities pavilion who had more than one costume, since hers took up less cloth. She reached into the steamer trunk she used as a bureau and put on her brown-and-yellow checked suit that drove Ernie "Hammer Toe" Morton wild.

Before a mirror hung six inches from the floor, she pulled the top off her lipstick tube and applied Damson Delight. She blotted her lips, tossed the hanky back into her trunk, and then climbed onto the straightback chair by the window. No sign of Hammer Toe. She hated waiting, but anticipation fanned the flames.

They had discovered the pleasures of pre-show *rendezvous*, excitement building as they snuck into a trailer midday.

A knock startled her. "Who is it?" she called.

"Earl."

Her stomach tightened. Quickly, she scanned the trailer for any tell-tale signs. "Come in."

He pushed the door open, his frame filling it.

"What brings you here?"

"Tell me the rumors aren't true." He stepped in and shut the door.

"What rumors?"

"It's a tight group. That's why I don't want any pairs. Mind if I sit?"

She shook her head. As he deposited himself in the straightback chair, she prayed Hammer Toe wouldn't show up now.

Earl looked like his eyes were about to roll off his cheeks. "Coupling can lead to hard feelings."

"More like sour grapes, Earl. There's no reason to make each piece of fruit sit in its own bowl." Only Tiny called him Earl. Everyone else addressed Big Earl as Mister.

"The rules are there to protect you. I don't want you at the mercy of some fella twice your size." Earl pulled at the crease in his trousers, then reached into his shirt pocket for a cigarette.

"What makes you think I need protection? I may be short, but I'm not a child." She stood tall as she could, puffing her chest, jaw jutting, hands balled into fists.

"Is that why the good Lord made you so short, Tiny? Because you can out-boss a man?" Earl cocked his jaw as he inhaled. A clump of ash fell like gray snow.

"Maybe I got bossy on account of being small. Folks run right over me if I don't speak up. Now what did Lizard Man tell you? I know he's the only one talking because that's the only thing he has to do." She watched the smoke waft toward the open window, grateful it wouldn't settle in her carefully curled hair.

"You're not the only midget, you know."

"I know that. I'm not stupid, and neither are you. We both know you aren't apt to find a midget and a nursemaid for Flipper rolled into one. How many dwarves you know want to wipe a seal boy's ass? You go hiring Miss Low and Mighty from the circus, I can promise she won't stoop to cleaning shit."

"You got a mouth more colorful than Tattoo's back." He had to admire the way she strung together her words.

"Well, give me a megaphone and I'll talk at the crowds, too. Then you can call me Miss Three-for-One. Meanwhile, you better keep that rat-mouth reptile of a man away from me."

Earl pushed the window open farther and flicked the ashes out. "You're the nerviest female I ever met. If I didn't know better, I swear you got balls under that dress."

"Too bad you got a policy that won't let you find out."

"I don't want you fraternizing with Hammer Toe."

"Why not?"

"Company policy."

"That policy already cost you a top-notch sword swallower. And an armless man with Hammer Toe's talents won't be so easy to replace." Tiny took a few steps back and then sashayed down an imaginary runway.

"You know the crowds love me, so why are you stirring up the pot?"

"We live too close for bad feelings. Season's just started. We got fifteen more towns to play. Word gets out one fella's getting something another's not, there's bound to be trouble. Not to mention a line outside your door, and believe me, I won't stand for that. In case you've forgotten, it's a carnival, not a bordello, I'm running here."

"You really believe all these healthy males gonna play poker all night for the rest of their lives?"

"They can go into town to satisfy themselves." He stood. "I got my eye on you, Tiny." His words were always bigger, higher, so they fell, fat drops of water on her head.

Soon as he disappeared from sight, she crept out, cutting through the web of trailers, thrashing through the weeds, infuriated by Earl's inability to fathom the same river of need coursing through a body half his size.

"Every animal mounts," Hammer Toe had announced during their first *rendezvous*. "Even snakes and mice. So why shouldn't we?" She wholeheartedly agreed, though the comparison to rodents and reptiles annoyed her. At three-foot-two, she got compared to low-moving creatures enough as it was. Besides, animals mounted to multiply, but people did it for pleasure. That's what elevated them.

As she neared Hammer Toe's trailer, she sighted Bettina, the Bearded Lady, in her oversized undershirt and cut-off trousers, coming down the path.

"Hey there, Tiny. Aren't you hot in that suit?"

"Naw. Cooler closer to the ground. You been down to the chow tent yet?"

"Yeah. Flipper's still there."

Tiny hadn't told Bettina about Hammer Toe, but she suspected she knew along with all the other oddities. Most didn't care or even comment, but Bettina had a way of acknowledging things sideways, as if the truth spoken directly would slice her clean through.

"I'll be back in time to get him ready."

"You didn't sign up to be his mother. You do more than your share."

"Breaks my heart to see him here. Course he'd be locked up otherwise, but he's such a sweet boy."

"He's lucky to have you." Bettina looked into the distance, above Tiny's head. "I got to help Beulah get ready. Have fun."

Tiny nodded, wishing she could say the same. It had to be ghastly emptying the world's fattest woman's slop jar. Not that Beulah wasn't sweet; she was. And patient, always waiting for Cheever and Ewell to wheel her around while they made snide comments about her size. How stupid could they be? Beulah didn't eat herself fat anymore than they'd made themselves black or she'd shrunk herself small. That's what she liked about Hammer Toe; he understood the mysteries of birth, how some were just destined to be different.

Her pace quickened as she neared his trailer. She scrambled up the steps and tapped on the door. He opened it with his right foot, balancing easily on his left. She scuttled in and struck a pose.

"You look ravishing, my dear. I love you in that checked suit, brings out the color in your hair." Hammer Toe lifted his right leg and stroked her face with his big toe. A smile fluttered across her lips. She held his foot like a goblet, sipping from the edges, then blowing tiny bubbles into the sole. Hammer Toe let her finish the greeting before suggesting they move to the bed, where he slid his toe along the collar of her jacket, nudging it from her shoulders. Sunlight doused them. "I wish we didn't have to work today."

She smiled at the thought of an entire afternoon luxuriating in his touch. On Sunday, when blue laws forced the show to close, they could disappear during "boil up," when everyone washed their clothes and bathed. Or maybe in Atlanta when Earl promised them all a few nights in a hotel. Meanwhile, Tiny lifted his left foot in her hands, each toe a grape she nibbled from the vine. She pressed her thumbs against his arches and fluttered her eyelids across his instep as if a thousand monarch butterflies had come to land. The heat rising, she slipped off her skirt and slithered up his legs, straddling his waist. Hammer Toe soughed. Tiny lifted his undershirt and nuzzled his belly, her kisses forming a trail up his chest. She traced the knobs of his shoulders with her tongue, fingers playing the keys of his back while her feet sought their own ledge of pleasure.

They purred and panted. Tiny let out the *ooo* of a cat dreaming deep as Hammer Toe stroked her feet with his, traveling up her shortened calves, over her soft behind, the length of his foot extending almost the entirety of her back. With his powerful toes he kneaded her muscles and tickled her neck. She rolled over, her soft belly an invitation. As Hammer Toe stretched across her to reach a jar of cherries he'd won in a bet, she felt weightless as lavender spanning the horizon.

Hammer Toe shut his eyes. The cherries Tiny hid in her crevices bled sticky juice, mingling with the sweetness seeping from her pores. While he searched for them, she dangled the ostrich feather he kept on the wall beside his bed, letting the plume whisper secrets into whatever skin it grazed. He joyously traveled the terrain, tasting yellows brushed with gold, the mossy dampness of ferns, the soft needles of fir, until he found the last sweet bulb tucked inside her own damp folds.

Tiny lay awash in a sea of azure and emerald as violet lapped at her head.

"You think Flipper Boy's all right?" Hammer Toe whispered, stroking the side of her face with his nose.

"Hmm?" The sound rolled out, her words suspended.

"The boy, you think he's all right?"

Her eyelids fluttered. She rolled onto her side, burrowing her nose in his ribs.

"It's almost one. I'm just wondering if he's all right."

Tiny stirred, his words a branch scraping the window.

"I'd love for you to stay a while, but if Ewell brings him back from lunch, and you're not there, won't he worry?"

"He knows I'll be back," she mumbled, still clinging to the last tendrils of pleasure, wishing she could stay and nap in the sunlight pooled on Hammer Toe's bed.

She could feel him nibbling at her neck, his breath warm.

She exhaled, letting herself drift back to shore.

When she approached her trailer, Ewell's whistle met her like an on-coming train. She darted inside and stood at the door waiting.

"Where you been, Ewell? Time it took, I thought maybe you'd carried Flipper on up to Memphis to eat."

"Mm-hmm. Wouldn't you have liked that?"

"What's that supposed to mean?"

"I got eyes in this colored head."

"Watch what you say."

"I watch what I say, you watch what you do." Ewell held Flipper Boy over the four-foot bed that matched Tiny's.

"Let me get the changing sheet." Tiny grabbed the tarpaulin from the crate of diapers on the floor, positioning it as Ewell lowered Flipper onto the bed.

"How you doing, sweetheart?"

"Okie-dokie-smokie. We had grilled cheese."

"That sounds good. I like pimento cheese sandwiches better. What about you, Ewell, you like pimento cheese?"

"That's cracker food, Miss Tiny. I'll be back at two to fetch him. You gonna be here then?"

"I'll be here waiting, just like I was now."

Ewell turned and crossed the trailer in one step, his broad back filling the two-foot-wide door. Tiny looked at Flipper Boy, body like a furless seal. Boy'd have prune skin by the time he was ten. Unfastened his diaper and slid it out from under him.

"What's black and white and red all over?" She patted him with a dry cloth and sprinkled powder all over his crotch.

"A newspaper."

"No, silly, a sunburned zebra." She watched the grin bloom, wishing she could humor him more. Not much to laugh at, sitting in a pool of tepid water all day, watching folks point and gasp in your direction. No life at all. At least she had Hammer Toe, but there were no mermaids for Flipper Boy.

She coated him with baby oil, then tugged his rubberized pants into place. His costume consisted of a one-piece suit designed to accentuate his fleshy fins. She climbed up on the bed and then stretched out beside him. "We got a few minutes before showtime. You want a story or a song?"

"A song, but make up the words."

"What you think I am? World's quickest wit?" She stroked his hair, then his face. "They pay me to be short, not fast." He smiled at her caresses. No different from her. Needed touch just like everybody else.

"Let me think of a tune." She shut her eyes and breathed a hum to her lips. She let it wind its way out like smoke undulating from a candle before she gave it any words.

> *Somewhere deep in the ocean*
> *Somewhere far out to sea*
> *I know Poseidon's a-watching*
> *his land-son take his leave.*
> *But one day, he'll rise up to meet him*
> *come rolling in like a wave,*
> *he'll hold him close to his bosom*
> *and take him back home to play.*

Tiny watched the oxygen fill his chest, hoping somewhere he still had gills. She kissed his forehead. His eyes fluttered shut, breath sweet. She sat on the bed with him, waiting for Ewell to return, wondering if Flipper Boy would ever find someone to frolic with.

As a child, she'd played with the crevices of another girl, where she learned the first two rules of sexual excitement: anticipation and friction. As a teenager, shortly after her breasts began to form, a friend of her father's, a man named Fred with thinning hair and yellowed horse teeth, used to pick her up and sit her in his lap as if she were still four or five. She always wondered why her father didn't intervene, tell him to put her down, that she wasn't some china doll, but her father just smiled limply and carried on the conversation, usually some prelude to a business deal. Her father operated a small but efficient still and distributed his liquor across the state. With most counties dry and the national temperance movement blazing beyond the soft Kentucky hills, he did a brisk business. Moonshining yielded more money than crops, and there weren't pickers to worry about. Just Fred and the other long or round-faced men who sat in the front room of the small log house her grandfather had built, swilling down the fiery liquid as if it were water, clutching her tender bosoms as if they were dice.

When Tiny overheard her neighbor Ma Bailey talking about the circus in some faraway city where her son had run off to join the sideshow, she sidled up to her and asked how she could join. Ma Bailey, so named for her thirteen children and the six or seven strays she'd gathered from her sisters or the orphanage, looked down at Tiny and then bent her crooked back so she could see into Tiny's eyes, a trait that unnerved most, but not Tiny, who rarely met an adult's gaze with her own. "What you want to join the circus for?" Ma Bailey asked.

"To get the hay out of here," Tiny whispered. With that, Ma Bailey scribbled down the name of the circus and the address where she wrote her son, who had somehow cashed in on his elastic hair. All of Ma Bailey's children boasted something different, but to her, the peculiarities didn't stand out. "You have enough of anything," Ma told her, "you get variety."

Tiny spent the next two years plotting her escape. Her mother, Henrietta, spent her days prone, an embroidered cloth across her eyes, the family quilt tucked under her chin. Bearing Tiny, whom she named Constance Grace Picklesimer, tuckered Henrietta out. When she realized her first child would remain small, she refused to have any more, afraid other afflictions might follow, like biblical plagues. She retreated to dimly lit rooms where her husband's curses fell soft as drizzle against the walls.

The house heaved under layers of dust that settled on surfaces above Tiny's head and beyond her father's scope of attention, so he hired any one of Ma Bailey's daughters to cook and clean. No one in town or along the row of farms that checkered the landscape she roamed cared about her size. They had grown accustomed to her, whispering at first, but Tiny developed a mean throw early on, rocks flying like buckshot from her small hand. She earned the distance the would-be taunters kept, and the other children who might have regarded her as the perfect companion—the one they could boss around—quickly learned she bossed them, as if from an invisible throne.

Help came in the shape of a sharply dressed man named Beasley selling patent medicines. Luckily, she answered the door. Her father had gone into town and her mother was resting like she had for the past twelve years. Beasley tried to sell her a tonic to increase vigor and height. Tiny knew better. None of the concoctions her mother had fed her as a child nor the root woman's conjures had made a bit of difference. She could smell the snake oil on him. He insisted she try a bottle of his curative free of charge. She thanked him, then watched him leave, the dust from the horses and wagon swirling like glitter before it fell.

She thought he was crazy the second time he knocked on the door three years later, grinning like a jackass when she opened it and he found her same as before. Told her least he could do since the remedy had failed was to hire her for his new endeavor, a traveling circuit of carnival amusements, complete with the South's largest assortment of natural wonders. He had already contracted the services of three previous customers, and he had more calls to make. He would provide her room, board, and a small wage, but more importantly, he gave her a ticket out.

She kissed her father's cheek and her mother's clammy hand and packed one of her father's wooden crates faster than she could wriggle her way out of groping Fred's lap. Better than any tonic was a chance to travel off the mountain in an automobile. On the brink of 1911, she took the stage name of Tiny Laveaux and rode off with a man who promised to make her famous, billing her as the world's smallest woman, although Ringling Bros. and Barnum & Bailey boasted a much shorter pair of midgets. Little matter to Tiny, who never made it to the circus, or to the throngs of farmers who would file past her. Located next to the fat lady's booth, Tiny appeared little enough.

ᘛ

At breakfast Lizard Man leered, then looked away. Truly reptilian. And bitter. There was nothing worse. Rumor had it he couldn't buy a woman's services with a whole month's pay. A whore'd have to be mighty hungry to rub her tired flesh against his scales. She eyed him suspiciously as the pool of grits and butter spread across her plate. He hissed at her. "I seen what you done."

"That makes you a lucky bastard then, don't it?"

"I'm gonna tell Mister Earl you leave that boy alone."

She studied his face: eyes the color of dirty dishwater, his putty nose flaky, hair combed back, greased to a viscose sheen.

"You'd best to mind your business, Lizard tongue." She thought of flicking a spoonful of grits in his face, but set her mind to plotting a much worse fate for him instead. If only he were bluffing, but she could sense he wasn't. He had squealed before, about her beloved Anders, the sword-swallowing Swede who used to lift her over his head and set her high on his broad shoulders, her short arms clutching his blond head.

Ace, who operated the penny arcade, had warned Anders not get distracted or look too happy in front of the others, but the noises emanating from his trailer enticed Lizard Man to sit outside, waiting to see who entered or left, and sure enough, when he spotted Tiny leaving at three in the morning, humming the melody of a Swedish tune, her compact body shivering with pleasure as she scampered back to her trailer, he ran off to tell Earl. By the end of the week, Anders was gone. Joined another show without so much as a farewell tryst.

She spotted Ewell wheeling Flipper Boy down to breakfast, strapped in his chair. She caught Lizard looking at the boy, then cutting his squirmy gaze over to her. "Think about it," he said, the words landing between them like cow flops.

"You're enough to make a person lose her appetite. Why don't you wander on over to the agricultural exhibit and find you a sheep?"

"Tiny Laveaux, you're in for it now." Lizard pushed the last triangle of toast into his mouth and rose, wiping his buttery fingers on his pants. Ewell brought Flipper Boy to the end of the table where Tiny sat.

"Good morning, good looking," she said to the boy.

"You talking to me?" Ewell asked.

"You wish. Hey Ewell, want to do me a favor?"

"Not if it means getting in the middle of you and him." He poked his head in Lizard's direction.

"Come on, when you were a boy didn't you ever like to yank a lizard clean out of its tail?"

"I know you freaks think us colored are dumb, but you're wrong. Nothing uglier than a freak sandwich with a poor colored man wedged as meat. No ma'am, Miss Tiny, I don't intend to get mixed up in your trouble. Ewell don't see nothing. Don't say nothing." He bent down and spoke to Flipper Boy. "You hungry, Flipper? You best tell your midget mama it's time to eat." Ewell turned on his heels, hands slicing through the air as if he were wiping them. "Cheever," he called across the chow tent and up the path, and then he was gone.

Now she was ticked at both of them, although she couldn't blame Ewell for steering clear. If she were in his position, she'd do the same thing. But Hammer Toe's kisses were far too sweet to lose on account of a jealous reptile and a spineless colored man.

She thought she had Ewell Sunday night when she heard him coming back to the fairgrounds, his familiar whistle wafting up the path. She had just left Hammer Toe's trailer and decided to walk back the long way to avoid running into Lizard. As Ewell neared, the smells of bootleg liquor, sex, and cheap perfume stretched between the two of them. She thought of trying to scare him, pretend she was a haint, but drunk as he was, he didn't strike her as that gullible. And much as she wished, she doubted he'd ever believe she was a leprechaun or a voodoo woman.

"Evening, Ewell," she whispered in the dark.

"Who's that?" He looked around but not down.

"Tiny Laveaux."

He lowered his gaze, pupils dilated enough to find her. "What you doing out here?"

"Same thing as you I reckon, heading home."

"They talking, you know. Liable to run off No-Arm the way they got rid of that big blond bohunk of yours."

She started to chide him, but she needed information. "It's Lizard, ain't it? Earl ought to paint him on his sign with a big forked tongue."

"He ain't getting any. You know that. Make a man like him even uglier not to sink his business into some sweet baby every now and then."

The crickets in the fields hummed behind them as they walked.

"I still miss Anders, even if he didn't tell me goodbye."

"I don't reckon he had much chance."

"You ever leave somebody behind?"

"Left me a no-good knot of a wife, skinny as string. Wasn't but sixteen."

"You or her?"

"Her. I was fifteen and a half. My Aunt Mary told me get one while they young. Get my babies early so I got help in the fields. But I didn't want them fields. Didn't want no babies either, not out of her. She too quiet. Set down my plate and stared like she seen Jesus, 'cept she might squealed at the sight of him."

"When'd you leave her?"

"Nineteen-oh-two."

"Nooo."

"Did too. Left her three months after we got married. Jumped a train to Memphis and never looked back. Ain't heard tell of her in fifteen years."

"You think she still misses you?"

"I hope not 'cause I don't miss her. Don't miss them fields neither." They reached the tent the colored workers shared. "Go on now, Miss Tiny, don't let 'em catch you around here."

"Night, Ewell." She scurried back up the path and cut through the field to the oddities' encampment. The moon hung like a cake pulled hot from the pan, its top edge missing. Her shadow fell across the steps of the trailer as she climbed them. She'd never tell so as not to swell his head, but she liked Ewell all right. Deep down she figured he wasn't much different, escaping some big-eyed, quiet girl the way she'd escaped her ailing mother and roving-hand Fred. They'd both signed on with Beasleys' in search of a little adventure and a better life.

Sticky from relations with Hammer Toe, Tiny dunked a washcloth in the basin of water she kept on the floor under Flipper Boy's bed. She unzipped her skirt and drew the cloth between her legs, then brought it to her nose, breathing in the scent of pleasure that lingered on her skin. Stepping out of her clothes, she pulled her nightdress from beneath her pillow but didn't put it on. In the velvet folds of night, she stood naked in the trailer for a moment. Her skin still fiery, she slid into bed, drinking in the coolness of the sheets.

The next morning at the chow tent Ewell wheeled Flipper Boy to the table. She could tell Ewell's head throbbed.

"Get you some Coke syrup from concessions. It'll ease the banging." She pointed to her temple.

Ewell started to nod, then braced his head.

"Go on, I'll feed Flipper Boy." Tiny gestured for Ewell to leave, but no sooner had he turned to go, Earl Sr. strode up.

"Why, Earl, you're just in time for breakfast." She smiled. He didn't.

"You can get yours later, Tiny. We need to talk." He motioned with his index finger as if she were attached by invisible string.

"Flipper needs to eat."

"Ewell can feed him, can't you?"

"Uh, yes, sir."

Tiny shrugged, head tilted in apology to Ewell.

"Tiny, you come with me." Earl Beasley marched toward his trailer. Tiny followed, certain he lengthened his stride just to make her trot.

He climbed the two stairs with one step, then turned and waited for her to hike herself up each one.

She hoisted herself on the chair in his office, trying to muster all of her charm. He stood in front of her, leaning against the edge of his desk, looming.

"I bet it's warmer up there, isn't it? It's cooler low to the ground."

"I didn't call you in here to talk about the weather. I don't want you wrecking this show's morale."

"Tell that to Lizard Man. He's the one snooping. Makes everyone nervous. He'll crawl right down your shirt into your drawers. Ask anybody else. They'll tell you. He makes stuff up. Has to amuse himself some way. Not a whore in town will touch him. I'm telling you, Earl, he's poisonous. You ought to advertise him that way. 'Previously unidentified species—half lizard, half man—from deep in the jungle of the Amazon with a bite that can kill. Step right up, but don't get too close.' Hell, Earl, you ought hire me to talk."

"Hire you, hell. I ought to fire you for instigating trouble."

"I'm not bothering anybody. He is."

"You're violating my policy."

"You got no proof. I'm telling you, Lizard lies. Ask anyone. He's lonely."

"That's exactly my point."

"Then hire a Lizard Woman. Or find some other oddity that'd cotton to the likes of him. Then you'll have a married pair like some of the other shows have."

Earl reached behind and pulled a cigar from the box on his desk. She watched as he bit the tip off and plucked it from his tongue. He had a way of staring down at her, the only time she felt small.

"I don't need you to tell me how to run my show." Earl lit the cigar, puffing till the smoke formed a cloud around her head.

Tiny stood on the chair seat. "I'm your best act. Folks love how lively I am."

"If I find out you're lying, you'll be vamping somewhere else."

"Go ahead, ask around. Meanwhile, just remember who's been bringing in the crowds for the last seven years. There's a war on, Earl. Folks need entertainment and you need a crowd."

"I could do with one less mouth to feed."

Tiny dropped to her rump and shoved off the chair. She straightened herself, eyes rolled up to meet his. "Then I better finish my breakfast while I can."

At the lip of the door, Tiny turned back. "You were singing a different tune when you lured me off the mountain, Earl. Just remember I knew you when you were peddling snake oil." She let the screen door slam behind her.

When she got back to the chow tent, Flipper Boy had finished breakfast. She spotted Ewell on the other side, talking to Ernie, one of the colored cooks. She sidled over and tugged at Ewell's trouser leg.

"What you want, short stuff?"

She smiled up at him, hand cupped over her eyes as a visor. "I reckon Earl might talk to you since you're around us all day." She bit the inside of her lip. "I'll owe you big on this."

Ewell looked down. "You ain't got to worry." Ewell winked at Ernie, half swallowing his words. "Just don't let me see the likes of you crawling on top of that no-arm man. Lordamercy, a sight like that could blind a fella."

Tiny let the comment pass unattended. She couldn't fault a man for a limp imagination. She just pitied him.

YOUNG BETTINA

The dreams started coming shortly after the hair. Initially, Bettina thought little of the whisper of fuzz across her upper lip, but once the hair darkened and spread from chin to cheek—in her sleep, old women with lined faces stared at her curling hair winding its way into her lap, creeping around her ribcage, weaving a tapestry across her stomach, threatening to grow between her legs and along her back. Children lurked near the penny-candy jars at the company store—boys pointing, lobbing taunts; girls whispering, turning away. Men blocked the doorway, even the windows, leaving no way out. The air lay heavy and hot, the sweat on her lip tangled in the hair.

When dawn finally broke outside the window, Bettina felt relief. She could wipe the perspiration on the sleeve of her nightdress and slip her feet to the cold floor. But once she was standing, the fog of sleep rolling away, she would always remember the hair. Without thinking, her fingers would travel up to her jawline and over her chin. She would feel a few more than the day before.

Luckily, she'd finished school before the hair had come. The coal company built the school same as they built the town, and her mother, Della, suspicious of anything connected to the mine, pulled Bettina out after eighth grade. She was glad to be done with school, the hours behind a tight little desk, staring at the backs of other children's heads, fingers sore from gripping the pencil, anxious not to make a mistake. The teacher had cut off all the erasers so every error had to be crossed out, then held up to the class.

She had still not gotten the blood like June, who was two years younger. June with her apple-smooth cheeks, who kept asking why Bettina had no bosom, only hair. June, asleep on the other side of the bed, her honey-colored hair spread across the pillow, her hand tucked under her perfect chin.

They lived beyond town on a swatch of land that had belonged to her mother's people for sixty years. Below the house were woods that stretched toward the hills. In the time it took the last evening light to leave the sky, she could make it to the creek in the woods that ran off the river. After her face began to change, she often found herself crouching on the edge of the bank, tugging up the roots that grew there, mirroring the dreams where miniature fairies yanked each chin hair, the pain making her call out "Mama," then "Jesus," though no one would hear. The Lilliputians stood on her chest, flat as it was, tying thread to each whisker, laughing as they went along. Their tiny feet would dig into her ribs and pinch her windpipe. When she woke, her fingers would travel the regions of her body to feel for bruises. Even when she was sure they had released her, the hair was still there.

It had been June who had shrieked one morning in bed, "Mama, come look. Bettina's got hair."

"Done cursed you, too," her mother had said, locking Bettina's face in her powerful hand, "unless this is His way of cursing me more." She'd turned her cheek as if inspecting a star dropped from the sky, and said, "Pray, child. Ask Jesus to wash your sins away."

So each night she lowered herself onto the roughhewn floor, imploring God to remove her sins and plaguing hair. Mornings when she woke, she got back on her knees, hands squeezed together till the tips of her fingers grew red and her knuckles glowed white. Visions of Eve throbbed in her head. That one minute in some garden biting into an apple, consigning women ever after to labor in fields of stone. Suffering passed from one generation to the next, a burden laid on each woman until she squatted and pushed it through her loins.

"God said 'Be fruitful and multiply,'" her mother intoned, face drawn like a wagon under a heavy load. "Then He give us the curse. Birthing children, our punishment for Eve's sin. Ain't ours to question. Just ours to bear."

The babies stopped coming after Arnold. Bettina watched her mother coil in pain, until Clem took her to see the company doctor, who told her she'd have to have her insides taken out. He explained the three miscarriages in between June and Arnold and told her to count her blessings because there'd be no more. She came from the hospital ragged as her worn coat. She whispered to Bettina, who was twelve at the time, "Won't miss my blood, but I hate not giving your daddy more sons." No mention of daughters, but then Bettina figured they were part of the curse, too. Why'd Eve make it so hard for all the rest? Didn't seem fair that she or her mother suffered for something someone else did, but the one time she asked her mama why God was so mean, Della had slapped her hard across the face and said, "He ain't mean. He's just God."

In the dream she could not see herself, only Him, tall as a mountain, white beard and robe flowing wide as the wind. "How dare you question me?" He boomed, the sound coming from all directions. She was smaller than an ant next to his sandal, and she knew His foot could come crashing down as she kneeled before Him, begging forgiveness, crying into the fabric of her own dress, snot running from her nose as she mumbled for mercy.

Before the hair, she asked God each night to forgive her for being made like Eve. When the hair came, and her chest stayed flat, she began to wonder if God was angry at her for something else she'd done. In her mind, she rattled through a catalog of possible sins: in school, she had taken a boy's apple after he threw it away half-eaten; she'd teased June and spilled her daddy's nails; sassed her mother and gotten slapped. But none of those seemed truly evil, just bad. Her mother had explained the difference: bad was naughty or unpreventable, a fib or a drought, but evil was blackness so deep that standing all day in the Jordan River couldn't wash the sin away. The mine was evil—gobbling men up as surely as they drew its riches out. Her mother came from farm people. To her it was evil to dig so far down that white men came up black, but she never spoke that way in front of Clem, the sixth man in his family to labor in the mine.

In another dream, Bettina rode down the shaft with him, miner's light strapped to her head, in coveralls, her face blackened by coal, listening for the canary he had told her about. Deep in the earth's private places, the hair began to grow. While the men chipped at the walls beside her, crawled through slender chutes, she crouched in the dark behind a coal wagon, feeling the stubble stippling the darkness.

She longed to slip her daddy's straight razor into her pocket without her mother noticing, but there were clothes to scrub, socks to mend, eggs to gather, no call for her to be poking around inside. Finally, late one afternoon, she managed to grab it and dart out to the creek. She reached the water winded from running so hard. A woodpecker hammered in the distance as she unfolded the blade. The metal glinted at her, its sharp edge beckoning. She rubbed her thumb across it, her mouth tightening at the thought of scraping it across her face.

Skin held taut, she lifted the blade. Unaccustomed to its heft, she gouged her skin along the jaw. Pain rose fast as blood beading on her cheek. The razor slipped from her hand into a clump of dried leaves. She wiped the blood but more took its place. Locking her jaw, she re-trieved the razor, raising it to her face. With her left index finger, she pressed the skin below her bottom lip, rolling it tight, and brought the razor down slowly over her chin. She guided the blade underneath and down her neck, where a few stray hairs had sprouted, then she set it down and ran her fingers over her skin. Except for the blood still oozing from the cut, her face felt smooth as the back of her hand. She pulled a kerchief from her pocket and leaned toward the water, dousing the cloth. The water stung, but she blotted the cloth against her cheek any-way. She had to get the razor back. Return before her mother's holler collared her. June would know instantly what she had done.

She kept the kerchief pressed to her jaw as she tore through the woods back to the cabin, one room with a curtain hung to make two. The wood smoke rose out of the chimney and hung in the crisp October air. She could hear Arnold sawing as she neared, his small arm bowing as the blade moved up and down. Unlike June, he would say nothing unkind. He still loved to run behind her, though he was catching up. In the evenings, they would arm wrestle and play a game of checkers while their mother sewed. Clem would play his banjo, and June would whisper to her rag doll, sitting on the bed.

The floorboards creaked as she entered the cabin. Her mother turned around.

"Where you been? Supper ain't gonna fix itself."

She held the kerchief to her face and prayed for God to take her then, to open the earth and swallow her deep inside, let her pass her daddy on the way down.

"What you done to your face, Bettina? Let me look."

"Nothing." She turned her face away. Her mother set down a spoon and approached like a cat twitching with the scent of mouse.

"You do that with a razor?" Her mother held her face, inspected it roughly.

"Yes ma'am." She stared at the floor.

"Damn fool, liable to slice your neck off. Better ask your daddy how to do it right." With that, her mother returned to the stove.

"What you want me to do for supper?" Bettina asked.

"Make biscuits. Wash your face first. There's some water in the pail over here." Her mother pointed. She followed her hands, pale as the lard she was spooning out. Chapped by lye and diapers, skin around the knuckles stiff and split. She looked at her own hands as she dipped them in the bucket. Skin smooth, nails clean, tendons jumping.

"You gonna stand there staring or get to work?" The words clunked against her feet, then skittered off.

"Coming," she muttered, wondering if her hands would stay the same.

In the dream, she did not recognize herself. She watched a woman with a billy goat beard sit crouched like an animal, scratching with her hind leg. Gray and white fur covered the young woman. Only her hands were normal. The barrel of a rifle extended out the window. She could hear her mother's voice screaming at her father. "Shoot the damn thing, Clem, before it tears up my garden." It wasn't until she sighted the bead at the end of the gun that she realized he was aiming at her.

The following Sunday, her father sat on the front steps made of flat stones he had arranged, while her mother, sister, and brother got dressed for church. Her father refused to go, which angered her mother no end, but he stood firm in his decision. He spent his days in darkness, returning home as the last light left the sky. Only on Sundays did he get the chance to sit outside and feel the sun on his skin. "No," he'd told Della the first time she asked why he didn't put his Sunday suit on, "I'll sit right here and say my prayers. He done said 'Let there be light,' and I aim to enjoy it." Her father used words the way he stacked rocks, each placed deliberately with as little wasted movement as possible. Her mother had *hmphed* and made her way down the steps in her good calico dress.

Bettina always accompanied her mother, her arms and legs gangly shoots that sprouted from beneath the plain cotton print that stingily covered her. The dress had belonged to her Aunt Lizzy, who stood half a foot shorter with an ample bust. On Bettina's shapeless torso, the dress hung like laundry, empty up top, too short on bottom. No one commented on the fit except her mother, who told her to stand up straight in the presence of God.

The morning sun fell generously on the front of the house. "I don't want to go today, Daddy. Let me stay here with you."

"That's between you and your mother," he said, eyes locked on the valley.

"Please, Daddy, tell her not to make me go. The other girls whisper things. And look at this dress. It's too short. They laugh at me, Daddy." Just once, she hoped he would speak up.

Her mother came bustling out the door with Arnold and June in tow. She and her father quickly moved to the edge of the stones. "Let's go,

Bettina. We ain't gonna get there with you hunched on them steps."

"Let me stay here with Daddy," she pleaded.

"I can't help that your daddy acts like a heathen, but I won't live to see my children take up his ways."

"I get one damn day of sunlight, Della. You can't begrudge me that."

"Church ain't but a hour and a half."

"By the time you get through gabbing it's longer than that."

"It's light in the church, Clem."

"I like the sun where I can feel it. Don't argue with me in front of the children. Just let me be."

Bettina watched her mother closely, the way her eyes squinted and her lips shrank.

"The day I see you in the mine, I'll go to church."

Bettina could almost see him brush his hands the way he did after setting the final stone in place.

"Come on, Bettina." Her mother beckoned with her hand.

"I ain't going, Mama. The others make fun of me."

"Ignore them. You need to hear the word of God."

"I'll pray here. I promise."

"Mama, we're gonna be late," June cocked her head to one side and set her hand on her hip like she was somebody important, not the younger daughter of a miner and his now-barren wife.

"Let her stay," said Arnold, tugging at the snug-fitting waist of his trousers.

Bettina listened to her own breathing, determined to wait her mother out.

"Suit yourself, but don't come near me with your devilish ways."

She watched her mother trundle off down the pike, handbag dangling from the crook of her meaty arm, broad feet wedged into her Sunday shoes. Della had insisted that the way one dressed in church would be noticed on Judgment Day. "The Lord God made the world and you gonna show up at His house dressed like you're slopping hogs?" she liked to say, arms crossed over her own full bosom. Then she would shove the dress at Bettina and wait right there while she put it on. She hated dressing in front of her mother, who stared at her chest, a popover gone flat. If only she had looked like June, she would have been spared her mother's glassy-eyed disappointment.

Bettina turned slightly to catch Clem studying her profile. "What you looking at me for?"

"Sorry," he said, yanking his head away, tongue rolling along the bottom edge of his upper teeth.

"I can't help it. It just started growing. I don't know why. I say my prayers."

He lifted his hand to his forehead like a visor and scanned the valley. The words unfolded slowly. "Your mama think everything got to do with that. Best not to argue with her, though."

"How come you don't believe like she does?" Bettina tugged the too-short dress toward her knees.

"Ain't got nothing against God. Just don't see why He save all the glory till after we're dead. Spend my life underground. One day of sunlight's all I ask and she calls me a heathen 'cause I don't go to church. Don't even know what it means, but it ain't nice."

"I think it's someone don't have God."

"Hmmph." The sound came out his nose. His mouth stayed closed.

"What do you do while Mama's at church?"

"Go into town."

"But nothing's open on Sunday."

"Don't matter. Peaceful just the same. I can walk around and look at things. Sometimes, though, I just stay here." He gave her a look like a boy at school about to ask her to dance. "Want to go for a walk in the woods?" It had been a long time, maybe years, since she had been alone with her father.

"Yeah, but let me change out of my dress." She rose to go inside. He slid over so she could open the door, and then sat there, waiting.

∽

As the summer foliage unfurled, the hair did too, thick as leaves. One Tuesday in July, she heard a car pulling up next to the house. Not too many folks had cars, and the ones who did used them to go far away, not across the hollow, so she crept up to the cabin and hunched behind it, listening. She could hear June pushing through the door and running into the yard.

"Compaannyy," June yelled, her voice extending like a kite caught on the wind.

A car door slammed. Just one. Then the sound of a man's voice. "Hi there," he said, sounding like he was from somewhere else. Bettina crawled to the edge of the house and tried to see, but the angle was wrong. Only the tail end of the car appeared in view. She could hear better, though.

"Hi there, yourself." She could tell June was trying her best to sound grown up.

"Aren't you a pretty thing. Mm-hmm. Tell me something, you got a sister?"

"Yeah. What you want to talk to her for?" She could tell June was aching to tell him what an ugly sister she had.

"Tell me something, sugar, that sister of yours got hair on her face?"

"How'd you know?"

"Word travels. Now tell me how much."

"A lot," June answered.

"We're in show business, my brothers and I. Beasleys' Traveling Amusements. We cover most of the South. Don't get up to Kentucky much. Lower states mostly."

"What kind of shows you put on?" asked June.

"Fairs, carnivals, and the like. We got rides, exhibits, and all kinds of attractions." He stretched his words like taffy. "Unusual talents, mysteries of nature, things like that."

"That's why you want my sister with her straggly beard. She ain't got no titties either." June sprinkled the words like she was feeding the hens. "I'll go get her for you." The gravel crunched under June's feet as she scrambled around the car to the back of the house. Bettina watched June look toward the woods, June's gaze traveling out and then down until it landed at her feet.

"There's a man here wants to talk to you."

"What for?"

"You know what for, squatting here listening."

"I don't want to talk."

"Why not? He might put you in a show."

She tried to imagine a circus, standing next to an elephant. "Tell him I ain't interested."

"Tell him yourself." June stalked off.

"Wait," she called. Her sister stopped, hand on her hip, all impatient. Bettina stood up and brushed off her hands. "You go first," she told June, "since you already met him."

She followed June to the man leaning against his car, his wavy hair the color of honey at the bottom of the jar. He had on fancy shoes coated with dust from the road, but she could tell they'd been polished right before. And he wore a brown suit fancier than any she'd seen. He smiled broadly but didn't show any teeth till he talked. "Well, hi there," he said, extending his hand. She wasn't sure what to do so she offered hers. He shook it hard, pumping like she was a man.

"Pleased to meet you. I didn't quite catch your name."

"It's Bettina," June answered quickly, like she was worried Bettina would swallow her own name and never get the word out.

"Ain't that pretty? Your mama name you that?"

"Yeah, Daddy, too," she said, just so he'd know she could talk.

"Well, Bettina, my name is Stan Beasley and I work with my brothers for the company our father started. I don't suppose you heard of us around here, but we travel all around the South—Mississippi, Georgia, Alabama, Louisiana, Tennessee—putting on fairs and carnival shows. We got all kinds of interesting acts."

"You got any animals?"

"There's agricultural exhibits. Livestock, horse pulls. We do have some animal oddities like the two-headed cow."

"What about elephants?"

"Why no, that'd be something you'd find with the circus. We got rides and a midway, not entertainment in rings. We got a Strong Man and a fellow who can knot himself like a pretzel and Flipper Boy and a fellow with lizard skin. Unusual talents and unlikely conditions. Folks pay good money to see that."

"Would folks pay to see me?"

"Absolutely," he said, fingering the lapel of his jacket, left eye trained on June.

"I better go get Mama," June said.

"You ain't got to get her yet." Bettina watched to see if he would keep eyeing June.

"How old are you, Bettina?"

"Sixteen."

"Well, in that case, might be best to speak with your mother if she's around. It would be a legal agreement, you know. If you want to join up."

"I'll get her," June volunteered as she bounced toward the door.

"What would it be like?" she asked.

"You'd have your own trailer to live in or maybe you'd share one at the start. You'd get a custom-made costume and on the days we travel, you get to relax. Mostly Wednesday through Saturday are performing days. You'd just sit there on a real comfy chair and let folks appreciate your unusual condition. No touching or rude remarks allowed. Strictly professional. You'd be a star attraction and we'd treat you as such."

The words fell over her. Before she could shake them off, he added more. "Let me ask you something while it's just you and me. Is folks here unkind? Any teasing?"

"Some. Mostly they stare."

"Precisely my point. Wherever you go, you'll be different and folks is apt to take a second look. So why not capitalize," he polished the word before he rolled the next ones out, "on your affliction? You see Beasley Brothers gives you a choice. You can stay here suffering, bringing shame to your family, or you can join up with us and meet other folks like yourself who've learned to make the most out of their misfortune. I can guarantee you, it's a better life than what you'll have here."

June returned with their mama. "After all," he continued, her wishing he'd stop, "what fella's gonna go for a girl like you? Your pretty little sister will be married in no time and you don't want your poor mother here having to fret over you her whole life." He turned to Della.

"Hi, there. Why, you look much too young to be these girls' mother. Allow me to introduce myself. Stan Beasley. It's a pleasure."

"What can I do for you?"

"Ma'am, my brothers and I run the largest traveling carnival show in the entire Southeast. As you know, most hardworking folks can't get to the city for entertainment, so we bring the fair to counties all across the lower South. We're always looking for new acts." He ran his hand over his hair. "I bet your daughter here hasn't been able to travel much, but she'd get herself an entire geography lesson firsthand. I already explained to her that she'd get private accommodations and a special costume."

"Would it be a dress?" her mother interrupted.

"Well, yes, ma'am, more of a gown, fancy-like. Probably red satin. Fitting for a motion picture star. Something Miss Joan Crawford could wear."

"I ain't see no Joan Crawford, but this girl could stand to appear more in a dress."

"You gonna let her go, Mama?" June asked, all bubbly.

"I don't see why not. Your daddy and I can't look after her her whole life. Can't get married with a face like that. Looks like a man. Might's well act like one and earn a living." Della took a rag out of her apron pocket and blew her nose. She looked right at Bettina. "I done told you the Devil took hold, and now you can see it's the truth. Sent one of his representatives to claim you." She turned to face Beasley. "You got carnal displays of the flesh?"

"We run a reputable operation, ma'am. Nothing unchristian about it."

"She was a real sweet baby. Always different though. Got along good with her brother. Ain't like her sister at all." She dabbed her eyes with the rag before she continued, "I thought the Lord had sent me enough, what with my condition. Must have done something terrible for her to turn out this way." Della sucked in the right side of her cheek and let her eyes drift toward the ground.

"If you don't mind me saying, ma'am, the Lord has His ways. Bettina here might just be one of God's mysteries, like that geyser they got in Yellowstone."

"I don't want her near anything carnal. Nothing nasty, you understand?"

"Ma'am, I wouldn't think of it. I promise. Did I mention my youngest brother preaches on the side?"

"Side of what? You don't do the Lord half-time. Now go on in and get your things, Bettina. We ain't got enough to feed this man supper. I'll wrap you something to go, unless you're going to feed her on the way."

"It might be a while till we stop."

"You letting her go without talking to Daddy?" June asked, her head turning from her mother to Bettina.

"What kind of life she going to have here? Won't go to church no more 'cause she thinks folks is talking. Christians ain't like that. Can't stop folks from staring. Might's well get paid."

"Can't I at least tell him goodbye?"

"You want to keep this fellow waiting?"

"I didn't know he was coming. Sir, you thinking I'd come along today?"

"It's a long way to Kentucky, so I was hoping not to make another trip."

"You heard the man. Now go and get your stuff." Della folded her arms tight across her chest.

Bettina filled an empty flour sack with some underthings and the old trousers Clem gave her to wear around the house. She took two shirts and a sweater her aunt had knit. She studied the small enamel box her mother gave her for her twelfth birthday, before everything soured. How could her mother give her something so precious and then send her away? She tucked the box in the bottom, wishing she had never caused her mother any grief. If only she could hug Arnold one last time. He'd gone down the road to play. She spotted his cap, wanting to take along something of his to comfort herself, but she couldn't take that. Then she noticed a small rag toy her grandmother had made him that he'd long since outgrown, a soft fox-like animal that fit in her hand. She grabbed it from the corner and wiped away the nest of dust. This way Arnold wouldn't have to grow up ashamed. What would the girl he'd marry think of having kin like her?

Her mother's voice splintered the quiet. "Girl, don't keep this man waiting." Bettina stuffed the toy in the sack and grabbed a handful of dried peaches from the jar above the stove. "Coming," she called back as she looked around one last time, wondering when she'd see the cabin again. Maybe Christmas they would send her home. Who went to fairs in the winter? Who went in the summer? At least she'd be far enough away from home none of the people she knew would come.

She pushed the screen door open and let it swing shut behind her. "All right, I'm ready. Can you tell Daddy and Arnold goodbye?"

"Yeah, I will." Her mother stepped forward and patted her on the arm, then leaned in close and whispered, "It's better this way."

June waved even though she was standing right there, a foot away. Glad to get rid of me, Bettina thought, wishing Arnold would come home. Maybe the man would drive by the company houses so she could look for him. But once she got in the car, she could feel his hurry.

"Got to reach the main roads before dark." He looked at her and then turned away.

"It'd only take a minute to tell Arnold goodbye. I didn't know you were coming. He'll be mad if I don't say goodbye."

"Where is he? I don't have time to stop at every shack we pass." The way he said "shack" gave her an uneasy feeling, like he was spitting out a peach stone before he'd sucked it clean.

"Just one row of houses where he'll be at, if we could drive by there." She pointed to the dirt road and he drove up it, scowling as if every speck of dust was scratching the paint on his car. She'd never ridden in a car, and at first the hurtling motion scared her, as if everything was disappearing too soon. He slowed the car to a crawl as she looked for Arnold, but he was nowhere to be found. He had probably gone off with the other boys to the gully or the gravel pit.

"You satisfied?" he asked.

She nodded, the words lodged in her throat. She missed him already and the thought of riding for hours, she didn't even know how long, with a strange man who was taking her far away suddenly overwhelmed her.

"Send him a postcard," he said as the dust rose behind them.

"I don't have money for that."

He reached into his coat and withdrew a wallet. It made her nervous that he took his hand off the wheel, but he pulled a dollar bill from between the folds and handed it to her.

She looked at the dollar, caught between the length of his fingers. "Go on, take it." He sounded irritated, so she pulled the bill toward her and folded it into the palm of her hand. She had never held a dollar bill. Her father had shown her a silver dollar, and on Sundays her mother gave her a dime to put in the basket at church. A few times, her father had taken her to the store and let her pick out five pennies' worth of candy. Now she was holding a whole dollar. Still, she wished, as her right fingers snuck up the side of her face and touched the hair, that her skin had stayed smooth like June's. She liked living with Arnold and June when they were all little, before her mother talked about the Devil and being cursed. Her mother cried a lot after she lost the babies, but it was Bettina's hair that turned her mother mean.

The car bounced over the bumps in the road, Stan Beasley muttering curses under his breath. The sky stretched black in front of her, with only the headlights piercing the dark. She prayed once more to wake from what felt like a horrible dream. Maybe she could run away when they reached Memphis and pay somebody to shave her beard.

In the car, she must have whimpered in her sleep. She dreamed of a man laughing as he drew the razor across her face, the dollar tucked in his pocket, asking what she planned to do the next day when the whiskers grew back. The men in the shop chuckled at the sight of her. The hoots and fingers pointing stung more than the tender skin splashed with aftershave. She gathered her coat and ran out onto the street, lined with people laughing. Never any escape.

She felt Beasley's hand on her arm shaking her awake. She looked at his profile and then out into the dark. Only then could she slip into the black, unnoticed as long as a bright moon didn't give her away. She looked at the floorboard and wiggled her toes to see if she could detect their movement. Barely. Somewhere, the Devil watched, laughing like the men in the shop. Soon, people would line up to laugh at her. Pay money, jingle coins in their hands waiting to see the girl with the hair on her face.

When they stopped for the night, pulling up in front of a rooming-house, she shut her eyes, hoping the darkness would shield her from anyone else's view. If she could not see them, maybe they would not see her. The woman who answered the bell didn't seem to notice. Maybe it had worked.

"Evening, Mr. Beasley," the gray-haired woman said. "Will rooms two and three suit you?"

"Be just fine." He smiled. "Don't worry about Miss Isabel," Beasley whispered as they walked down the hall. "She's seen some of our best acts. Here's your room. There's a toilet at the end of the hall. Now sleep well because we got a long day ahead."

She stood there for a moment, the night suddenly empty of the place where her family used to be.

"Go on then." He waved like he was shooing flies.

She entered the room. It seemed half the size of the cabin, with even surfaces and plumb lines. A bureau to one side, a freshly made bed pointing out from the wall. She stood in the smooth darkness, imagining what life would be like living in such a house with a flush commode at the end of the hall. She undressed quickly, afraid someone might come in, push the closed door open and see her standing there, spindly as the bedpost. With her nightshirt on, she knelt by the bed, hands clasped, head bowed. What was left to pray for, alone in the darkness in somebody else's fancy house? Much as she could feel her eyes pulled to admire the furnishings and the size of the place, a knot of terror thudded against her chest. She squeezed her hands tighter, her tongue searching for words. None came, but the fear crept around her ribs, tenacious as vines.

Peeling back the blanket, she lay beneath the sheet, head nestled in the feather pillow. She shut her eyes and hummed quietly, the notes of her mother's favorite hymn, "Old Ship of Zion," filling her head.

In her sleep, men lined the streets to see her, carrying flowers they tossed at her feet as she rode by, standing on a float pulled by her uncle's mule team. Little girls called her name, sending shimmering sounds into the sky. Arnold ran alongside tossing her candy, his cap waving in his other hand. Her father drove the mules, and when he glanced back to look at her she could see he'd scrubbed his face and ears till all the traces of coal were gone. He was wearing a Sunday suit with a dogwood blossom in his lapel, his cheeks floating above his smile. She held on to the wagon railing with one hand and waved to the crowd with the other. Below her, June stood on the street, scanning the crowd, her own dress plain, a single braid falling unadorned onto her back. At the end of the street, she could see a huge arch made of flowers and ribbon with a banner declaring "The Kingdom of Heaven," her mother standing to one side. As the float drew closer she could see her mother crying, throwing kisses as she watched her oldest daughter rolling in.

CHEEVER

Cheever arched his back, hands clasped behind, stretching as if he could loosen the muscles tight as the packed clay beneath his feet. He twisted his neck to the left, tilting his face upward until he heard a pop. "Ahh," he said, the tent light catching the blue and purple dust motes settling on his close-cropped hair. He'd been up since six. By the time the gates opened at noon, he'd worked the better part of the day. Everyone at Beasleys' Traveling Amusements pulled a long shift, but the seven colored workers who pounded stakes, set up the tents, assembled displays, tended the oddities, limed the privies, and climbed the tallest ladders toiled the longest. Ernie and Martha, the common-law married cooks, rose before dawn to feed the shifts of workers: first the midway hands who operated rides and game booths, then the sideshow attractions, followed by the colored workers who lived together under one old army issue tent, furnished with cots and a heavy canvas partition for Ernie and Martha. They were the only hired couple in the Beasleys' employ. Martha's parents had worked for the Beasleys before the carnival business started, back when Earl Sr. and his brother sold patent medicine. If it weren't for the other colored folks, Cheever wouldn't have stayed. Glad as he was for steady employment away from cotton, he missed eating among a passel of cousins, uncles, and aunts.

He left Sweet Water, Alabama, at fifteen, to work with the Beasleys, who offered him three meals a day and life free of farming. Cheever's father and his seven uncles were sharecroppers, and after watching their toil fatten the owner's children instead of their own, Cheever decided to join the carnival. He and two of his younger cousins had watched the traveling show chug down the railroad tracks, then snuck to the edge of the fairgrounds, where Earl Beasley spotted him. Four days later, when the show rolled out of town, Cheever rode with it. For months he missed his mother's cooking and his sisters' loving slaps on his head as they urged him into his pre-dawn chores. His three sisters were all older, and though his father said he hated to see his oldest son go, he slipped him a buffalo nickel and told him to spend it when he crossed into the promised land.

The lights of the midway from the top of the Ferris wheel seemed extraordinary at first—bulbs glimmering below like fallen stars caught on a fence. But he quickly realized he had not found paradise as the churning motor suddenly quieted and the car he sat in lurched to a halt. He peered down through the gears and spotted the white undershirt of the ride operator as he straightened himself, his hand rising from the lever that locked the engine into its stillness.

"Hey," he called out, as the man drifted away, "bring me on down."

The man looked up, laughing. Slowly, the other ride operators, who had shut off their machines after testing them for the next day, gathered at the base of the Ferris wheel. Recognizing that he teetered on the edge of becoming an amusement himself, Cheever scooched down on the bench and settled in for the night. He knew the car that contained him would circle downward in the morning when the patrons came. He had only to wait out the night, too hot for sleeping anyway, the humidity clinging to his skin. Deflated by his willingness to stay perched above the fairgrounds without complaint, the ride operator shoved the switch. As the car rotated toward the ground, Cheever knew the glittering city was no promised land. A dozen years later, he held on to that nickel, his days no shorter than a field hand's, his back no straighter than if he'd been walking behind his daddy's plow.

The cavern of mouth opened, jaws extended as the yawn broke, lengthening his face.

"You freeze like that we'll move you in the tent with us." Lizard Man smiled.

Cheever squeezed his eyes and pushed the yawn to its edges, his jaw popping.

"I can see it now," Lizard continued, "a booth right next to Stony: Here go Cheever, the Yawning Man."

"And to think all I thought I's good for is pounding stakes and shoveling shit." His jaw widened again. "Damn," he said as another yawn progressed, "I got me a case of them."

"Better be careful. Next you might get a case of scales."

"Then get away from me before I catch something serious." Cheever stepped back, caught at the knees by a tent pole guy wire. He stepped forward and shook his head. "You sure you ain't no leper?"

"I done told you, I ain't contagious and it ain't leprosy. It's just one of them skin disorders with a long-ass name."

Lizard wiped his forehead with a rag. Cheever watched the greenish smudge come away on the cloth. "Makeup. Earl calls it 'enhancement.' Supposed to make me look more like a lizard. Otherwise the scales are pale and flaky."

"You put that shit on your face every day?"

"Face, chest, back, arms. Lucky they let me keep my shorts on."

"Damn, man, you freaks is something else." Cheever yawned again. Lizard pointed and smiled.

"Ain't nothing but a sign of too much work. Now go on and get your peely ass out of here so I can close up and take Miss Beulah. Got to round up Ewell for that."

"He's over taking Flipper out of his tank."

"I gots to say, some nights that boy looks blue. Time for them Beasley brothers to rig a heater up to that boy's tank."

"I know. Poor kid, it's no kinda life to be a boy without friends."

"Who'd play with that?"

"Just his limbs are missing. He's regular inside, not dimwitted. You know, Yawn Man, just 'cause we look bad don't mean we have shit for brains."

"I got to get Miss Beulah. You see Ewell, tell him to get his ass over here."

"And if I see Brother Earl I'll tell him about your act."

"Bad enough to be born colored. Ain't about to be no freak. We done stood on the auction block too damn long to be caught standing any-where else."

Cheever heaved with all his might, but the wheels on Beulah Divine's rolling throne wouldn't move. Stuck again, the mud gobbling the wheels quicker than he and Ewell could push the massive load. His own feet sank into the goo, each step stickier than the one before. The rain pelted his forehead. He and Ewell covered the fat lady with her poncho, a piece of leftover tent flap with a hole cut out for her head. She wore a yellow rainhat, like the girl on the salt box, while the two of them got soaked. The water seeped into his scalp and ears.

"Man, I hate water. I'm apt to drown standing on my feet."

"We got to get a board to push her on. She's sinking fast."

"There're those planks under her trailer."

"Yeah, but we'll be here till morning laying them end to end."

"We're still closer to the chow tent. Why not leave her there?" Cheever wiped the water off his face. Two seconds later his eyelashes were misted over again.

"Ain't no place for her to sleep."

"So I gotta lose mine pushing her all night? Damn, that's backwards. Them tightass Beasley brothers oughta buy a Massey Ferguson to pull her around."

"Team of mules would be cheaper."

"Shit, let's go see if they got them oxen in the agriculture show."

"They ain't gonna let you use their prize bull. Shit, that thing's worth more than she is. Besides," Ewell continued, "even if we had a pair, we ain't got a harness or a wagon. That's what we need, a wagon."

Cheever looked at the path to the trailers. He felt like Moses crossing the desert, or Noah herding those animals onto the ark. "Lordamercy Ewell, what if it don't stop raining?"

What if it were some kind of test from God? His mother was full of those stories, had her a mind full of hymns praising His glory. If only he had bothered listening.

"Ewell, you think God's looking down saying, 'See them colored men pushing and pulling on that fat woman's throne? They ain't had enough, colored people. Hundred years of slavery. Jim Crow. Pecker-heads telling 'em when to breath and how loud to do it. Shit. They ain't had enough tribulation. I'ma gonna send my fattest angel down to test them.' Godamighty." Cheever squinted through the sheet of rain. "That's it, ain't it? That's why they call you Beulah Divine."

"Must be." Funny how such a big woman mumbled such tiny words.

"Shit," said Ewell, "we in trouble now." He cocked his head down low in front of her face. "If you an angel, you want to make some miracle so we can get you up to your trailer?"

"You best do something, Miss Beulah, 'cause this here colored fella's about to drown." The rain had saturated Cheever's shirt so that the yoke lay plastered on his shoulders. The sleeves clung on his arms, a second layer of skin.

"What about that truck they use with the winch?" she asked.

"What we gonna raise you into?" said Ewell.

"Nothing but the bed of the truck. We could run the ramps up it and set her in the back." The prospect heartened Cheever.

"Them tires'll spin with all that weight. You talking damn near a ton with her in that chair. Well, half, but that's too much."

"Wait a minute. We thinking itty-bitty instead of a lot. They got to have that bigass trailer to haul them rides in." He could feel himself scaling the walls of this test, the blood pumping, water rolling off.

"Man, Beasleys hire that flatbed truck."

"What, you think they hire a new one in every town? That one rides on the rails with the rest of us." After twelve years with the Beasleys, he knew what there was to know.

"Then where is it?"

"Parked down by the midway so they can haul out the rides."

"Which one of them crackers gonna give us the keys?"

"Damn, Ewell, the way you mouthing quit-talk, the Devil licking his chops."

"Stop that shit, now. Ain't got nothing to do with God."

"This got to be some God-sized joke. Ain't neither of us could have made something so big we got to move knee-deep in mud."

He knew the ride operators better than Ewell. They'd long since laughed at him stranded in the air. They'd probably laugh just as hard at the sight of them stuck, with the fat lady sinking fast.

"I'm gonna go find one of them Beasleys then. She their freak. Ain't mine." He could barely hear the suck of mud at his feet over the sound of rain.

Cheever came back with Randy, a Beasley cousin driving a flatbed truck with two steel ramps in the back. Ewell came trotting out from under the awning of the popcorn stand where he'd been waiting. Beulah still sat in her chair, covered by her own poncho tent. Randy pulled the truck up behind Beulah, who was parked in the middle of the path.

"You think you can wheel her around or do I gotta back this thing up?"

"I s'pect we can wheel her that far. Course we could put them ramps down to wheel her over."

"That'd coat them with mud. Try pushing her first. Ewell, get on over here," Randy hollered from the truck.

Cheever opened the door and got out. Dumb sonofabitch gonna sit there and watch the colored do it. He spat into a puddle.

"All right, Ewell, it's you and me." He lowered his voice in timber and volume and spoke directly into Ewell's ear, "Massa's gonna supervise."

Together, the two of them pushed the great iron throne, but only the oozing mud moved.

"She ain't budging," Ewell offered. "Go tell him he gonna have to move the truck."

"The fool wouldn't be wasting his time if he trusted a colored man to drive."

"Go on, I'm getting drenched." Ewell tilted his head upward in the direction of the truck, rivulets of water cascading down his temples.

The mud swallowed Cheever's feet as he tugged himself over to the truck cab.

"Them wheels of hers sunk deep. Ain't no choice but back around."

"Well, go on. Stand over there and make sure I don't hit nothing."

Randy ground the gears into reverse. The truck lurched backward. Cheever guided him out and then watched him back in. Beulah sat out of sight on the other side of the truck.

"Damn man, Ewell, she all right?" Cheever strained to see, but Ewell had turned his attention back to the midway. "Beulah," he hollered, hoping she could hear through the rasp of the engine and the rain. He listened for a thread of her voice, but heard nothing. "Stop," he screamed, waving his arms wildly, hoping Randy would double-check to make sure the truck cleared her.

He caught Randy's eye and pointed in the direction of Beulah. Randy waved like he was whooshing a basketball into the hoop. Cheever watched him crank the steering wheel to the left and ease backward. Cheever kept dodging to catch a glimpse beyond the truck. He saw Ewell turn back around and throw his hand up.

"Stop," Ewell called, waving his arms. The truck jerked and shuddered to a standstill. "Tell him to cut the wheel hard and pull up. The edge of that flatbed's about six inches from her head."

Cheever pulled his feet across the mud taffy and motioned to Randy to roll the window down. "Ewell say you 'bout to take off her head with the corner of that bed. Best pull up and cut toward me."

Randy shook his head like Cheever had told him a colored man had just been elected president. The truck sputtered momentarily and then burped forward in the mud. Cheever could see Randy turning the wheel, mud flying. The truck stopped, Ewell waved, and Randy jerked his head back, indicating for Cheever to attend to Beulah while he waited in the truck.

Beulah sat beneath her mud-spattered poncho, water dripping off her hat. Her eyes looked closed but he couldn't tell from that angle.

"Miss Beulah, you all right?" Cheever asked.

"Mmm," she exhaled like a sleeping cat.

"Guess so," said Ewell, who was lifting one end of a steel ramp. "Come get the other end and hitch it to the truck."

Cheever obliged. They set the other ramp in place. Beulah sat entrenched several inches from the planks, their bottom ends oozing down into the mud. Cheever took his post behind the right side of the throne and Ewell manned the left.

"Wait a minute, we gonna have to get something under her wheels," said Ewell. "Go see what he's got in the truck."

"Not me. I'm tired of dealing with that cracker. Won't even get out of the damn truck."

"Come on, you rode with him. Just ask do he got any wood or something stiff."

Cheever eyed a shovel in the bed of the truck. Nothing one shovel could do. "Where the hell's Muscle Man when you need him? I reckon us three could tilt her back enough to wiggle them rear wheels onto the ramp."

"Wait another minute. Hey, Beulah," Ewell called. "Miss Beulah Divine, I'm talking to you."

She tipped her head upward, the rain rolling back.

"Can you walk at all?"

"A few steps. Hard on my heart."

"Don't even bother, Ewell. She'd sink sure as shit in this mud. All I need's for the fat lady to drown out here. There goes my black ass."

"What I want to know is why the hell this throne ain't got wagon wheels in front."

"Well, next time she's out, we'll put some on, but for tonight we got to get her and us out of the rain. Jesus, I ain't been this wet since I got baptized."

"I didn't know that."

"What?"

"You got baptized. You don't never talk about God."

"For Chrissake, Ewell, I wasn't but ten and it was my mama's idea. She had a thing for that preacher. Not nasty. Just wanted to show him her younguns was children of God. Lot of good it's doing me out here, stuck in the rain with a fat lady. Leastways Noah had an ark."

"Ain't nothing to do but try to tip her back, get them little wheels up, and roll the big ones to the edge of them planks. Then we set her down and roll her up." Ewell wiped his rain-soaked face with a wet shirt sleeve. "I say we go get Muscle Man, no joke."

"Let's us try first. If we can't tip her, you can get him." Cheever resumed his position.

"On the count of three. Miss Beulah, we going to tip you back, but don't worry, we ain't going to let you fall."

Ewell shot him a look that asked how he could make such a promise. Cheever shrugged. What else could he tell her?

"Alrighty, one, two, three." Together they pulled, but the leverage wasn't right. "Wait a minute. Let me get it front, between her feet. I'll lift up and you pull back." Cheever pulled a foot out of the mud.

"Man, you gonna tear up your back."

"I ain't got no choice. We got to get her out of this mud. Now, on the count of three."

"Why we ain't got animal duty I'd like to know."

"Stop asking questions and push." Cheever positioned himself in front of Beulah, his knees bent, praying not to feel anything tear. "One, two, three." Cheever hoisted with all his might. He even asked Sweet Jesus to let him pick this woman up. The muscles in his flanks burned, his arms quivered, and with all the rain, he couldn't feel the sweat beading on his head, but the smaller front wheels lifted out of the goo. "Praise God," he grunted.

"Now, come round here while I hold her steady so we can push them big wheels forward," Ewell said. Cheever could tell he'd had enough.

"You sure you got her?" Cheever asked before he moved.

"Yes, now get over here."

"Wait, wait, I'm going to pull on this here ramp and see if I can inch it closer."

"It's hitched up top. Now come help me push."

Cheever tugged his feet once again. Exhaustion rode heavy on his shoulders, pushing till he felt his knees threaten to buckle.

"I can't hold her forever," said Ewell, balancing the weight of Beulah and her throne.

Cheever summoned his strength, yanking his feet. He moved around back. Both men crouched down low, their shoulders pushing against the high back of the throne. The wheels rolled ever so slightly.

"Again," said Ewell. "On three." Ewell gave the count and they pushed again. It seemed to Cheever that the whole contraption was sliding forward in the mud, not rolling, but he didn't care as long as the front wheels landed on the ramp.

"Did we get it?" Ewell asked. Cheever looked down, the water traveling down his scalp and dripping off his forehead. Half of the front wheels fell on the ramp, enough to gain traction.

"Finally. Come on, let's push it the rest of the way." Cheever resumed his place at the back of the throne. Together, they heaved their weight against hers until the smaller front wheels rolled fully onto the ramps. "Praise God and pass the whiskey. I thought we'd never get her on this thing. You all right, Miss Beulah?"

"Tired." Her voice came back limp as thread.

"We about got you, now. Just got to roll you on up here. Up to the truck. Then Mr. Randy going to drive you home."

"We got to try to lift up a little on the back," Ewell said. "On three." Ewell counted and this time the chair moved forward. Once the front wheels rolled, the back ones drew through the mud and caught the lip of the ramp, rolling onto the steel.

Cheever quickly realized the next challenge. Each ramp was no more than a foot wide. He and Ewell would each have to follow behind on a ramp, balancing and pushing up the incline with all their might. Now, if they had a rope, they could winch her on up, but they'd have to figure where to hook onto her chair. If they hooked on too low, she could flip backwards and break her neck. There'd be no way to hook onto the high part without hurting her head. Nothing to do but push. Exhaustion drove across him in circles and he could feel every tire mark.

"Ain't much to balance on, is it?" Ewell asked.

"We do this, we can join the circus. Push her across a tightrope." A chuckle slipped out of Cheever's lips. He was getting punchy.

"Tighten up now. Let's push," Ewell commanded.

One foot forward at the base of the back wheel and the other foot cocked behind, Cheever pushed against the great throne and its contents with all the force he could muster. He wished for Muscle Man and even the Geek, anyone else who could relieve him of the final agonizing stretch. He shut his eyes against the strain and listened to his own breathing, mirrored by Ewell on the other side of the gulf. If either one failed to keep full pressure against the throne, the weight would surely crush them.

"Ranndeee," Cheever yelled, feeling the expenditure of air deflate him. Surprisingly, Randy peered at them through the back window. He must have sensed their predicament, or recognized the Beasleys' potential loss, because he jumped out carrying a coil of rope, which he wrapped around the back of the chair and tied in a knot around Beulah's tented frame. Then he climbed up on the flat bed with the end of the rope, which he slid through the opening in the back wall of the bed, and brought the rope back down again.

"Should have brought the damn winch truck after all, but the bed's too short. All right, you boys push."

"We already is." The words tumbled out before Cheever could stop them. He knew not to antagonize Randy. Without his help, they were sunk, smooshed, buried eyeball deep in the mud.

"Well, push harder, darkie, and I'll pull. Leastways, she won't roll back on your black head."

Why'd it always have to do with color? Seemed like crackers couldn't get a sentence out of their mouth without slamming the darkness of the colored man. Shit, what he'd give to paint their lily asses black and send them through the world.

The anger stoked the fire just enough to heave Beulah over the top. Cheever opened his eyes as he and Ewell pushed the front wheel onto the truck bed. With a final grunt and Randy's tugging, they brought her flat up and ready to ride.

Randy kept her tied in to the back panel, but told the two of them to make sure she didn't roll too far. Ewell slid a piece of scrap lumber the size of a cotton candy roll under the front end of the rear wheel.

"She ain't going anywhere else," Ewell said, hands still mounted on the handles of the throne. Cheever sat down at Beulah's feet, covered by the rain-slickened poncho. He lifted the canvas and squinted to glimpse her shoes, black oxfords with rounded points. The kind old ladies or little boys wore. She hardly ever walked. Why didn't she wear moccasins?

"Miss Beulah." He tilted his head back so the sound would carry, but he got a faceful of rain. "Why you have to wear them shoes? Injun moccasins be softer on your feet. They line 'em with sheepskin if you pay extra."

She didn't respond right away. Must have dozed off with the rain pattering on her roof.

A *hmm* floated up, nestling in his ear.

"It's all right, Miss Beulah. You rest."

The truck bumped along up the path. Cheever imagined soaking in a bath filled with Epsom salts. The only tubs he'd been in since the aluminum one at home were the occasional ones he found in whorehouses. He hated to admit it, but at that moment, the thought of a woman drawing him a bath was even more compelling than what she might do to him afterward.

"All right, let's go," Ewell barked. "Been way too long a night. Time to get the fat lady to bed." Cheever blinked, inhaled jaggedly, and rose. Randy had pulled up a little past Beulah's door so they could extend the ramps and there she'd be.

He and Ewell set the steel planks down. He untied the rope from the back of the throne.

"You think we can hold her going downhill? Maybe we should leave her tied in. There enough length in that rope?"

God, he was sick of rain. Every inch of him was wet and even though it was probably sixty degrees, the dampness turned to a chill. He eyed the rope and then the distance it would have to travel. He fastened it back onto the throne again. Ewell took his side of the chair and nodded at Cheever. Weary done stole the words right out him, Cheever thought. Been way too long a day. Times like this, he wished for something beyond the shape of his own imagining. He knew his daddy and the other farmers were long since tucked into bed, but their days were no easier, rising before dawn and toiling till dusk. He wondered what colored men escaped the fate of such toil. He remembered his mother telling him about colored doctors and teachers, but he could conjure their existence no easier than he could conjure Mars.

He gripped the right side of the back handlebar, which ran the width of the throne. In between his hands and Ewell's, the thick cord of hemp coiled around still lashed to the opening in the back of the truck bed.

"Let her down easy," Randy called.

Cheever was too tired even to mutter the *shit* that formed at his lips. He held on tight as he could as he and Ewell pulled against the half-ton that gravity was tugging down. Once the back wheels rolled over the lip of the ramp, the throne rolled hungrily toward the ground. Cheever could feel his feet trotting and tried not to stumble. He barely caught himself a couple of inches from the bottom when the throne thwacked into the mud. For once he was grateful for the goo, but then again, without it, they wouldn't have had her up in the truck anyway.

"Shit," Ewell said, "we should've had him back up so we could put them ramps right out onto the ramp into her door."

"Well, I ain't pushing her back into that truck. Front wheels ain't but an inch or two from her ramp."

"Why's everything have to be so damn hard?" Ewell asked.

Cheever was too tired to answer so he began pushing instead. Ewell's question dropped somewhere in the mud, where, no doubt, they rolled over it. Ewell tugged and Cheever pushed and the smaller front wheels reached the reinforced ramp in front of Beulah's extra-wide door. After struggling so long, Cheever felt his muscles snap at the last push. As soon as they were through the door, the strain, the rain, the length of the day congealed at once. He felt his legs turn to jelly.

"Whoa there," said Ewell as he caught Cheever.

"Man, I got to get my sorry butt into a bed."

"Beulah got room," said Ewell, a grin winding across his lips.

"Get me out of here, Ewell." He let out a sigh wide as the Mississippi.

"You all right?" Ewell asked, his fingers still tentative on Cheever's elbow.

"Yeah, but I'm tuckered out. You think old Randy give us a ride?"

"Shit, only if we pay him." Ewell moved to the door. "He's still there. Let's go."

"We got to get her onto the bed." He looked at Beulah, only her shape visible beneath the canvas poncho. "Come on, help me get this off her head."

Cheever inhaled deeply and let go of the throne. He began gathering the bottom of the rain tent on the left side as Ewell worked on the right. Together they lifted it off of Beulah.

"Where we going to put this thing?" Ewell asked.

"Best to hang it outside. Otherwise, it'll drip in here."

They carried it out and draped it on a boot hook coming out of a nearby utility line.

"Tell him we'll be right out," Ewell said, nodding at the truck.

"What I got to tell him for? You got lips." Cheever let the air collected in his cheek escape in a *ppfff*. Ewell tapped on the passenger side window. Best not to get up in a cracker's face, 'specially to ask him something. Instead of watching, Cheever slid the long ramps they'd used back onto the bed of the truck. When Ewell stepped back on the short ramp up to Beulah's door, Cheever joined him.

"He going to wait?" he asked.

Ewell cocked his head and mimicked Randy: "I'm still stalling here, ain't I?" A stream of saliva burst from Ewell's mouth. "Why can't he just say yes or no? Jesus, them crackers born talking crooked."

"That's so's they can get it out both sides of their mouth." Cheever shook his head, water spraying as he crossed back into the trailer. "All right, Miss Beulah, time to get you on this bed."

"I'm more'n ready tonight, Cheever. You fellas are awful sweet, standing in the rain with me like that."

"Can't let the fat lady drown. Shoot, the midway wouldn't be the same," he said, fixing his right arm around her back.

Ewell mirrored him, and together they lifted as Beulah stood. Cheever tried for a moment to imagine being so fat he couldn't propel his own bulk out of a chair. He felt the weight of weariness ready to glue his skinny ass down, but that would pass. The way she was, her body'd never quite be her own. Like her will got dunked in blubber and couldn't get up. The thought of it sent a shiver through him.

"All right, we going to step and turn." The words came out unassisted. He and Ewell had been getting her onto her bed for years now. Cheever remembered when she'd first come, she could still walk, not very far, but the Beasleys had insisted she get fatter so they could advertise her as *the* fattest woman in the world.

A pain shot through his shoulder. His back seized. Fire coiled around his spine.

"Damn," said Ewell, "I believe we finally done." Ewell stood straight and then arched his back. "Let's go."

"Night, Miss Beulah," Cheever said, following Ewell toward the door. "Is Beard Lady gonna help with your slop?"

"I reckon she will, though it is kinda late." He was too tired to see if Beulah was fretting. "Go on. I reckon she'll come."

"I'll knock on her door. Let her know you're in."

"Thanks. You all sleep tight."

"Yes, ma'am," he mumbled. "Sleep going to come easy tonight."

Cheever didn't have to summon the Beard Lady. She was at her door waiting for them to leave.

"She's all yours," Ewell called as he opened the passenger door of Randy's truck.

"I was getting worried. It's past eleven," Beard Lady said from behind the screen.

"You try moving six-hundred-fifty-seven pounds on top of a cast-iron chair stuck in the mud. Shit, it be easier to move a herd a cattle in a thunderstorm," Cheever responded, waiting for Ewell to slide over in the cab. No doubt old Randy's skin was crawling with the thought of two colored sitting alongside him. Cheever slammed the door to the truck. He could smell Randy: Four Roses, Camels, and the boiled egg odor of his sweat. Too tired for a glass of whiskey, though the thought of a pair of soft brown hands moving across his back awakened his senses, setting his tongue to trace the line of his teeth.

The truck lurched forward and rolled easily through the mud. In less than a minute, they had traveled further than the distance they had covered in an hour and a half. Across the field, beyond the colored workers' tent, Cheever glimpsed the Ferris wheel, its empty cars hanging in space. He'd had no idea that first night, stranded in the top car, what lay in store. His days tugged just as hard as any plow. He had stories to tell, but no audience. Ewell and the other colored workers saw much of what he did, and the women he found in town listened politely for a drink, but no one really cared if he spent a wedge of night in the pouring rain trying to get the fat lady out of the mud. His nieces and nephews, even his own daddy, might laugh if he got home to tell them, but they had seven more towns left in the circuit and by then, he could see his own likeness painted on the fairway—legs and arms dripping, body coated with mud like some creature crawling out of dinosaur ooze, mouth wide as a cavern, locked in an endless yawn.

NAMES

She could hear their grunts outside her window, as Cheever and Ewell heaved Beulah's rolling iron throne up the ramps to her trailer.

"Mm-hmm, she sure ain't getting lighter, are you, Miss Beulah?"

Bettina recognized Cheever's gravelly voice.

"Godamighty, with this here throne she must weigh a ton." The still air effortlessly transported Ewell's voice. He heaved hard as he'd lift a boulder crushing his chest. "Shit," Ewell paused to breathe, "I wish I could make a living just being fat."

"Why, if you that fat what you gonna do with a paycheck besides buy your food?"

"Build me a platinum trough." Ewell's chuckle rolled like clouds colliding.

She wanted to holler out the window at both of them, talking so cruelly in front of Beulah, as if she were made of cast iron too, unable to hear their taunts. Her fists tightened as she watched. She could feel the muscles in her forearm, the blood pumping to her fingers, but even with all her strength, Bettina doubted that she could ever land a blow either man would feel. Beneath the sheen of sweat glistening on their ebony skin lay deltoids and trapeziuses that split wood easy as kindling and raised tents like she might lift a lampshade. Ewell and Cheever were raised on toil. The broad lats of their backs spread wide as wings, and their arms hung crooked from the tug of biceps tight against the triceps that powered sledgehammers and twenty-pound mallets several hours a day.

The string of lights hung above the row of trailers barely illuminated Ewell's face, the color of blackstrap molasses, but she could imagine the strain lifting veins to the surface as he and Cheever heaved the iron throne on the final roll, tilting it back and setting it down so as not to jar

Beulah. They had sawed a new opening around the doorway to accommodate Beulah's massive chair. Without the greater expanse, neither she nor the throne would pass over the threshold, but now they could ease her into the trailer and lift her onto the specially welded bed frame. After they left, Bettina would come over and ready Beulah for bed.

"Nighty-night, Miss Beulah," Cheever offered as he and Ewell lifted the ramps and set them under the edge of the trailer.

Bettina watched as they disappeared, their broad hands waving in the darkness, their voices trailing behind like puffs of breath on a frigid day. Bettina grabbed her brush and crossed the dirt patch between their trailers. She knocked and Beulah beckoned her in.

"Evening, Beulah," she said, stepping into the trailer. The last sideshow closed at nine thirty. By the time she came over it was close to ten. Beulah looked over, warm butter melting into a pancake.

"You know what happened again tonight? Some wise-ass tried to pull on my beard. The Beasleys oughta put barbed wire up instead of rope." Bettina tugged at the whiskers protruding from her chin. "What is it with people? They gotta touch something to believe it's real. If all I did was glue it on, it'd be a sorry way to make a living." She studied the streaks of mud on the floor. "Not that it ain't a sorry way already, but you know what I mean."

"I sure do. If this isn't the boringist job in the world I don't know what is. Don't take long for all the gaped-mouth people staring at you to look the same."

As much as Bettina hated being gawked at, it was better to have them pay to do it instead of sneaking a look on the sly or stopping in the middle of town, bags heavy in their arms, like Jesus had just asked them for the time of day. She sat at the end of the bed and unlaced Beulah's shoes.

"Yep, folks like to stare, but they don't never look at your eyes. I bet not a one of 'em ever noticed Stony's is glass."

"Were they like that when he came?" Bettina asked.

"Naw, he just came fossilized, stiff as rock from the chest down. Fell off a horse when he was ten and his folks couldn't keep him. Eyes must've rotted right out of his head. Or maybe he got wall-eyed or something. I just remember hearing Earl Senior say those eyes of his were ruining the act."

Bettina moved up near the head of the bed and leaned behind Beulah, who shifted forward so Bettina could reach. As she unfastened the buttons on the backside of the gown, Bettina marveled at the mammoth breasts let loose, great waves of flesh spilling out undammed, feeling the dearth of her own flesh—the lanky limbs, the waist descending into hip without notice, the stingy chest full of emptiness. The shapeliness she enjoyed in costume disappeared as she slithered each night out of her padded red sequined dress.

She spread her hands across the soft terrain of Beulah's back. The great rolls of citrus-scented flesh called to her, lured her fingers in. The gypsy woman who traded in tarot cards and potions had special essences she added—almond, orange, sandalwood—to the oil Muscle Man kept in rich supply. Each morning, Beulah dabbed orange oil under her arms and between her bosom to override the smell of sweat trapped in the layers, baking under the lights and the weight of the shimmering gold gown. The gypsy woman had mixed a concoction for Beulah to make her perspire less, but when it failed, she declared the spirits had cast Beulah into that body in praise of their own countenance. Hence, the origin of her stage name—Miss Beulah Divine.

With a dab of the oil, Bettina's fingers glided over Beulah's skin, her thumbs sinking into the shoulders pliant as putty on a hot day. She drew great swirls and kneaded up and down Beulah's back. Her hands grew warm as she rubbed, etching messages deep into sacred ground.

A moan akin to a sleeping cat's escaped from Beulah's lips. "Darling, you keep rubbing and I'm likely to fall asleep."

"How about I brush your hair?"

"You don't mind?"

"Not at all." In fact, she loved touching the soft auburn curls that bounced back from the bristles as if they had a life of their own. "You got such beautiful hair."

"Part of why they took me, I suppose. Earl Beasley said 'twas a shame God wasted such pretty hair on a woman so fat, and Tom corrected him right there in front of me. Said he was missing the whole point 'More's the pity she's fat,' he said. That's what makes the freak show work with women, that little shred of pity. If they just see you as homegrown ugly, oh well, but if you got a feature they can relate to, then it really gets in and breaks their hearts."

Bettina knew without padding there would be no thrill in seeing her. A beard on a body that otherwise looked like a car stripped of its parts—no tragedy there. She wished she had enough fat on her so that someone would long to rub her body. She envied the curvaceous figures of the dancing girls, though she knew they grew tired of shaking their hips and pastied breasts, of having to roll their tongues like cows as they lifted their long tresses onto their heads while clots of farmers pawed their creamy smooth skin.

Where to find caring caresses amid the sideshow? Like Noah's ark severed down the middle with one of everything—God forbid any of these creatures reproduce. The absence of touch ached like a phantom limb. She longed for a cat to curl on her chest or stretch out by her side, but there was no way to keep one. She couldn't confine another animal to life in a cage. She had seen the five-legged calf being herded into one after the show. What a bleak life. She prayed for it to die young.

She looked down at her own fingernails. Sassy red. A red that talked back, that said, "Lookahere, get a load of me." Red to match the dress. Every morning she checked her polish, reapplying it over any nicks or chips. She hated the polish, especially the color. It did not belong on her hands. Enough of her screamed "look at me" without having to wear such a garish color. Her hands were the only part of her body that suited her. They looked like anyone's hands. They betrayed no one. They had lifted branches and carried stones and stroked a wounded raccoon she had found while walking in the woods. Hands that had tended fires and kneaded dough. Hands she had lain on her mother's fevered forehead, hands that had lifted to it a cool cloth. Hands that had felt the first hair protrude from her chin.

Every Saturday night, she plumbed the bottom of her toiletry bag for polish remover. Nothing pleased her more than wiping the red away, draining the lifeblood right out of its screeching color, returning her nails to their natural state. She had grown accustomed to disguising her body, but not her hands—the only part of her that experienced gentle touch.

A soft rain started falling shortly before eleven. The drops struck like the pads of fingers drumming lightly on an empty can. Ewell and Cheever would no doubt moan about pushing Beulah in the morning, the wheels of her rolling throne gumming up in the mud. Bettina peered out the window of Beulah's trailer and saw Cheever heading back up the path. As she moved toward the door, she heard him rap on the side of the trailer. She opened the door as he approached.

"I just come back to empty her pot before I turn in."

"I'll do it, Cheever. I'm helping her get ready for bed."

"Alrighty then." He called in to Beulah, "Get thin by morning, Miss Beulah. Otherwise me and Ewell's liable to lose you in all that mud."

"Hard to lose something my size," she called back, her voice wafting through air.

"You might not sink, but them iron wheels ain't gonna spin."

"Night, Cheever." Bettina closed the door. "Black bastard," she muttered, watching Cheever recede down the path.

"I don't reckon they fancy being here anymore than we do."

"At least they can leave. Most of us, we ain't got no place else to go."

"World still ain't too kind to the colored."

"They may be black as night in Wonder Cave but they can still get a regular job. Nobody's branded them a genuine oddity of the natural world."

"That's true. Folks don't blame you for being colored the way they do for being fat. With all them trough jokes, Ewell acts like I got this fat 'cause I wanted to. He knows I got a condition. Even the doctors say so. I known that since I was fourteen. He knows 'cause he brings my food, it's Beasley Brothers that make me eat. Want more pound for their dollar."

Bettina pushed her shirtsleeves up.

Beulah's head darted to the side slightly, like a question mark. "Mind if I ask you something?"

"No, go right ahead."

"I noticed when you come over that it's only your nails got the same shape, after you're outta that costume."

A puff of laughter passed through Bettina's throat. "Padding," she answered. Bettina leaned in close. "I don't know what got messed up on the inside, but whatever's outside don't look altogether right."

"You mean to say most of you is made up of removable parts?"

"Yeah, the padding's sewn right in my dress. If I didn't look all curvy and feminine, wouldn't be as big a shock, me having the beard. Heck, it'd almost be easier to pass as a man and get a job on the railroad except I'm not that strong."

Beulah looked rapt as a girl being courted.

"None of this happened when I was little. Wasn't till I was fifteen and I still had no kinda figure and the hair started growing on my face and I got to wondering if something went wrong. You grow up thinking you're a girl so you just expect to turn into a woman. All those gawkers pay to see the bearded lady, perfect except for a single flaw. If they knew what they were really getting, I reckon them Beasley brothers could charge more."

Beulah leaned back, wide-eyed. "You mean you's really more a half-and-half?"

"Kinda."

"You got a wiener?"

"No, not exactly." She nibbled the inside of her bottom lip. No one had asked her about it.

"What you mean, 'not exactly'?"

Bettina looked at Beulah, inert, trapped by her own weight. "My pink spot's kinda large."

"Large how, like a grape?"

"Yeah. I ain't never told anybody before."

"Honey, you just offered to tote my slop. It don't get much more personal than that. Now tell me something, you got balls?"

"No. I got a hole inside same as you."

"Any blood?"

"No."

"Ain't you lucky. I had my parts removed when I was fourteen. Doctor said fat as I was, it'd be dangerous to carry."

"They took everything female out when you was a girl?"

"Mm-hmm."

"How come you ain't got a beard?"

"I don't know. All I know is I had a operation and when I woke up the doctor said I couldn't get pregnant not even if I had relations with an entire baseball team."

"Don't seem right doing that to a young girl."

"They figured I was too fat, you know, but it just made the boys more likely to try, knowing they couldn't get me pregnant."

"How would they know? Did you tell them?"

"No, but somehow word got out. I weighed two-hundred-eighty-seven pounds and everybody knew that, too."

"Don't you hate the way folks talk? Like they ain't got nothing better to do."

Bettina conjured the sight of Beulah as a girl. Already something to laugh at. At least she had been given childhood before the stares and comments had come. "So'd you run away?"

"I didn't run nowhere, honey, but later on, much later, I took me a train to meet Mr. Beasley. The daddy. I'd heard tell they was signing on acts. I missed them when they came through the county, but I rode right on up from Georgia and they signed me up. Made me ride in the colored car. Bless they hearts, this little girl and her mama sat nearby. I know that child's eyes kept twisting to see, but her mama kept her faced forward the whole time. Mama weren't so tiny herself. Nothing to compare, but not skinny. That's the thing. They made me promise to gain more weight. Said three-something wouldn't do. They wanted the world's fattest fat lady so they fed me about six times a day, but I don't eat that much, contrary to what Ewell says."

Bettina lifted a small enamel basin half full of water left to warm that morning and carried it to the bedstand. She removed a bar of soap from the drawer and retrieved the washcloth, dried like a slice of cured meat, from the curtain rod that spanned the window, thick with grime. She lathered the soap on the cloth and then wrung it out so the water wouldn't run down Beulah's back. She swabbed her, gently lifting the layers of flesh, eyeing the plump nipple, soft and drawn across its pink disk. After she washed her arms and the top of her torso, she retrieved the flannel gown from the dresser where Beulah kept her underthings.

Once the gown was on, Bettina handed Beulah the bedpan from under the bed and the washcloth. Bettina stared out the window to allow Beulah some privacy. She did it more for her sake than for Beulah's, since Beulah, who'd been with the Beasleys fourteen years, was used to being handled, gawked at, even pried apart. Beulah had told her the stories of the early days, when she'd been treated like some heifer at the agricultural exhibit.

As she watched the drizzle, Beulah began to hum.

"That sure is a pretty tune. Does it have any words?"

"Mmm, somewhere," Beulah said, lightly as butterflies waiting to land. "Sometimes things is just prettier without the words."

Ain't it the truth, Bettina thought. All those hymns rising like smoke from the fires of eternal damnation. She'd loved the music, but some of the words had scared her. There were songs that sang God's praises, but then there were the others, the ones her mother sang at home full of impossible routes to glory. Then the hair came and her mother pronounced her Godless. Maybe it was because she hadn't embraced the words, or taken up the fight.

"Beulah," she turned, almost breathless, "You think God made you fat?"

She let the hum run out. "God made us all the way we are. Why'd you ask that?"

"My mama thought I turned out this way 'cause I took up with the Devil."

Beulah wriggled off the bedpan. "My mother explained it this way:

some's fat, some's thin. Some got born with the cripples, others get born straight and cripple up later, and some don't cripple at all. Told me always to look at a meadow. Some weeds, some wildflowers, some hay. All God's. We ain't got to know the purpose anymore than we got to know the plan."

"So you don't think me not wanting to learn the words to all those hymns turned God against me?"

"Honey, you was born how you was born and there ain't no fat lady can tell you why, but if you a child of the Devil, you wouldn't be sitting up here worrying about them hymns."

Bettina stepped over and lifted the pan that Beulah had covered with the cloth. She dumped the contents in a five-gallon drum Ewell or Cheever would haul away, then rinsed the pan and set it back under the bed.

"Now come sit in front of me and I'll brush your hair for a while."

Bettina looked at Beulah the way dew gathers. "Really?" No one had offered to brush her hair since she'd been about ten, when she could still get June to do it. Bettina climbed on the bed and wedged into the space where Beulah's calves parted.

"Lean on back. Fat won't bite you." Bettina felt Beulah's hand on her shoulder. "Scooch back some more. Push them blubber legs apart so I can reach your hair."

Lacing her fingers beneath Beulah's ankle, she lifted the left leg and set it down a couple of inches over. Next, she moved the right one, the weight pulling on her spine. She offered an inchworm of a smile, slightly embarrassed by the prospect of tucking herself into the opulent vee of flesh.

"All right, now try," Beulah insisted.

Bettina slithered back, putting her hands under her own rump and sliding, until she had wedged herself in, appreciative for the first time of her narrow hips. A chill tingled at the nape of her neck as Beulah lifted her long straight hair, which the Beasleys had made her grow out enough to pin on top of her head. "You sure you want to do this?"

"Why in the world not?" Beulah replied, the brush already firmly planted in her hair.

The sensation of the bristles gently tugging against her scalp opened her body in a way she had never felt before. The first things to go were the words. Warmth spread from the tingle as each stroke pushed open the darkness, casting light into the forgotten world of touch. As the soft folds of Beulah's flesh pressed against her backside, enrobing her hips, Bettina shut her eyes. Tears pushed forward. The rise and fall of Beulah's breath pushed the worry right out of her. Left alone with sensation, devoid of thought, she lay back into the welcoming cushion of Beulah's body, wishing the feeling would never end.

Beulah brushed until they both fell asleep. When Bettina woke and saw that it was well past two, she eased up off the bed and turned down the lamp. In the near darkness, she let herself out, still feeling the tingle in her scalp.

Across the path, she slipped into her pajamas and under cold sheets. The rain pattered all night, the tinny sound playing over and over like music from the carousel.

By morning, mud yapped at the heels of the fairground. Bettina woke to the banter of Ewell and Cheever as they heaved barrels spilling sawdust across the gooey flats.

"Wake up, Miss Beulah. Another day, another dollar," Ewell yelled, waking Bettina. "Ain't no point sleeping when you can earn money being fat."

"What I want to know," said Cheever, "has she got any titties under all that fat?"

Ewell snorted. "Maybe she could give some of hers to the beard lady. She ain't got but raisins on a board."

"Hush your nasty mouth, Ewell," Bettina hollered as she threw back the covers. The cold floor bit the soles of her feet. "Damn," she muttered, crossing to the door. She pushed it open and called after them, "What do you work here for anyway?"

Cheever turned around and spotted her so he nodded to Ewell. "Uh oh, she done heard you now."

"Sorry 'bout that." Ewell's apology dribbled out.

"The hell you are. You know, just 'cause we're different don't give you the right to be so mean."

"Times is hard, Beard Lady. I didn't mean no harm." Ewell spit into the mud gumming up his shoes.

"Crackers ain't much fonder of colored than they are of freaks," said Cheever. "I been setting up midways since I was fifteen, and I can tell you them no good sorry sonofabitches coming in here look at me like I'm a steaming heap of that five-legged calf shit, but I got news..."

She shut the door before he said, "I ain't no freak." She knew it was coming. It was the rung of the ladder every normal person climbed onto, thinking it kept them high, dry, and out of harm.

All the way to the privy she walked gingerly on the sawdust trail. No getting around it, they were just plain mean. She wanted to tell them to trade in their black hides for hers, or Beulah's, or Tiny's, or Stony's, or, even worse, Flipper Boy's. Let them spend their lives making so little they couldn't afford life on the outside even if there were someplace else to go. Try a life of watery soup and runny grits and leftover hot dogs and the endless aroma of cotton candy and popcorn. She stepped into one of the stalls on the women's side. She could hear Tiny the midget singing in the next stall. Where did Cheever bathe? Did the seven colored workers have their own facilities or did the whites share with them? No, they wouldn't share with the colored anymore than Cheever would share with Flipper Boy. Folks stuck with their own.

Back in her trailer, she filled her washbowl with water from the faucet near the chow tent. On Sundays they all bathed in makeshift showers, but the other days, folks had to make do with washrags and bowls in their trailers. The soap lather frothed in her hands. She rubbed her armpits and quickly moved over her chest. She wondered every morning how it would feel to let her hand slide slippery over a breast, firm and plump like a pear, instead of the tiny burps of flesh she had. She knew it wasn't right to think of other women that way, but she imagined the showgirls with the coppery colored hair in a neat triangle down below. Her soapy hand traveled between her legs and around her behind, skinny as her brother's.

Too bad she couldn't borrow a cup of Beulah's fat. She dunked the cloth in the washbowl and wrung it out to rinse herself. Patted dry, Bettina let her fingers slide over her beard, easing them back up to the top of her cheeks, to the soft patch right below her eyes. She could no longer remember the feel of a smooth face. If she took a razor to her beard, it'd be smooth for a day, but then what good would it do? She'd just be an ironing board that shaved.

She'd never dreamed of this. She'd just taken the only way out she could find.

Cheever would laugh out loud at her nakedness. For that, she wanted to kill him, bring one of those mallets he used right down over his head. She slipped her underdrawers on, then her trousers, wondering if this was this the life he had dreamed of. Had he sat in church next to his mama waiting for the day he could ride the rails with the likes of her?

The breakfast bell rang from the chow tent. The vision of the food line stretched across her mind like the afterglow of the midway lights when she shut her eyes. The Beasleys fed them three meals a day, though dinner came at three thirty when the sideshow closed for an hour. After the break, they were back in the display tents till nine thirty. For supper, they ate the overcooked ears of corn and hot-dogs that had steamed on a roller since early afternoon. On travel days, they actually ate a little better—two meals, a snack, and no midway leftovers. On Sundays, the colored cooks would bake a cake or a brown betty. She wondered what Cheever did on his day off. Did he go into whatever town they were in and find a diner or a juke joint? Did he carouse with colored fellows or find a woman to keep company with for the night? Had he wanted to settle down, get married, have children? Did he tire of the travel, the stale air and endless scroll of scenery that always looked the same? Did he dream of going home at night, resting his feet on a hassock, patting a dog, and having someone who'd been waiting to untangle the knots tightening his shoulders?

On her way to breakfast, she followed him as he made his way down the path between trailers, arms swinging, sweat already spreading like petals on his shirt. His day began earlier and lasted longer than her own.

No wonder he and Ewell acted ugly. They were stuck in the same boat, paddling furiously in the waters of unbelonging, all the time muttering about some invisible shore.

The day wore on like plaster wrapping, encasing Bettina in her own thoughts beyond the mumble of the crowd. She fixed her eye on the far tent wall as the people filed in to see her. She kept seeing images of Cheever at fifteen: smaller, perhaps still not yet shaving, taking orders from the Beasleys and the white workers there. Focusing on him made it easier to dull the banter of the patrons who always wondered if her beard was real. She stifled the urge daily not to yell back, or even to whisper. The Beasleys had a policy about that. No interchanges with the customers, except of course for the dancing girls, but even they got reprimanded if they did any more than accept tips. Even saying "hello" was discouraged; it just led to more conversation and the line had to keep moving in and out. No dawdlers. Customers paid for one viewing. If they wanted another look, they paid twice.

For each attraction, a small curtain opened and then closed. Usually Ewell and Cheever operated the curtains, along with a younger colored fellow who went by the name of Tyrone. The pulleys were rigged together so that they parted simultaneously as viewers proceeded down the line. Beulah had told her that in the early days, there were no curtains, but the Beasleys had trouble with folks carrying on conversations, trying to paw at the performers and figure out the tricks. Someone had even tried to open the jar holding the two-headed baby. That's when Earl Beasley moved the inanimates up on a stage with the live exhibits. The curtains came after Tiny complained she couldn't even scratch herself once in six hours, but Beulah told her she'd made the same request months before, and it wasn't out of compassion that the Beasleys acted. Stan Beasley decided curtains gave the show a more theatrical feel, along with stage names and tinny music that played inside the exhibition tent. He insisted they were not freaks but performers, whose natural oddities could be used to entertain. And performers, he lectured them, did not chat with the audience during the show. Since none of them were permitted to talk to customers on break or afterward, the wall of mystery and interest remained intact.

At quarter to five, a guy smelling of cheap liquor snuck under the rope line used to herd the viewers through and jumped onto the platform to yank at her beard. Damn fool peckerhead, she wanted to call, I wear all this padding and you tug at the only thing on me that's real. Instead, she squeezed the buzzer attached to her chair, which signaled Cheever to come and escort the roustabout out. Cheever quickly dislodged him, tugging and flicking him like a tick. She watched as he pushed the man out the exit, telling him not to ever come back, sounding fierce and protective—the way her father had the time he'd screamed at a boy who had teased her at school. She'd thank him later, even though he was just doing his job. He'd acted like she mattered, treated her like a fancy monument some drunken farmer had tried to deface. Sitting in her chair on the platform, she spent the rest of the evening pretending she was a statue instead of an oddity of nature, and while it didn't change the way the viewers saw her, it allowed her to believe their comments came not because she was hideous, but because they misunderstood.

That night as she left the sideshow tent, she found Cheever with Ewell shoveling out the two-headed heifer's stall. The pair of them, their broad backs bent, arms extended, cleaned up behind a rigged-up cow—anyone who looked closely could see how someone had stitched on a taxidermied head. "Hey, Cheever," her words like coins tossed over the fence. He turned to look at her.

"Thanks for rescuing me this afternoon."

"No problem, Beard Lady. Tell you the truth, I get a kick out of pitching them peckerheads."

"Hey, Cheever, you think you could call me Bettina?"

"That your name?" He lifted the last shovelful into a wheelbarrow.

"Yeah. I wasn't born with a beard, you know." She turned, churning the silt of memory as she glimpsed her own life before. On the walk back to the trailer, the mud gluing her feet to the ground, the smells that had become so familiar suddenly seemed foreign. Gone were the fragrant basswoods and black locusts, the aroma of rabbit cooking in her mother's stew, even the acrid odor of the mines—scents that rose from the earth, so unlike the manufactured smells of the fair. Her nostrils filled with the smell of corn dogs, cotton candy, and the sweat of machines and people up and running too long.

The sounds of the midway followed her back to the trailer, where she tugged on the door. She unzipped her dress and let it fall to the floor. All she wanted was a dish of her mother's dumplings and a bottle of birch beer. The hardest part of the traveling was the sameness of it all. Every fairground looked the same, along with the people who filed by. Only on the train she glimpsed the mountains she had left, since the circuit covered mostly the Deep South, with only a few stops in East Tennessee.

She could hear them coming, the cadence of their voices familiar as the heat. "Lordamighty, hot as it gets I come to hate the rain. Pushing her through the mud just about killing me."

What would they do if they didn't complain? She picked her dress up off the floor and draped it on the wooden hanger that lived on the hook riveted to the inside wall. As soon as she slipped her jeans and undershirt on, Bettina opened the door. Cheever and Ewell were hoisting the iron throne up the ramp. "S'posed to be dry tomorrow," she offered, like chucking a chicken a handful of corn.

"Is that so?" said Cheever, opening the extra-wide door. He and Ewell both grunted as they pushed Beulah across the threshold. She let her own door slam behind her as she crossed over to Beulah's.

"On three," directed Ewell, as he and Cheever each wrapped an arm around Beulah's midsection. Ewell counted and together they pushed as she called her weight up from the seat. She teetered for a moment before pivoting just enough to land on the bed. Cheever walked around and tugged as Ewell pushed until Beulah sat spanning its width.

"Thank you kindly," Beulah said.

Cheever straightened up, his broad hands splayed on either side of his spine. "Mm-hmm. Another day, another dollar."

"Ain't it the truth," said Beulah, her curls smiling against the pillows. Ewell winked at Cheever and then got caught by Bettina's glare.

"We'll bring you your supper directly," said Cheever, as he made his way around the bed.

"I'll bring it up, Cheever. Save you another trip."

"Thank you, Miss Bettina," he said, dipping his head on the way out.

She clung to the doorway, watching his long legs swallow the length of the ramp as the sound of her name hung in her ear.

She turned slowly, feeling the pull of a knot tightening inside.

"You think Cheever's his first name or his last?"

"I got no idea. It's the onliest name I heard him called around here." Beulah leaned forward, her eyes widening. "If you come close I got something to tell."

"Before I fetch your supper?" Bettina scratched the side of her neck, the part that remained smooth.

"Lord, yes, because today I had me an encounter. Come sit on the bed." She patted the sliver of mattress left on the side.

Bettina sat at the foot of the bed. Out of habit, she began untying Beulah's laces.

"Child, that can wait. Listen here to what happened."

She'd never seen Beulah so excited. "All right, I'm listening."

"I know you're not going to believe me, but it's true. Something came over me this afternoon. Outta nowhere the words came out."

"Somebody talked to you?"

"Yeah, and I talked back."

"How come?"

"Well, it'd just been one of those days when you half wish the roof would fall in. All of a sudden there was this little boy, nine, maybe ten, hanging on the rope. Stood there right through two viewings so the second time the curtain opened, I said 'hello.'"

"Why?"

"I told you, something just came over me, so I asked him his name."

"Did he tell you?"

"Yeah, but that's not the important part." Beulah's head moved forward like a turtle. She whispered, "I told him mine."

"But it's right there on the sign. Miss Beulah Divine."

"No, you don't understand." Beulah's cheeks flushed like a ripe pear. "He asked me did my mama give me that name. I motioned for him to lean in real close and he did. Crawled right under the rope so I could whisper it to him. He's the only person I ever told."

"How come you never told me?"

"Because we go by stage names. It's all we ever use. But having him tell me his name all proud-sounding made me miss my own. So I told him and you know what? He came back later, after dark, and gave me this coin." She lifted her right fist squeezed tight.

"Can I see?" She waited for Beulah to uncurl her fingers.

Beulah kept her hand close, like she was afraid the coin would fly away, so Bettina leaned forward, supporting her weight with her arm. "Ida Mae Appleby," she read aloud. "That your real name?"

Beulah nodded, a tight-lipped smile forming to catch the tear rolling down her cheek.

"What a pretty name, Ida Mae Appleby."

"Say it again, if you don't mind."

"Ida Mae Appleby." She tried to mouth each word as if she were polishing gold.

"And look here, it's got his name, too." Beulah extended her hand, the coin held tight between her fingers.

"Oden Fenton Parks. That's a fancy name."

"He was such a sweet boy." Beulah cupped her palm and ran her other index finger over the letters. "Ida Mae Appleby and Oden Fenton Parks."

Bettina watched the deliberateness of each syllable forming on her tongue.

"Been so long since I heard it. Almost forgot it myself."

Bettina reached over, her palm resting on Beulah's hand. "I'll fetch your supper."

"Bring yours back, too, and we can eat together, if you like."

"All right, Ida. Or do you like Ida Mae?" said Bettina, rising off the bed.

"Ida Mae, but you know what, let's just keep it our secret, 'cause I don't want the name my mama gave me rolled with me through the mud."

On the way back from the chow line, Bettina stopped at her trailer and pulled the small enameled box her mother had given her out of her drawer. She placed it on Beulah's tray, and when she took supper next door and set the tray down on the bed, Beulah lifted the box right away.

"Only thing Mama gave me."

The tears welled again in Beulah's eyes as she turned the box all around, the colors of the enamel lighting her face. Slowly, Beulah unfurled her fingers and set the coin inside. She looked up at Bettina, her eyes full, but instead of speaking she brought her teeth down on her bottom lip, giving her mouth the shape of a sideways exclamation mark. She lifted the box and held it out to Bettina, who placed it in the dresser drawer next to a photograph of a baby swaddled in a woman's arms.

"Me and Oden, we know who you really are."

LEROY HAINES

From the time he was a boy, Leroy Haines's height made him utili-
tarian. He grew taller than anyone in his family by the time he was
twelve. He could count the thinning hairs on his father's scalp, and his
mother, who stood five-foot-three, called upon Leroy to fetch things,
to reach behind furniture and generally make himself useful around the
house. He didn't mind reaching for jars on the top shelf, and he liked
placing the star on the Christmas tree, but inside his elongated frame,
the same shy heart pattered, the same fearful eyes darted, and sometimes
his long legs ached.

At night, he would lie on his pallet since his legs extended beyond the
foot of even his parents' bed, dreaming of mysteries he could not imagine. Machines yet to be invented, or whose discovery he had yet to hear
about. He stared at the rafters, pretending the rest of humanity paraded
around on stilts and only he could lift them up or set them down. Without him, they were doomed to wander awkwardly, lurching, swaying,
balancing precariously as thinly rooted trees laboring under ferocious
winds. As he drifted, his thoughts strayed like clouds sweeping across
the sky, puffs of matter too delicate to hold in place.

After school, he spent afternoons in the stable caring for the horses he
climbed atop with ease. His father worked him as he did all his sons, but
unlike his brothers, he grew gentle as he grew tall. His brothers, two
younger and one older, thought his stature would protect them, a walking wall to encase them from bullies, but Leroy proved them wrong.

Soon after the growth spurt at twelve, his brothers, anxious to cash
in on his staggering height, hurled taunts and stones at other boys in
school, assuming Leroy would come barreling out of the building,
ready to pummel them. His brother Louie whistled shrilly to signal Leroy, who slowly lifted himself from his own table and chair, no longer

able to stuff himself into a child's desk seat, moving like a wobbly colt when he first rose, the cells in his legs multiplying and dividing faster than he could track. By the time he reached the yard where the other children were playing, his stride had steadied, balancing his bulk as he eyed the pack of boys his brothers had roused like angry bees. A great ball of molten lead formed in his stomach, dripping hot globs of metal into his feet. The soles burned as he stood, hoping movement would cool them. He stepped forward into the fray.

"If it ain't Jack and the Beanstalk," a boy called.

"Jack's not tall," a younger boy corrected. "Was the giant you're thinking of."

"Shut up, Harry," the first boy spat.

Leroy could see his brothers watching, waiting for him to avenge the taunt. He wanted to chase them all away, but the weight of the lead anchored him.

"Whip him, Leroy," Louie called, eyes lit up in desperation. Scotty, his youngest brother, boasted to the crowd, "He could whip you with his pecker, it's so big."

"Then let's have a look," the beanstalk boy jeered. "Whip me with your pecker, you big dufus. Got all that height and shit for brains." The boy laughed, small mouth pulled back, head tipped, cap gripping his recently trimmed head.

Sammy, Leroy's brother who was older by a year, pleaded, "Go on, Leroy, kick his scrawny ass," but Leroy stood trapped in the doorway, feet welded to the threshold. The look in his older brother's eyes seared him. He remembered a time when they were both small, years ago, when a bully had chased Leroy, and Sammy had helped him out. But now it felt different. They had stirred the clump of other boys into a frenzy just to brandish him like a giant club. He had been practicing long division. He ached to return to the paper dotted with his computations, the numbers drawn in orderly rows. What gave them the right to use him as their weapon? He looked at his shoes, already two sizes bigger than his father's, and wondered why he had no interest in lifting the wide-mouthed boy who hurled insults and dropping him on his head.

He could hang him by his ankles over the well. Scare him till the stink of his own shit flowed out the collar of his shirt. In that moment while the crowd waited, he tried to summon the fury or the taste for such an act, but he couldn't. The scarred-up table and straight-back chair in the classroom called to him. Leroy turned, the molecules of air losing contact with his face as he ducked back inside.

"Yellow-bellied chicken," the boy called, his words spitballs that fell short of the target. Leroy had almost reached his table when he heard his own brother's voice.

"Stinkin' coward. Henry's right. You got shit for brains and less for guts. You big lump of dog turd," Scotty spat. His own brother turned against him. Hard as he gripped his pencil, the point poised above the divisor, the numbers blurred, the multiplication tables evaporated, the air expanded in his lungs. Leroy Haines, all six-feet-two of him, softened, hoping he could pour himself under the table and then seep into the floor. When he failed to liquefy, he set his head on the table, right cheek against the worn wood, and whispered into stoic lumber—*make me small.*

That evening at supper, none of his brothers spoke to him. They exchanged looks like the ones they swapped when their mother cooked liver or tongue. Clearly his cowardice surpassed even the most objectionable organ meat. The thought of facing the others at school weakened his appetite, but it was the glares and quickly turned looks from his brothers that forced Leroy to excuse himself. He rose, head hung like an empty bridle, and slouched away.

"What's got into him?" he heard his father ask.

"He's a yellow-belly scaredy-cat," Scotty replied.

"Pathetic's what he is," said Louie, two years Leroy's junior. "Got less guts than a milk cow."

Each footstep took Leroy further from the sound but not the words. They lingered, spoken as if he weren't there. He knew they considered his kindness a waste. Had they been endowed with his stature, they would have wielded it over all the other children. But in all the new inches, he could find not one bit that longed to trounce someone else just because he could.

His father, unable to understand his tallest son's fear and sensing the division among his sons, asked his brother to speak to the boy. So the following Saturday, Leroy's uncle Louis took him to the great stand of trees and, without ever saying anything, he showed Leroy beings that grew even taller, the guardians of the earth. On the way back, riding next to Leroy on the mule-drawn wagon, the uncle let his words pass as quietly and quickly as the trees swallowed the sun below.

"The trees will outlive us, my boy, so they command our respect. They see what we do, sense it with their branches, feel it with their leaves. To waste a tree is unforgivable. To ignore one is a loss."

Leroy studied his uncle's face as he spoke in the dimming crimson light, the shape of his head almost a silhouette against the beet-water sky. He could see the solemnity. His uncle spoke about trees the way his Aunt Mary spoke about God, as guardians whose shadows painted the earth with shade, who sacrificed limb and trunk for shelter, and then offered their stumps to the insects and animals small enough to call the mighty remains home.

When he returned to school that Monday, he imagined himself a mighty old oak, impervious to the taunts of the humans who rustled below his branches. He let the spitballs ricochet, the words slide down his trunk the way a hurled egg would. Even the mound of dog turd in his chair passed without comment. He simply lifted the chair, hewn from his brother oak, and carried it outside, where he shook the drying stools from the seat and then wiped it with his handkerchief. Without his response, the taunting lost its fun. Soon the contempt of his peers and siblings bubbled with the quiet consistency of a deep stream. Each time a boy eyed him, deciding whether to throw a punch or huck a gob of spit at his shoes, Leroy remembered his uncle's reverence, and summoned the spirit of his forest guardians. Only when he imagined the smell of evergreens or the grain of maple did the sting of his brothers' disappointment fade away. By the time he reached twenty years and almost eight feet, only the trees rose above him, so he took to invoking them as God.

The cloud cover shone gun-metal gray as the afternoon sun dipped beneath, showering the trees in the distance with golden light. Leroy Haines stood at the far edge of the fairgrounds, hands jammed deep in his pockets, wishing he could touch the sunlight spilling into the leaves. He stood watching the sky for a long time, noting the subtle shift in color as the sun slipped closer to the horizon. Leroy looked over his shoulder and scanned the ground around him. Satisfied no one was looking, he bent over and unlaced his mammoth shoes. Specially made by a deaf cobbler he knew in Talladega. Size eighteen. Then he peeled off his socks, which left tiny white clouds of cotton on the soles of his feet and in between his toes. The cool earth beneath his feet calmed him. He let his eyes close and, slow as a crane lifting off, he raised his arms upward, inhaled deeply, aware of the air as it passed through his nostrils and into his lungs. Toes burrowing into dirt, fingers tickling the belly of sky, he once again imagined himself the great oak towering above him in the forest when he was a boy.

He sought a job at the school for the deaf and blind, figuring if he surrounded himself with those who couldn't register his height visually, he would escape the gawks, the spinning heads, the fingers pointed upward in disbelief. But before he could convince the school of any particularly useful skill, a man named Beasley, who had once sold his family patent medicine, offered him a job in his traveling show.

"There's more to being a giant than your height," Earl Beasley Sr. told him as he unfolded a contract from his pocket. "People pay for the story—in your case, the tall tale." Earl snorted just a little at his own wit. Leroy bore down on the pen, anxious to line his letters up right. Writing had always buzzed around him, a fat fly that landed close enough to swat, only it darted away as soon as a thought slipped into his head. By now, numbers and letters felt too small, like the tiniest pebbles that slipped through his massive hands. He liked the things he could hold firmly: poles, boulders, calves. But Earl had other ideas. He was searching for the angle, he told Leroy, the details that would make his stature even more intriguing.

Earl decided he could intensify the value of two acts if he placed Leroy in the same booth with Tiny the dwarf. Other shows had all the oddities line up on stage, but that never made sense to Earl, who had folks pay twice just to get a second look. Why give them the whole feast for the price of an appetizer? Earl heightened the excitement by allowing the patrons only a brief look. But he made an exception with Leroy, with his personality dull as tarnished silver, assigning him to share Tiny's booth.

"What the hay am I supposed to do with him?" she demanded as they both stood in Earl's office, Leroy teetering on the edge of one chair, Tiny standing on the seat of another chair turned around so that she peeked through the back rungs like a convict trapped behind bars.

"Don't talk about him like he's not there. For God's sake, Tiny, he's a lot harder to miss than you are," Earl said, pulling out one of his cigars.

"Save that smelly thing for later," she barked. "No offense to Leroy, but folks'll get the contrast if you set him in the next booth."

Earl stared at her, his irritation apparent. "Leroy, would you excuse us for a moment, please?"

Leroy rose slowly, careful not to bang his head on the ceiling, a foot and a half lower than his full height.

"Wait right outside, would you?" Earl said as Leroy lumbered out.

"Yessir," he answered, soft as cotton candy.

Earl rose, his movements angular, working his way around the desk, buttocks leaning against the carefully turned rim of wood.

"Now listen, Missy, I've had about enough from you." Earl paused to light his cigar, brandishing the lighter on his desk, drawing in the smoke, then letting it billow out of his mouth, watching as she stepped aside to miss the cumulus rolling toward her head. "Why are you causing a stink? Every other show in the world has you all on stage together."

"What am I supposed to do with him? You're the one likes us viewed apart. Why not keep it that way?"

"Because it'd make him look even taller."

"He's eight feet already."

"Make you look smaller."

"I'm small enough."

Neither Earl nor Tiny noticed Leroy's shadow fall across the window.

He listened intently through the screen, wondering what he'd let himself in for.

"Well, I've been thinking I might want to change the show. Have somebody inside to tell the stories like other shows do." Earl sat on the edge of his desk. Tiny stood on the seat of the chair.

"Look, Earl, folks already file in and out of the oddities tent, so why mess with it?"

"Because we could do more to maximize the oddities."

"Well, I'm maximized enough. I ain't going to stand there all day next to Leroy. Just build him teeny weenie furniture. Stuff him behind some little desk."

Leroy peered in the window watching her. She made him nervous, all mouth and hardly any body. He tilted his head sideways and bent at the waist to get a better view inside. Earl waved his cigar as he gestured.

"I was thinking of dressing him like some Russian prince."

"Folks in Biloxi don't care a rat's ass about Russia. Just give Leroy a sack of suckers to hand out."

Odd that even here people talked about him like he wasn't there. Hardly anyone ever addressed him directly. He felt like a monument being discussed.

Earl began to pace. Leroy stepped aside and pressed himself against the outside wall. Earl's words skidded around the corner of the window frame. Leroy sighed, resigned himself to waiting. Mr. Earl and the dwarf would decide his fate. He wandered away from the trailer and dropped to his haunches to look at a clump of dandelions clinging to the safety of a utility pole.

"Hey, Leroy," Earl called, his head poking out the trailer door. "Come back in here." Leroy rose as if summoned to his execution. Inside the trailer, Tiny still stood on the seat of her chair.

"Tiny here has agreed to share a booth, on a trial basis. You and she can work out your stance and get ready for tomorrow. Any questions?"

Leroy shook his head, wondering what had transpired in the conversation during the moments he had stepped away. Tiny hopped off the chair and he followed her out.

"Sorry if I messed things up," he offered.

"It ain't you. Earl's always trying to steal my thunder, or lightning. Whatever he can wrestle away first. How about I latch onto you like a parasitic twin?"

He'd never seen one and he didn't know if she was fooling, so he stood there, blankly wishing he could fit in. The others all seemed to like to perform.

"How about I play with your rod?" She winked. "What's it take to turn your crank, Leroy?" She eyed him squarely.

He squiggled his lips, his mouth a flattened worm.

"That's why he wants me in your booth, because you just stand there." She kicked a discarded roll emptied of its twine.

"I can't help it. I don't know what I'm supposed to do."

"You dance? How about a little soft-shoe shuffle?"

The weight of the world creased the muscles in his back. He thought joining the show would ease his troubles, allow him to slip into a crack where no one expected much. He thought he could just be tall, but then he recalled Earl Beasley's words. The only giant he knew about was the one in Jack and the Beanstalk.

"Just what's a giant supposed to do?" he looked down, hands shoved in his trouser pockets, cuffs riding up toward his ankle bone.

"Entertain 'em, buddy, just like we all do. Folks are bored. These farmers plant and pull and pick all day. They don't have time to read stories or go anywhere. This here's their big treat. You and me and the other freaks. Natural wonders. Takes their mind off their sore legs and spent backs. Listen, walk around this place and see what amuses you. Learn how to do a back bend or jump rope. Anything that fools them into seeing something that ain't there."

"This is harder than I thought." He tugged his right hand from his pocket and scratched the back of his neck.

"Dress up as Jesus. That ought to get them. Ask one of the colored fellows to build you a cross."

"I don't have long hair."

"Well, grow it. The younger Beasley, Tom, he's all wrapped up in

God. He must figure himself a walking Jesus sandwich, he's in so thick with the Lord."

"You don't believe in Jesus?"

"Doesn't matter whether I do or not. This here show ain't nothing but an act. So play along. Choose a part. You're enormous. Who's gonna argue with you if you say you're Jesus?"

He thought about it. If he could pretend he was a tree, could he pretend to be Jesus? Anyone who hadn't met his brothers might think his strength matched his height, the same way they figured his father's mutt was vicious as he was big. "But who's gonna believe Jesus would work the ten-in-one show?"

"Where else is He gonna find the true heathens, the sinners, the lost lambs who've strayed from God? Where else but in a tent with those rubes happy to pay to gawk at God's mistakes? Why, think of the nerve involved. Our Creator in His infinite wisdom has made us unusually small and tall. Instead of seeing the beauty in that, the hidden value we possess, these yokels line up and stare, thinking themselves a damn sight better. Pitying us is nothing more than sullying the Lord." Her eyes blazed with fire, fist balled in the air, words spraying like buckshot.

She had him there. "What'll I do till my hair grows?"

"Get one of them girlie-girls in the dancing tent to lend you a wig, or tell old Earl to have his sister Emma buy one." She pointed her stubby index finger toward his nose. "See, Stretch, we found your calling. Leroy the Giant just turned into the recently located son of God."

They found Tom, but he didn't buy the pitch. "It's sacrilege," he sputtered, walking away from them both.

"But wait," Tiny persisted, running after him. He waved her away without even turning back. "How do you know what shape a prophet takes, Tom? Won't you feel bad if you meet Saint Peter and he says, 'Too bad, Tom Beasley. You had your chance and you turned Jesus away.'"

"Wait a minute." Tom spun around. "You got something there. He ain't no Jesus, but he sure could be a long-lost prophet or some kinda angel fallen to earth. Yes, it's coming to me now. The Good Lord sent Leroy to warn the masses. The Gentle Prophet Giant. A latter-day Isaiah."

Tom's glare landed on Leroy, who bit his bottom lip and hoped God wouldn't strike him down like a shagbark hickory for impersonating a holy man. But once a Beasley settled on an idea, the valise slammed shut. No discussion, just a fitting with sister Emma, who designed his new costume.

"Something biblical," she said, words squeezing around teeth clamped down on several straight pins. She stood on a small wooden step ladder Stan had built, pinning a sheet of muslin around Leroy's shoulders. Mouth emptied, her speech loosened. "You reckon we can find you some sandals in your size?"

"I don't know, ma'am," he offered, head drooping, a wilted sunflower.

"Well, we'll find out. I can always ask Jimmy to make you some. Man can sew a moccasin like you wouldn't believe. Now you better start growing your beard."

Draped in unwashed muslin, he felt like a tent pole. Suddenly it occurred to him that he wouldn't get to wear his pants underneath. The thought of bare legs in front of strangers flushed his face.

"Miss Emma, what would I be wearing under the robe?" He looked straight ahead at the molding.

"Your underdrawers, silly." She stepped down from the ladder and began pinning above his ankles.

"Won't I get cold? I suffer from poor circulation." He tried to pretend she wasn't inches from his stocking feet.

Emma looked up, her gaze searching for his faraway eyes. "Leroy, prophets were desert people. The Lord didn't come from New York City and neither did all them fellows roaming around before He got here. From what Tom told me, I'm supposed to outfit you as the second Isaiah. We're talking way before Christ. You ever read the Bible, son?" she asked, her gray hair coiled atop her head like a bird's nest.

Leroy dropped his head even further, ears burning with embarrassment. "No ma'am, not much, but I reckon I should. Who's gonna believe I'm a prophet?"

She stepped back from him, her eyes traveling the length of his body.

He ached, waiting for an answer. They always saw him, but they rarely heard.

"Something's missing. I just can't tell what. A sash?"

He started to answer, but her expression signaled that she was talking to herself.

"I'll have to ask Tom. He's up on biblical dress." She circled around him. "I reckon I got to get those sandals custom-made. Now what was it you asked?"

He hesitated, wondering whether to repeat the question. Would it evaporate the moment it reached the air?

"Did you ask something or not, son?" She cocked her head back, as if setting her sights on his chin.

"Do you think anyone will believe me?" he blurted out.

"Some folks would believe you were Jesus Christ. It's all in the telling. And their need to believe. You got to go into your own trance. Conjure the hottest heat you ever felt and let your mouth go dry. Feel all that dust blowing at you, see the sand rippling as people gather to hear, waiting for that moment when you speak, clasping their hands in prayer."

People actually listening. That would be a change.

Sometimes, because of his extraordinary stature, they initially thought he possessed Herculean strength, periscopic sight, equine masculine endowment. Once they realized he was neither miraculous nor invincible—only tall—their disappointment eddied around him. He understood there was more to gianthood than height, but he had not imagined such an outlandish ruse.

The night after his costume fitting, Leroy sat hunched in his trailer, reading a Bible Tom had lent him. He found the Book of Isaiah, but wondered if he had to read all the books that came before in order to understand. He hadn't opened a Bible since childhood, when he still fit in a Sunday school desk. Outside he heard hissing, followed by a man hollering something rude. He let the sounds fall without catching them. The knock on the door a moment later startled him. He shut the Bible and slid it onto his lap. "Come in," he called, assuming it was a Beasley brother or Tattoo Man, since no one else had ever come to call.

The screen door pushed open and Lizard Man appeared. Leroy felt badly he didn't know his real name. "Good evening," he offered as Lizard Man stepped inside.

"I hear you're starting a new act."

Leroy nodded, embarrassed to be impersonating a prophet.

"Mind if I sit down?"

Leroy shook his head, his shame compounded by his lack of manners. "No, of course not. Nice to have someone call."

"You only been here a couple of weeks?"

"Ten days. I hadn't never done nothing like this before. What about you? You been performing long?"

"Since I was four. My mama had me in front of her church lady friends, convinced I was a messenger from God."

"So you do this act already?"

"Not anymore. Now I'm plain old Lizard Man. When I signed on with Beasleys', I insisted on that."

"Why'd your mama think you were an angel?"

"It was her way of accepting my terrible skin. You read the Bible?"

Leroy searched Lizard's eyes for judgment. Finally, he shook his head no.

"In the Bible, leprosy, skin lesions, stuff like that's nothing but trouble. Sign of being spiritually unclean. Now here was my mama, figuring herself a good Christian woman, and out I come with this ugly-ass skin. Far as I can figure, she had two choices: believe she birthed some kinda evil or some kinda good. She picked the latter. Dreamed up her scheme that I was her little messenger from God."

Leroy bent forward, as if closer proximity to Lizard's mouth would afford him a better understanding of the words.

"You got any religious training?" Lizard asked.

"Not directly. I quit going when I was a boy. But I don't mean to be a blasphemer. I don't want to offend anyone." He looked down at his hands, hidden under the table, still clutching the Bible. "Before you got here, I was studying." He pulled out the book, his finger still marking his place.

Lizard nodded toward the text. "You know Isaiah suffered even though he was good?"

"What for?"

"I'm talking about the second one. There's more than one Isaiah, you know."

Leroy didn't, but he nodded anyway. "Why'd he suffer?"

"For the sins of others, like that could make things right again, through God's grace. Gotta have God's grace in there so folks will be redeemed."

"Suffered for no reason? No cause he brought on himself?"

"That's right."

He looked at Lizard's arms, the skin all patchy scales. "You ever feel like you was made to suffer, on account of being different?"

"Hell, yes. I was no angel—just a scaly little boy. She paraded me around in those angel wings from the time I could walk. I'd been training for this show all my life. Least now I get paid and don't pretend I hear anything from God."

"But you know all about the Bible." Leroy extended it to Lizard, who took it and flipped through the pages until he stopped and read:

so marred was his
appearance beyond human
semblance and his form beyond that
of mortals—
so he shall startle many nations:
kings shall shut their mouths
because of him:
for that which had not been told
then they shall see.

Leroy leaned forward into the verse, his arms sprawled across the table between the two men. "Could you read that again?"

Lizard read the passage over. "You get what it means?"

"He was ugly, kinda odd..."

"Beyond that of mortals."

"And he suffered even though he was good?"

"Yeah. God's a pisser, but then He might go and serve you up grace."

Lizard set the Bible on the table. Leroy could hear the long breath he drew in through his nose. "Well, I should get going. You play poker? Tattoo's got a game going in his trailer."

"Not much of a card player."

"Oughta give it a try."

"Sometime I will."

Lizard rose. Leroy realized he hadn't even offered him a cold drink.

"I'll be seeing you, then. Good luck tomorrow." Lizard moved toward the door. Leroy stuck out his right hand.

"Thanks so much for coming over. Come again." The scales felt dry under his fingertips. He pumped Lizard's hand hard.

As soon as Lizard left, Leroy sat back down and read the passage over. Isaiah 52:14–15. He read the words so many times he could shut his eyes and hear them in his head. Leroy lowered his windowshade till only a sliver of light peeked in. He lit a candle next to his bed and read the rest of the chapters slow as a trickling creek, his mouth swallowing each word. In a dream, he knelt on one knee at the edge of the stage, tears streaming down his face, arms swaying like branches, explaining to the audience they had broken their covenant with God.

The next morning Leroy sat in his trailer, hands clasped around his biceps, arms folded across his chest, the muslin toga bunching underneath as he peered at his mammoth feet, nails trimmed. Unshaven for a week, his bristly face itched. Had God moved through Tiny, insisting he have his own booth? Had his suffering—the disappointment and insults—spared others? Is that how the great pine and mighty oak felt as saws bit into their flesh? The questions sent shivers up his arms.

"Leroy!" The voice punctured the moment. "You gonna sit in there daydreaming, or you gonna help me?" Stan Beasley called. He lifted his head to see Stan standing at his door, hands on hips, mustache inching like a worm.

Leroy sighed, exhaling the last particle of solitude.

"For God's sake, put your shoes on and let's go. I need your help, man."

He hopped up and scurried, as best an eight-foot-tall man could, to retrieve his shoes from under his dresser. He sat on his bed, pulling the sandals off with one hand, reaching for his socks with the other. He had stashed the white cotton socks into the toes of his specially made shoes. He yanked out a sock, scrunching it first and then rolling it over his toes. The damp cloth, pregnant with sweat, seemed to struggle as much as he did, the sock and his skin both gasping for air.

"Ain't got all day," Stan said.

"Yes, sir," he mumbled, trying to envision the child who needed rescue. Some rascal must have shinnied up a pole. He tugged the sock on the rest of the way and slipped his foot into the shoe, lacing it quickly. Then he pulled on the other sock, covering his foot the way a parent might hastily wrap a coat around a frisky child. The second shoe in place and laced, he exited his trailer and stood ready to follow Stan Beasley, who had begun walking away. With each stride, Leroy could feel his left sock gobbled by his heel. By the time he caught up with him, the wind chomped at his bare skin of his ankle. The bunched sock lapped at the sole of his foot, collecting in the hollow of his arch. He bent down to retrieve it, but caught his employer's glare. He lurched forward, fingers unable to find the sock, hands splaying as he lost his balance. The child, he must think of the child. Someone needed help. His gobbled sock could wait. He lifted himself, a kiwi on the runway imagining flight. When he tried to run, his hips ached, so he concentrated on elongating his stride to swallow as much of the worn ground as possible. *March, march*, he mouthed to himself, *you must cross the fiery desert with no regard of your own pain.*

He followed Stan Beasley into the heart of the fairground, behind the midway and the concessions tent. "Look, Ma, it's the tall man," a boy yelled. Leroy jerked his head down, as if turning his face away would make him disappear. Caught offstage in his costume, legs like a heron's ending in mammoth oxford shoes. A sight too painful to imagine, his breath rattling inside his chest, growing hotter with the effort of moving quickly and trying, however futilely, to blend in.

So marred was his appearance. "Somebody in trouble?" he muttered as the middle Beasley brother led him along the edges of the fray.

"Just come on." Stan's words scattered like popcorn, leading him across the midway to the trailer where the Beasleys slept. "Watch your head," Stan reminded him as they approached the door.

Leroy ducked as he entered and stayed curved, a lower case *r*, waiting for Beasley's direction, confused as to where the child in distress might be hiding.

"See that spot on the ceiling? It's leaking."

Leroy craned his neck and rolled back his head. He felt like a broken *s*. A discolored spot came into view. No child swaying on a pole or caught in the rafters of a tent. No frightened parents standing nearby. A brown spot on the ceiling of a trailer. Stan Beasley pointed, his own fingertips touching the offending stain.

"You gotta be kidding," was all Leroy said.

"No, damn things aren't built to last. I thought you could putty it or something."

Leroy unfurled himself as far as he could, shoulders still hunched, head twisted to one side. The words got caught around the bend so he backed his way out and then turned to step out of the trailer. This time, Beasley followed him.

"Mr. Stan, a prophet does many things, but fixing your leaky roof is not one of them. Those folks are waiting to see the return of a holy man, *his form beyond that of mortals—so he shall startle many nations: kings shall shut their mouths because of him: for that which had not been told them they shall see.*"

"You been reading the Bible, son? What, did Tom fill your head with all that talk?"

For the first time he could remember, Leroy breathed into his full height, the words flowing from his mouth. "A man whose height reminds them of towering trees, whose outstretched arms are branches they can come to, a man who watches like the great sequoias and sees far across the horizon of time."

Leroy followed the length of his outstretched arm. Could this be him? Were these his words, stored for years, centuries, even?

"I'm terrible sorry, Mr. Stan, but I have to go."

"What about the roof? Can you come back later on your dinner break?"

"I got visions to reveal, hope to offer." Leroy glanced at his feet. "Sandals to fetch." Without looking back, he walked across the midway, head swirling with words, glorious words, their soft edges and long, sonorous curves bellowing in his throat. As he reached the back entrance of the oddities pavilion, he loosened his laces and stepped out of his shoes. The bunched sock slid off immediately and he slipped off the other, setting them both in his shoes, which he left by the exit flap. Striding across the tent, he took his place in the booth next to Tiny's, stepping into the sand that covered his platform, the grains moving between the hourglass of his toes. He'd fetch the sandals later. Feet planted on holy ground, he gazed across his own desert, shoulders arched, neck straightened, arms outspread.

STONY

Jim Edward Cartwright fell from a horse when he was ten and broke his back. His parents bundled him in the back of the wagon and carried him into town, figuring they'd save time. The ride jostled things further and the doctor at the county hospital politely informed them that Jim Edward would never walk. He wouldn't even crawl. Paralyzed from the waist down. Being of modest means, they packed him up at the end of his long stay and brought him home, where he either sat in Grandpa Willis's wingback chair or propped in bed all day. His mother had chores and his sisters either helped in the fields or went off to school, depending on the season, which left him to leaf through the Sears Roebuck catalog his mother placed in his lap.

He liked to study one picture of an object—a pair of men's workboots, a lady's bonnet, a maul—and invent a story whereby he would find the object and return it to its rightful owner. After a few days studying the wish book, he jumbled the letters on the tool page and pretended he'd discovered a new country. Nobody walked there, and all the people who scooched around on their bellies or rocked on their backs cheered when he rolled in, riding on a carved walnut throne drawn by two black steeds. He sat above the wriggling subjects as they called up to him and pronounced him king. Then he would get two helpings at breakfast with all the blackberry jam and biscuits he could eat. His mother would have to ask permission from the palace guard, who knew to admit her only if she brought more biscuits.

Worried he would get fat, his mother rationed his food. Unable to reach the food unassisted, he studied the pages of utensils, imagining something to eat. His mother, looking over his shoulder at spatulas and whisks, quickly flipped to pages of flannel shirts. Plaids and checks did not console him. He wanted smoked ham with red-eye gravy and grits with pools of butter melting under his fork, instead of the stingy portions his mother doled out.

Two years after the accident, his father sought the advice of the town fathers, six rusty old men who rocked on the porch of the general store. When his father returned from town, he told Jim Edward about a man named Beasley who ran a show featuring unusual people.

"What would you think of joining the show?" his father asked, breath sweet with whiskey.

"How would I get there?"

"I reckon he'd fetch you. Don't expect you to walk."

His father knelt down beside him. "You'd get to see things I never seen, travel in a fancy automobile, ride the train. It's a traveling show." His father pulled out a knotted-up hanky and wiped his nose. "It's not that we don't want you, boy, but your mother and I's busy. The bigger you get, the harder you'll be to keep."

Jim Edward looked past his father, imagining the kingdom of crawlers who'd coronated him.

"Think of all you'll get to eat."

He gazed at his drunken father, tiny veins exploding across his broad nose.

"If it'll make you happy, I'll go."

"It's for you, boy, not for me. But it's best that way." His father wobbled upright and patted him on the head. "He'll be coming to fetch you the end of the week. I best tell your mother."

What if he hadn't agreed to go? Would the old man have slipped him in an empty grain sack and loaded him on the back of a wagon? It wasn't his fault he fell off the horse. She'd gotten spooked.

Earl Beasley Jr. drove up the road to the house in a new Studebaker, direct from South Bend. Jim Edward strained to peer out the parlor window so he could see the man in the fancy automobile arrive. He stood taller than his father, though about the same bulk. Beasley's hands weren't rough when he reached out to shake Jim Edward's hand, and his nails were clean.

"Been all across the South. Folks come looking for me now," he explained. "Our traveling circuit offers an honest living to anyone whose misfortune or unusual appearance draws a crowd. Beats sitting home feeling useless, son. Draining your parents. Running a farm's burden enough, isn't it?"

By asking it like a question, the man with the mustache and the Sunday suit made it seem like the right thing to do. And by the time he got through reassuring Jim Edward's mother what good care they'd take of him, she looked ready to pay Mr. Beasley instead of the other way around. Before they left, Mr. Beasley made a point of giving Jim Edward's father his calling card. "Any questions you've got concerning the well-being of your son, you contact me. Directly." As if *they* had a way to call.

His parents hugged him and stepped back to watch Mr. Beasley lift him into the front of his automobile, secure him in place with packing straps, and tie the wheelchair to the back, careful to put a blanket around the wooden frame. Wouldn't want to scratch the paint on his fancy new car.

The transaction happened so quickly he could hardly believe he was sitting in a stranger's automobile, on his way to another state, with nothing more than a suitcase and two hugs. For the first twenty miles, he relished the ride, until he realized that Mr. Beasley had not anticipated the effect of a saturated diaper on his leather seats. After his accident, the doctor had inserted a catheter, which remained attached to a bag tied to his leg, but since his mother couldn't hoist him onto a pot every time he needed to pass solid waste, she made him wear diapers instead.

"Christ almighty, boy, what you doing over there?" Beasley's look frightened him.

"Didn't my mama tell you? I wear special underthings." He couldn't bring himself to say diapers aloud.

"We got a long ride." That was all Beasley said. They drove in silence for a long time before the man pulled the car off at a roadside store. Jim Edward wondered where the man could clean him up in a place like that, but he sat quietly and waited for Mr. Beasley to help him out.

"Wait right here," he said, as if Jim Edward had a choice.

Beasley returned with two pieces of smoked ham and a half sour pickle wrapped in white paper along with a bottle of Coke. No fancy dinner. No clean drawers, just hours more traveling through the dark. He wanted to turn around and go home, return to his life of gazing at pastry cutters, imagining a kingdom where he never had to bear any shame. But his father had signed a contract and collected a payment. Jim Edward knew even if he persuaded Mr. Beasley to turn around and take him back, his father would stand in the doorway, head drooping like their old cow.

To pass the time, Jim Edward dozed until he felt a hand gripping his shoulder.

"Wake up, son. We're almost there."

"Where's that?"

"Family homestead. Memphis. You're in Beasley country now."

Jim Edward peered through the windshield into the night.

"Now listen here, every act's got a stage name, something to accentuate your condition. Seeing how your attraction is sitting still, we have to capitalize on that. Make it seem miraculous. Folks don't pay good money to see a boy who fell off a horse. But a bona fide living fossil, some kind of dug-up creature, mysteriously turned to stone, now that's worth leaving the farm to see. So from now on, you're Stony, understand?"

"Yes, sir." He shut his eyes and imagined the slitherers folding his Christian name like a scrap of paper, tucking it in a drawer.

When they reached the house, Mr. Beasley's sister greeted them.

"Evening, Earl, who you got here?"

"Our new fossilized boy." Beasley carried Stony across the threshold.

"Pleased to meet you," Miss Emma offered. Luckily, she looked like a grandmother, her gray hair fastened in a loose knot, hands much softer than his mother's, her features firm but not sharp. He wished she would carry him, hold him close so he could smell her. He imagined she smelled faintly of vanilla and cinnamon like his mother at Christmas, or a hint of his sisters' lavender water. Mr. Earl set him down on a bed in a small room at the far end of the hall, but not before Miss Emma laid down a piece of oilcloth underneath. He looked up at the tin ceiling painted white, and then rolled his eyes to catch the top of the rose-papered walls. He detected no familiar aromas: no animals, no hay, not the smell of grease heavy in the air. Not the manure on his father's boots nor the cracked corn for the birds nor the biting scent of lye. City folks, he reasoned, had no smell at all.

"Pillows," he sputtered. "I need more pillows under my head." At home, his mother had made large feather pillows and covered them with soft flannel cases so that he could lean back into softness. Without them, he had to prop himself up with his arms, which grew tired from his weight. Mr. Earl lifted his shoulders while Miss Emma slid two pillows beneath his upper back. He suddenly worried they would kill him. Ordinary carelessness could be fatal to a fossilized boy. He didn't really feel like a fossil because he wasn't old, but he did feel trapped in a stone body he could barely move.

Since his accident, he had been propped, moved, positioned, dressed, bathed, and wiped like a baby without so much as a vote. Even more than he missed riding horses and petting the cow, he longed for the chance to decide when and how to move. One fall had locked him into a world of other people's intentions and convenience. Mr. Earl had let him sit in shit for hours because he didn't want to stop long enough to haul him in somewhere and clean him. Now the gray-haired woman with the tin of powder in her right hand stood ready to suffer the unpleasant task. Stony had to endure lying there while she unfastened his trousers and slid them, soiled and smelling, off of his motionless legs. He could have wiped himself, but she would have had to roll him over and spread his legs apart. The thought of asking her to help him seemed worse than allowing her to do it all.

As he watched her hand bring the washcloth down over his private parts, which for him were never very private, he shut his eyes and pretended her hands traveled somewhere else. Since he could not feel her touch, he found it easier to imagine that he was far away, riding with his grandfather's cavalry unit, upright on his sorrel steed, hands tight around the reins, ready for battle. With a quick kick, the horse exploded into a gallop as the unit advanced on the Yanks. Just as he was ready to draw his carbine, helping to secure victory at Chickamauga, Emma

Beasley lifted his legs and slid a clean diaper underneath. He tried to pretend the horse had jostled him, but she pulled a nightshirt over his head. He wanted to tell her he was busy, that there were Union soldiers to kill, but she had her own plan and he knew, just like with his mother, some things were better left unsaid. He pushed his arms through the sleeves and propped himself against the pillows, wondering if the sounds in a city would be as absent as the smells.

She offered to read to him, but he declined, preferring to draw the darkness around him as if he were lying in a tent with his comrades, absolutely still. He conjured pictures of all the soldiers' faces he'd seen in the pictures his grandfather had shown him, all the names in the stories he told. He thought of his hero dying bravely. Suddenly, Stony appreciated his new name. Whether or not Mr. Earl knew about Stonewall Jackson, so named because he stood like a stone wall, Stony knew he had been called upon to do the same, sitting still as stone, unflinching, watchful, waiting for the perfect moment to order the attack. From that moment on, blanket drawn up under his chin, Stony accepted his orders as a latter-day spy for the Confederate Army, assigned to travel with Company B.

Miss Emma sewed Stony a gray suit, though she did not faithfully reproduce a Rebel uniform. Mr. Earl instructed her to make a costume that conjured the image of a stone so she made him trousers out of gray flannel and tunic that slightly resembled the top half of a uniform. Stony implored her to use gold buttons, and he explained how a cap would bolster the effect. She asked Earl about the cap. He liked the idea, but thought one that looked like the Confederate Army would detract from the idea of a fossilized boy.

"No," said Stony, pleading his case at breakfast, "don't you see, if you dress me like a Rebel and I'm supposed to be fossilized, folks might think I'm a fossilized soldier. Boys my age fought in the war. My granddaddy told me so. You could pretend you dug me up and dusted me off." He was so excited, head lurching forward, arms waving. "Petrified things, they don't rot, right? That's what I'm supposed to be. If people ask me things, I can answer. I know all about the war."

"You don't talk to the audience, you understand? Rule number one. There's always tricksters out there who try to bamboozle you. You don't move. You don't talk. You just sit still as a stone. That's your attraction."

"But how will they know I'm not faking, Mr. Beasley?"

"I told you, you call me Mr. Earl. I have two brothers so it gets confusing."

"But if I dress up like a soldier, and you put up a sign declaring I'm fossilized, folks'll think I am some kind of miracle, being perfectly preserved, like them heads Miss Emma said you keep in a jar. I'll sit still 'cause I can't move, and they won't even know I'm alive."

"The boy's got a point, Earl. If you just sit him in a chair, not much odd to that."

"If he looked like a stone there would be."

"But he doesn't. He looks like a boy. I can make up his face and hands so he looks ashy, like he came right out of the ground. Get one of your fellows to build him a display box."

"You could put a rifle in it or a sidearm, so it'd look real."

Mr. Earl bit into a piece of toast, gobbling half the slice. His eyebrows slid toward his nose as he chewed. "Hmm. Stony the Fossilized Soldier. Mysteriously preserved for fifty years." He pushed the remaining half into his mouth. Miss Emma took a sip of her coffee, her eyes trained on Mr. Earl.

"All right, by God, we'll try it, but boy, this means you're dead. You got to fix your gaze and not blink, you hear me. I don't care if a snake gets loose and wraps around your neck. You got to stare straight ahead and act like nothing's changed. You sure you can do that?"

Stony smiled. He was going to be a soldier, after all. If only he was missing his arm, he'd pretend to be Stonewall himself. He could still pretend. He'd just be Stonewall, the boy soldier. "Yes sir," Stony said, straightening his shoulders. "I can do it, sir. I promise."

"All right, then. Go on and fix up that costume. Give him a Rebel cap. But let me tell you something, boy, don't you let out one of those stinky doos while you're propped up there like some petrified soldier. If you're a fossil you best not smell of shit."

"Earl, hush now. Don't hurt the boy. He can't help his bowels."

"Well, then, we'll see to it he don't eat till after the show."

"You can't starve him. It takes hours to pass. I'll watch his schedule. See when he goes."

If Stony had known he'd have to endure Miss Emma checking his behind every hour for two days, he might have reconsidered the whole plan, but it was too late. She kept him in an old nightshirt and diaper to more easily ascertain that he emptied his bowels twice. Next, she experimented with different foods. On the third day of the great shit trials, his rump was so raw, she put a stop to it.

"Most of the time, your business don't stink, so don't mind Mr. Earl."

The signpainter depicted him as a Rebel soldier standing at attention under a Confederate flag. In black letters, the sign read: STONY, THE FOSSILIZED SOLDIER—MYSTERIOUSLY PRESERVED. The colored fellow, Cheever, winked at him as he built a coffin-like box lined with leaves, with a ledge for his feet. They tipped it back thirty degrees so people could see into it. Mr. Earl instructed Cheever to stretch a Confederate flag across the back of the cubicle for effect. He spat, mumbling something about President Lincoln while putting up the flag, but Stony, who lay in the box, was too excited to catch what Cheever said.

He spent his first day on display staring past the viewers. Miss Emma had scrubbed patches of the uniform so it wouldn't look brand new, and Cheever had scuffed up Stony's boots and coated the soles with mud.

In the battlefield of his mind, the steeds stomped red clay into great clouds, particles glinting in the late afternoon sun, casting the air bronze, as if they were all statues, frozen as they rode courageously into battle. Suddenly, an interruption. Stony squiggled his lips, trying to dislocate the fly that had landed on the tip of his nose. He recalled Mr. Earl, finger wagging, and quickly set his mouth in place. He could see the fly's wings, filigree connected to the stout body, the large green eyes peering into his own. Stony blew a column of air upward, but the fly remained. He rolled his eyes up just enough to lose sight of the fly and returned to Chickamauga. The horses thundered, dust rose, and the smell of the dry earth, dirty uniforms, and fear jammed his nostrils.

The fly crawled to the bridge of his nose. For a split second, the path of his vision crossed, then he quickly looked ahead. Stony blew more air but there was no way to direct it. The fly clung to its post, tiny legs adhering to the smooth terrain. Behind the rope that separated viewers from the stage, a boy jabbed his father. "He's got a fly on his nose."

"Dead things always attract flies." The father sounded unimpressed.

Stony knew the boy would be watching, so he concentrated on the image of a fallen Union soldier about to be trampled by scores of hooves galloping by. His breathing hardened as the fly crawled onto his forehead, then buzzed, lifting itself to land in the valley between cheekbone and eyelid. The tickle taunted him, but Stony resisted the urge to blink. He heard the boy's voice again, this time farther away.

"If he's dead, how come he don't stink? Remember that opossum we found by the barn?"

"Cause he's fossilized. Ain't really a fossil. More petrified. Like underneath that skin makeup he's nothing but stone."

"Oh," the boy's voice trailed off, "that's why he got that name. I thought he was related to Stonewall Jackson."

Stony felt the tug in his chest. He wanted to get up and run after him, trade Civil War stories and play with the soldiers he kept in an old cookie tin. He lost the sound of the boy's voice in the patter of the crowd.

Though he missed home, he acclimated to his new life after a few weeks. The routine comforted him. He savored the time spent fighting Civil War battles. In those moments, all he needed was his imagination. Even movable legs could not have transported him to the war. He had been born too late; too many decades had elapsed, but he was grateful time circled back and stretched before him in long afternoons that allowed him to recreate the very battles he had missed.

Cheever and Ewell occasionally told him stories about the different oddities. The Geek struck Stony as the strangest among them, since he chose to bite heads off of live chickens instead of just getting a job. There was nothing odd about Muscle Man; he was just magnificently strong. Pretzel Man told Stony he was born limber and blessed with double joints. For a while, the Beasley brothers had a thin woman who hardly ever ate, starved herself as part of the attraction, but according to Cheever she got so skinny fur started growing on her. Mr. Earl got excited about that, but right before he could augment her banner, the fuzzy-looking skeleton lady died. That's when Mr. Stan said a fat lady would be better in the long run. More expensive to feed, but less likely to cash out earlier. He had a peculiar way of talking like that. The youngest Beasley, Mr. Tom, said Mr. Stan always saw things in terms of currency, either flowing in or rushing out, and that's why he handled the money. The midget lady told Stony to stand his ground. Otherwise, the Beasleys would find some extra way to profit off him. The only human attractions treated like people instead of pickles in a barrel waiting to be sold were the dancing girls who got tips and their own tent.

Stony had never seen the likes of them, with their slender waists and bosoms so full they made his insides ache. They looked nothing like his doughy mother or his sisters, stout as oaks. He glimpsed the dancing girls only fleetingly when Ewell wheeled him by their tent, but Mr. Earl noticed his gaze one afternoon.

"You want to see them titties up close? That what you want, Stone Boy?" Mr. Earl rustled his hair and offered to take him backstage.

"You think they'll mind?" he asked as Mr. Earl pushed his wheelchair, Stony lashed in tight.

"Are you kidding? These girls spend their nights wiggling away from guys a lot quicker than you." Mr. Earl brought him in through the rear exit flap and parked him near a shiny-haired woman applying her makeup.

"Give the boy a thrill, will you?" he said, winking at her as he left.

She set down the brush she was using to rouge her cheeks. When she looked at him, he dropped his head, embarrassed to be caught staring.

"It's all right sugar, you can look. That's what I get paid for." She stood and his eyes traveled the length of her legs up to the tiny swatch of fabric wrapped around her hips like no skirt he'd ever seen. "I bet

you won't say anything half as nasty as the men who come to see us."
She walked over and put her hand on his shoulder. Stony looked down
at the sight of it resting there and bit his bottom lip. "You poor thing,
you're all strapped in."

"So I don't fall out, but you could loosen the top one so I could move
my arms."

She leaned over so her face lined up with his, her breasts straining
against the bustier. "What's your name?" she asked.

Caught in awe, unsure how to answer, he peered into her eyes. "Folks
call me Stony. It's short for Stonewall Jackson."

"That's nice."

He could tell she didn't recognize the name. He let his gaze fall, heavy
as overbeaten flapjacks. How could anyone not know?

He reeled his head back up. "To my mind, Stonewall Jackson was the
greatest Civil War general that ever lived." She looked at him, her face
suddenly serious, so he whispered, "Do you believe in ghosts?"

"Why?" She tilted her head.

"Because if there are any, I might be his."

She stood back up. "You don't look like one to me."

"Could you loosen the strap, ma'am?"

"You don't have to call me 'ma'am.' Just call me Lisabelle."

"That your real name or did Mr. Earl name you that?" He watched
her fiddle with the top strap. "The knot's in the back." She moved
around and untied it.

"My mama named me that. Mr. Earl, he calls me 'Tits.'" She rolled her
eyes like his father used to when he complained about the price of mash.

"How long you been here?" she asked.

"Two months."

"You miss your family?"

"Yeah, but they couldn't really keep me, not for much longer. Mama
said I weighed more than a full flour sack, and it hurt her back something awful every time she lifted me."

She smiled at him, straightening herself up.

"Mind if I ask you a question?" he asked.

"Go right ahead." Her permission, a feather light on his skin.

"How tall are you?"

"Five foot, eight inches. Some girls say they'd hate being tall as a man, but I like being able to look them right in the eye. Course most of the ones I see got their eyes focused somewhere else." She bent over to face him. Her bottom front teeth were a tad crooked, but overall they lined up nicely.

"You ever seen a naked tittie?" she asked, not even shrinking her voice.

"No, ma'am. I ain't even seen my sisters in their underdrawers. They're a lot older than me."

"Would you like to?"

"Sure." He looked to see if Ewell was around, or if any of the other dancing ladies were watching, but no one appeared to be paying attention. Lisabelle leaned in close and unfastened her top. He watched as they fell only slightly, released from their binding. Instinctively he lifted his hand to catch them.

She smiled and took his hand in hers, placing it on the soft mound.

"Go ahead, hold it, get a feel. Never know when you'll get another chance."

It was heavier than he expected, the skin so smooth, the nipple slightly bumpy. He slid his thumb across it a couple of times and watched as it tightened, looking just a little like the skin of mock oranges that fell near his house.

"Does the other one feel the same?"

"I think so, but you can make sure."

He wondered if she thought him foolish. With his other hand he lifted the right bosom. It felt the same. He tried to imagine what it would feel like to have appendages like that, soft and pretty to look at, but not good for much else. Not much different than his legs, except the bosoms looked far better than the pale bark-stripped sticks of his withered limbs.

"Want to kiss one?"

Her question caught him off guard, and once he realized what she had asked, he wasn't sure if he wanted to, but he didn't want to seem rude so he nodded.

She leaned in closer. What if Mr. Earl or Mr. Stan caught him? Ewell or Cheever? She seemed to detect his concern. "Nobody's looking. Might never get another chance."

He hesitated, overwhelmed by the prospect of putting something so forbidden and mysterious in his mouth. Had Stonewall Jackson ever done such a thing? He leaned forward, and imagined catching a raindrop on his tongue as he felt her nipple, but it made him nervous so he let it slip from his mouth.

She stroked his cheek. "I am glad I got to meet you, Stony. You're a sweetheart. Now I got to put my tassels on."

"What's a tassel?"

"They cover my titties. When we jiggle, the tassels sway and it drives the menfolk wild."

He watched her cover them, blinking, not quite sure he had just taken one in his mouth. He shut his eyes for a moment, wondering what his mother would say. Suddenly, he knew he could never face her again. He had sinned against her and God and probably everyone else, and he hadn't meant to—he was just curious, and the lady had offered and it wasn't his fault she had taken pity on him, stuck in his chair.

The slitherers and crawlers hissed. He opened his eyes and blinked them away. "It wasn't my fault," he called.

"What the hell are you doing?" Mr. Stan yanked his chair. "Aren't you supposed to be on stage in the other tent right now?"

In his mind, he called after his subjects to rescue him, but the king's carriage failed to appear. Mr. Stan's face filled his view. "What's that I smell?"

Just when Stony imagined the firing squad, Cheever burst in.

"Coon, you're not allowed in this tent."

"Mr. Earl sent me after Stony."

"Well get him out and clean his sorry ass. I ought to fire you both." Mr. Stan stalked off.

Cheever turned his chair and shoved. Stony flopped forward as the front tire dipped into a rut.

"Godamighty, you ain't tied in. Who untied you?"

"Lisabelle."

"Who's she?"

"One of the dancing ladies."

"This day's turning from bad to worse." Cheever wrapped the packing strap back around his shoulders and off they went.

"I think my britches is dirty."

"I don't smell nothing."

"But Mr. Stan said..."

Cheever yanked the chair backward and pulled Stony into the oddities' tent. "Soldier boy, I don't see Mr. Stan. All I hear is them crackers lined up to see your ass in the box." Cheever untied him and scooped him out of the chair, dropping him into his display like a sack of potatoes.

"Ouch," he whimpered as his elbow hit the side. "Damn fool coon." The words hissed out.

"What'd you say?"

"Nothing."

"Don't lie to me, boy. You better watch your mouth, 'cause the war's over. I don't care what you think you is, you ain't nothing but a shit-stinking freak, gotta beg mercy for someone to wipe your ass. So you better watch who you call a damn fool coon." Cheever spun around, his beige work shirt a flash against the darkened tent.

"My cap," Stony muttered, the words hobbling out. "I need my cap." But there was no one to fetch it as he heard the crowd gather on the other side of the curtain, about to go up.

He prayed the smell in his britches would not pass over the crowd. Though he tried conjuring images of battles, he thought of slave uprisings instead. He didn't trust Cheever anymore.

Tears gathered but he knew not to blink. He tried harder to summon his comrades, wishing for all the world he were crouched in the woods, ready to blast the Union forces drawing near. When no soldiers came, he summoned his subjects, but they'd left the kingdom. He'd been dethroned.

❧

The Beasleys didn't fire him and he might have remained a Confederate soldier forever, but much to everyone's dismay, he grew. Not a lot, but enough to be noticed by a family that came back to view the oddities each year. "If he's a fossil," the red-faced farmer asked, "then why's he bigger than the year before?" The man's wife, a sausage-looking woman with her hair in a net, stood alongside him bobbing her head. "See, she seen it too, how that boy done grown."

Mr. Earl told him the soldier act had to go. They'd have to create a new ruse. All entertainment, Mr. Earl explained, was an illusion, like the dancing girls who were right there shaking and kicking and swinging, luscious as could be, but they weren't going to dance into some fellow's living room and let him do whatever he pleased. Mr. Earl insisted that too many people had seen him dressed as a soldier to let him continue on like that, so he had to change his appearance altogether.

By the time he turned sixteen, he was just a paralyzed man with a repainted display sign that made him look more like a stone. Tiny made up his hands and face to look ashen and dead, and Miss Emma sent a striped shirt and trousers to demonstrate how the lines never shifted, but Stony felt more like a runaway from the chain gang than a carnival performer. For a couple of days, he imagined returning to his parents' farm, but there would be no fanfare upon his return—no parade, no legless wonders calling up to him, only his mother grown too weak to lift him, and his father, weary from the farm, slightly liquored up, gazing at the lump of a son he'd sold four years before. His sisters wouldn't want to take him, nor would he choose to live alongside them with their robust husbands filled with a sense of purpose and the means to carry it out.

Strapped in his new chair, turned to stone, he drew in breath, somber as a white winter sky. He never again saw Lisabelle though she danced less than a hundred yards away. He traveled back to those sensations: that first look, the heat in his fingers, the feel of her nipple against his tongue. But the memory ached as it crossed the long hallway between once and never again, so he retreated to his early years on the farm, helping his father in the field, getting the hay in, riding the horse, the reins familiar in his hands. But suddenly, he was falling, the mare rising up on her hind legs, his feet sliding, crashing to the ground, the snake that had startled her slithering away.

Earl himself yanked Stony by the back of his shirt. What the hell was he doing closing his eyes and tearing up in the middle of a Saturday afternoon show? How was it, Mr. Earl demanded to know, he could sit in shit without blinking, and then shut his eyes for no reason? Behind the closed curtain, listening to the hum of the audience on the other side, Stony didn't bother to explain how he'd stumbled on the fall that would always haunt him, the spooked mare dragging him back into the endless pasture of the loneliness he had tried to escape.

The battles over, the sight of any pretty woman a cruel reminder of the touch he'd never have, Stony stared into a future that burned his eyes. They began to water constantly, and Earl threatened to yank him from the show. That or get the sorry orbs cut out. What good were they in a body tethered to a chair? A weepy fossilized man did Earl no good, so Stony made his choice. Mr. Earl let him pick the color of the glass ones. He chose the gray of his beloved uniform, and on the eve of his seventeenth birthday, Stony had his eyes taken out.

He couldn't feel the emptiness in his eyes anymore than the weight of his legs. He stayed with Miss Emma while the sockets healed. She fed him and changed his dressings, and read to him every afternoon. The words formed a blanket he gathered close to his ears, the warmth of her voice the only real comfort he had known since the early days of his boyhood kingdom, revered by his loyal subjects. What would they make of him now? Worse than the fly he could not swat were the tears still leaking, ducts unaffected by the removal of his eyes.

Still, he welcomed the blindness, enveloping him like a great quilt, shielding him from the women he would not touch, the horses he would not ride, the parents he would not see. It was better without his eyes. Mr. Earl said he'd display them in a jar along with the other preserved attractions: the two-headed pig fetus, a bull penis, and a twelve-pound tumor removed from the stomach of a man who swore he was the first male to become pregnant. Upon hearing that, Stony couldn't help but worry, now that he provided them two exhibits for the price of one, what else they'd cut out.

LISABELLE

She'd run straight through night, slipping into an empty boxcar as the train slowed near the ravine. Luckily, her brother had shown her how to hop trains as a child when the steam engines rolled by. She slept for the first leg of the ride, but when the train stopped and she heard grunts outside, she wished she'd picked another car. She heard the voices of two men driving the hogs up the ramp and she panicked, thinking they would shine their light and spot her. Of course then she'd be spared riding with the hogs, but there'd be no telling where she'd end up, tossed out of a freight car well after dark on a Tuesday evening; so she crouched down, tucking her head between her knees to avoid the bristly hides rubbing against her skin. The grunts turned to squeals as the men outside brought a lash down on the backs of the pigs who tried to turn around on the narrow ramp. Soon, the space was filled with snorting beasts, their bladders letting go, the warm liquid rolling toward her feet.

When the train stopped again, she edged her way along the inside of the car, listening for the sound of the railway men unlatching the door. A pig pressed its weight against her, snorting wildly. Sweat beaded on her forehead, straw plastered to her skin. No voices. Only the sound of agitated swine. Perhaps the train had stopped to load more pigs into another car, or some other cargo traveling south. She swallowed, the dryness in her throat scraping against itself, her nostrils filling with dust and the stench of frightened hogs.

She had no idea where she would go once she got off the train, but she would be farther away from her father, with his angry pink stump of a hand gobbled at the sawmill. He had grown tired of striking her mother, who had taken sick; the smell of her illness infuriated him. Lisabelle and her sister cared for their mother until she died. Two weeks after the burial, his anger turned to advances: grabbing her apron with his good hand, his reeking breath hot in her ear, the pink stump waving in her face. Five years of that sent her reeling into the airless night. Much as she hated to leave her brother and sister behind, she had to go.

Her hand cupped over her mouth, as if she could filter the smell and dust out, Lisabelle waited, the sweat trickling down her ribs. The snout of a particularly large hog rooted between her legs. The sound of human footsteps crossed through the walls.

"Get that ramp in place," a man called. She stepped back as she heard the iron latch lift. Suddenly, the door slid open and the hogs shifted. She worried how to exit without getting caught. She needed no scolding for being foolish enough to ride for hours in a boxcar of swine. She watched the clot of hogs push their way down the ramp as she sidled around the inside wall. When the man monitoring the pigs turned to spit, she leapt, landing with a thud, hands scraping the gravel. Hair loosened, heart pounding, lungs gasping, she scrambled behind the train.

Edging her way along the small building next to the tracks, three silver dollars snug between her breasts, she gazed upward, hoping the rising sun would orient her as its amber light spread across the sky.

"What's a pretty girl like you doing in a freight yard?"

Startled by a man dressed in a suit and Sunday shoes, watch chain dangling from the pocket of his vest, Lisabelle stepped back, fingers working the seam of her skirt. He approached, his hair the color of hickory bark combed back, mustache still dark, eyes unafraid of morning. He looked like a man reaching for a stalk of fresh-cut sugar cane. Then he caught a whiff of her. "Sweet Jesus, missy, you smell like hogs."

She wanted to say, *you would too if you rode with them all night*, but instead she glared, the ache in her back pushing tears to her eyes.

"Where you heading?"

"I don't know."

His eyes traveled the length of her. "Don't you have lovely hair."

Hard to imagine her auburn tresses looked becoming after the night she'd just had.

"What you fixing to do?"

She was fixing to cry but she knew not to tell him. "I'm not rightly sure." She looked for a sign, some indication of where she was. "What brings you here, Mister?"

"Pick up a delivery. Got a two-headed heifer supposed to be coming in from Johnson City. Wanted to get the old girl in the Knoxville show."

She studied him the way her brother inspected plugged nickels. "What you want with a two-headed cow?"

"Got to replace the one that died." He winked. "I'm Earl Beasley Senior, president and founder of Beasleys' Traveling Amusements. I run the best darn fair on the circuit. Travel all over the South bringing folks top-quality entertainment, and if you're looking where to go next, I can solve your problem." He extended his hand and waited for her to take it. As soon as her fingers grazed his, he kissed the backs of her fingers and gazed in her eyes. "I got a job for you, young lady. Make you feel special in a way you never felt before."

She rubbed the back of her hand against her skirt. There was a distant cousin in Kentucky, but she had no way of knowing whether he'd take her in. Her mother's sisters had all passed, and she didn't dare contact her father's remaining brother. "Doing what?"

"You ever hear of burlesque?"

"No, sir."

"You sing?"

"Not really." The songs had vanished when her mother died.

"Dance?"

"No, sir."

"Anybody pretty as you can learn. We're talking artful entertainment. You come with me, and we'll get you cleaned up and smelling like roses in no time."

The smell of the leather seats and their relative comfort eased the muscles in her back long enough to believe God had not utterly forgotten her. She couldn't tell where they were going, only that she was traveling away from her father, her mother's absence, and the cabin containing both. She closed her eyes, the blackness filled with her sister's face, a flash of her brother running toward the train to find her.

By the time the shiny blue Studebaker drew to a halt, she believed every word Earl Beasley told her about a life filled with adventure and satisfaction. Meals, a warm bed, travel, money of her own—he promised it all with a stroke of his mustache at the wheel of his fancy automobile. At the fairgrounds, he showed her to a trailer that looked to her like a pioneer wagon, but inside, it was set up with a bed, a bureau, and a small desk. "Guest quarters," he told her, and then led her to the chow tent.

The dancing girls were the most popular feature of the show. Every night, farmers and occasional tradesmen would pack the tent, the stench of their toil and desire rising in appreciation. Behind the stage, a tiresome phonograph played while each woman shimmied across the stage. When all of them were there, they would link arms over shoulders and lift their legs as if they were in some Parisian dance hall. After the line dance, they would perform a few choreographed numbers designed to stir up the crowd, so that by the end of the show, the men would stuff coins in the tops of their G-strings, giving utterance to their lewdest thoughts.

Her first night performing, Lisabelle could scarcely believe what came out of the customers' mouths, with their tobacco-stained teeth and cheeks permanently bulging with pinches of snuff. Even her father had not spoken as crudely as some of them. The words left welts. Did they talk that way to their wives, grunting ugliness into soft-lobed ears, silently cursing the stinginess of their bodies, while envisioning the dancing girls?

The thought of her own movements lingering like the taste of smoked meat caught between their teeth disgusted her. With each gyration, she imagined them grunting against their wives with her body swiveling in their brains. Sickened by possibility of her presence in their fantasies, she sought solace conjuring color, great swirls of lilac and lupine blue. Goldenrod and Joe Pye weed, the green of mayapple leaves. As their eyes traveled across her, prodding her private places, she disappeared into the colors of her girlhood blooming across the mountains and along streams. As a child, she'd learned to go outside to find color, to hear sounds kind to the ear. Inside there was precious little from which to spin richly hued dreams.

By her second night, she realized she had simply traded the familiarity of her father's intrusions for the lasciviousness of unfamiliar men. When the lights dimmed, she could smell sweat and tobacco, whiskey, and a hint of manure clinging to boot heels. As her nose filled, she summoned greens fresh with the scent of pine and fir. With each step, she stared into the lights, the red-black emptiness filling with the blue of summer sky. Earl Beasley had warned her not to catch any man's eye. Obviously, Old Earl had never stood on stage, drenched by the lights that blotted out everything else, except the smells and the words, coated with more than desire, coated with a kind of taking that fell like ash through the air.

Though she hated their hands grazing her thigh, she knew accumulating tips was the only way she could afford to leave in pursuit of a more dignified living. One of the other dancers, a dark-haired beauty named Tracy, told her that if she were lucky, she'd meet the man of her dreams right in the tent. Sheila Marie had found herself the son of a railroad baron. He'd paid the man working the door five dollars to let him stand there all night and admire her. The next Monday, when the show was fixing to leave, Sheila Marie left on the arm of her prince. From that moment on, Tracy confided, she'd started studying the crowd, looking for that fellow with the scrubbed face and collared shirt who would spirit her out of there.

Unlike Tracy, who passed the evenings on the wings of hope, Lisabelle had to resort to other means. Salvation in the form of any man, no matter how good-looking or sweet-smelling, held no appeal. Though she had no idea how to find a better life than the one Earl Beasley delivered, she learned to let the leers and words bounce off, pathetic lumps of longing left to roll across the ground. She had to pay attention to the other girls on stage, but their locations became predictable, and unless someone fouled up, she could depend on her body to carry her through the motions. By staring at the string of lights hung above the stage, she pretended to be gazing into the crowd, while launching herself into her swirls of color. She assumed the other dancers would laugh at her if they knew she escaped into the palette of the mountain, with its flowers and trees, rich hues she carried in her mind's eye. She dared not risk their teasing, so she told no one, but to her it seemed safer to seek refuge in the fire pink that blazed in the woods rather than the eyes or arms of a man in a carnival tent.

Mornings before the show, she ventured through the midway, snagged by the painted banners advertising the oddities. How could the people inside truly resemble their pictures? Did the fat lady really have a snout? She thought of going in, but the ten-on-one didn't open until the afternoon, when she went on. The oddities ate at a different time and their trailers were on the far side of the lot, so Lisabelle had not encountered any of them. One of the other dancing girls, named Emmaline, rolled her eyes when Lisabelle asked if she'd seen them.

"The freaks?" she said, as if the word itself tasted putrid. "Hard to imagine who would pay to see the likes of them." Emmaline squinched her face and adjusted her cleavage. "Pathetic, really."

The attractions or the patrons, Lisabelle wondered.

As her curiosity intesified, Lisabelle roamed the edges of the fairground, hoping to glimpse the oddities around their trailers. She caught sight of the midget, whose arms and legs bowed as she walked. Even if the tiny woman had noticed her, Lisabelle would not have known what to say, or even how to address her. Everybody used either a stage name or a first name, rarely their own, and Earl Beasley Sr. did nothing to encourage the various acts to become acquainted. In fact, he forbade the workers to socialize with the attractions. Rumor had it that a dancer had been compromised early on by an unidentified laborer, who barely escaped intact. According to the story that circulated, Earl Sr. was ready to place the worker's scrotum on display to make up for the revenue lost on the rapidly expanding girl. After that, the workers went outside the fairgrounds to satisfy their carnal needs, and each constituency kept to itself. The Fire Eater and the Strong Man liked to make eyes at the dancers, but they knew not to transgress beyond that.

Beasley and his three sons watched over them, herded the dancers like prize sheep, as if any misplaced attention might sully them. It was a form of protection she wasn't used to, which made her feel freed and confined at the same time, but she accepted her strangely cloistered life and took advantage of the hours during the day when she was not on display. On a trip into town on a day off, she bought a set of colored pencils and a small pad, which she carried with her on her morning walks. Though the fairgrounds rarely offered flora, she drew what color she could find: the reds of the banners, the brown, black, and dapple gray of carousel horses, the gold of the lettering. Her sketches began to evolve from swatches of color to shapes, to dimensioned objects, and before long, she tried to hold the details of people long enough to transfer them to her pad.

One setup day, standing beneath the painted panels lining the midway overhead, she finally realized why the oddities were depicted so strangely. The dwarf lady's sign pictured her eye-level with the seat of a dining room chair, and having seen her from a distance, Lisabelle knew the sign exaggerated her shortness. People paid for Odd, and the Beasleys went all out to please them. Every night she performed, the announcer introduced "the world's most beautiful girls," and she knew that wasn't true either. But how many farmers would line up to see women advertised plain as their wives?

As she walked back up the midway, she wondered about the oddities: what their lives had been before they became performers, or attractions, when they were no doubt the objects of taunts, whispers, and cruel stares. She hurried toward her tent, chill bumps rising on her skin, horrified by the thought of childhoods more isolated and terrifying than her own.

When she first saw the colored man pushing the boy in a rolling chair, she half expected to see his head fall off or arms unbutton or some equally bizarre trick. She couldn't imagine how he entertained the crowd, but she didn't dare ask as the pair passed by, and though she could have sought out the colored man who tended the oddities, if anyone caught her talking to him, they'd assume he was talking to her, and that'd be the end of that colored man. A white worker who approached any of the showgirls was apt to lose his job, but a colored fellow was destined to lose a lot more, so she let her curiosity simmer, wondering who would give up their child to a traveling carnival. Then she thought of Earl Beasley pulling out his wallet, offering her father a handful of bills. How many would it have taken for him to let her go?

A week later, Earl Jr. approached her in the dancing tent an hour before the first show. Said he had a visitor. Then he'd winked and mumbled something about giving the boy a thrill. She looked past Earl to the boy strapped in the rolling chair, not even a hint of whisker on his face, sandy hair cropped short, looking skittish as a startled deer. Earl disappeared, leaving the boy stranded there, lashed to his seat, eyes big as nickels that kept darting away. Embarrassment reddened his ears and flushed his cheeks so much she felt compelled to set him at ease. No doubt it was Earl's idea to bring him in. Probably had to think of some way to keep him from calling for his mother, a boy living on his own with strangers like that. So she mustered her best showgirl's voice, full of pomp, and assured him it was fine to look. It's what she got paid for so there was no sense pretending the idea of it shocked her anymore. What difference would it make if she spoke kindly, even a tiny bit alluringly to a shy, lonely, homesick boy?

Seeing him strapped in a chair, knowing he would never be able to walk or court a girl or even look her way without her or some relative hollering to stay away, saddened her. She couldn't improve his lot or hers, but she could do what Mr. Earl had suggested. She could give him a thrill, a chance he deserved but otherwise would never get.

That was enough to make her happy, something she hadn't felt since she'd arrived. She'd felt relief amidst the loneliness. Less anger, and less fear. But not happiness, not the feeling she got as a girl when her mother made pudding for Christmas and she got to lick the spoon. For that one sweet moment, the world melted into that mouthful of fragrant vanilla, her mother's hand tousling her hair, winking as if the lick were a sacred secret only they shared.

Lisabelle asked his name, wondering if he had secrets that made him happy. If not, maybe she could provide one. He told her he was named for Stonewall Jackson, the greatest Civil War general that ever lived. Thought he was Jackson's ghost. Maybe believing that worked the way her colors did. Freed him from a tethered body the same way blue lupines freed her from the stage. She leaned forward so the boy could reach. She unfastened his straps and guided his hand. He hesitated. She smiled and brought it to the top of her breast, heaving in its scant covering. He touched her the way a baby bird had once fluttered in her hands.

"It's okay," she whispered, her eyes locked into his. His fingers tickled without meaning to, but when he finally smiled, she felt the urge to let him feel more. She undid the top and removed it slowly. "Go on," she urged. He traced her nipple with his finger until it stood erect. When she moved closer and leaned over him so he could take it in his mouth, she surprised herself as much as she seemed to surprise him. She suddenly wondered if she had scared him, waved that nipple the way her father had brandished the stump. But the boy's face softened, and she exhaled the bitter thought that she had frightened him. She let herself feel the gentleness of his touch, the first she'd felt since her mother had become too ill to brush her hair. Eyes shut, all sensation filtered through one nipple, a shiver ran through her—feeling pleasure at the touch of a half-scared, half-amazed, fossilized boy.

She thought of him every now and then, though she never saw him again. She could have wandered up to his trailer, though he had to live with someone else and there'd be no way to explain what she was after. There was just something about him, maybe his innocence, the way he imagined himself the ghost of a general. Much as she wanted someone to talk to, she knew the Beasleys would frown on her visiting him. She could hear Emmaline telling the others, "Lisabelle talks to the junior freak." How could she explain his appeal without revealing too much of herself? Somebody had loved him once, too—at least she hoped so—

somebody who wished him a better life than the one stretching before him now.

As the weeks yawned into months, Lisabelle wished for some sort of companion, someone to talk to or even dream about. The other dancers nattered over fellows they spotted on their forays into town to buy nail polish and stockings. They cracked jokes and chewed gum to get back at the youngest son, Tom, who chided them for any unladylike behavior. Strange how his family paid them to strut and saunter in front of men, but if they laughed too loud on their day off, or chomped like horses, he acted as if they were the ones compromising their character instead of his father's show. She noticed Tom gazing slack-jawed at Tracy, toting that Bible and gawking just the same. She was tempted to ask the other girls whether he'd ever whispered any lustful intentions, but she didn't want them thinking she was interested in him. Better to remain invisible. Even miserable. Better to imagine herself a ghost.

One night deep into summer, she lay on her bed, the sheets clammy, the heat of the nightmare still coursing through her though she could not quite recall what she had just dreamed. She woke with a start, jerking herself awake, heart pounding. In the charcoal wash of the room, she could discern the shapes of the others sleeping. Apparently she had not spoken or uttered a half-swallowed sleep scream, because Emmaline didn't stir. Lisabelle longed for her mother to hold her, though for most of her life, it would have been her sister who would have rolled over and shushed her, or if she were lucky, shaken her lightly, brushing a sweaty tendril of hair away from her face. But in the trailer, or across the fairground, there was no one to hold her. She thought of Stony, arms freed, reaching over to stroke her face, his little boy smile shy as a whippoorwill. No one to comfort him either. A starless sky stretched overhead, its darkness descending. She could crawl into the great field of black and disappear, but the morning always dumped her back, small, visible and afraid. What did the others do to shake themselves free of a bad dream that left no pictures, only the prickle of fear and longing?

If she'd known when she crawled into the boxcar that she'd end up in a field full of people, surrounded by just as much loneliness as before, she might have kept riding past the first stop with an open door. But at the time, the stench propelled her. The taste of her father's mouth and the feel of his stump not yet faded to memory when she crept out of the car, certain the dark morning promised a better fate.

Every Sunday, the colored workers hoisted a row of water barrels with taps up on racks, each with its own muslin curtain drawn around. As Lisabelle approached, the bearded woman, dressed in a large jersey and a pair of men's faded workpants, lowered her head and scratched her jaw, the dark hair twitching as her fingers moved. Lisabelle tightened the sash on her robe and nodded at the bearded lady, whose name she didn't know. She tried to force a smile but she could feel her lips drawing into that thin line crossing from pity into the unimaginable horror of thinking what her own life would be like inside a face as wretched as that. The fat lady was huge, and Stony was paralyzed, but at least they could look in the mirror at their faces and see some semblance of who they were beneath the oddity. But not the poor creature who stepped outside the shower. She could fool no one, least of all herself.

As she showered, Lisabelle could not get the woman's face out of her head. She wondered what her father would have done to a daughter like that. Had her parents sold her to the Beasleys? Did hair cover the rest of her? There was nothing to do but try to catch her next Sunday. It would mean rising early, an inconvenience on her day off. If it hadn't been for the humidity that kept her tossing all night, Lisabelle would have slept till ten. Usually, morning made for the best sleep, the hours furthest from her father's midnight prodding, from the catcalls that still rung in her head.

The next Sunday in Hattiesburg, hoping no one would see her crouched behind the privy near the shower tent, she waited beneath the first wash of slate blue light. As soon as she heard the trickle of water begin, she crept up to the curtain. Heart pounding as she squatted, Lisabelle studied the feet: longer than her own, narrow—the water bouncing, trickling over the nub of little toe, draining into the sodden ground below the line of pallets that formed the floor. She could barely hear her humming a tune she did not recognize, a worn pebble of an old hymn. Magnetized by the woman's feet, she stared at the line of the curtain, as if her gaze could melt it away to reveal the body behind it. Lisabelle imagined the last bead dripping off her breasts. Did she have them? Were they shaped like her own? Did the back of her calves arch in the same way? Did the triangle of hair between her legs cover the same parts? Hearing the shower stop, she scurried to the other side of the privy, then waited for the woman to leave. She counted to sixty and then started over again. At the end of the second minute, Lisabelle peeked around the privy and saw the woman heading down the path. The way the woman looked sideways, checking to see who was around, made Lisabelle uneasy, as if the woman sensed her lurking, curiosity deep as a coal seam and just as dark.

Nagged by the questions that whirled in her head, the uneasiness persisted. She kept seeing the feet, wondering about the life she'd left behind.

Three days later, Lisabelle woke, restless, shaking sleep like a dog scattering water. She slipped on her robe and hurried to the privy. The mugginess still weighted the air. Once inside, she could hear someone walking, humming a hymn. She hurried to finish her business. Soon as she could, she pushed open the door and spotted the figure making its way back up the path. In the first shadow of light, she could barely make out the figure, but she knew. She waited until the broad back of the bearded woman grew small enough to follow without being heard. Lisabelle wanted to see which trailer was hers.

Intent on the outline of shoulders draped in the same jersey she had seen the woman wearing before, Lisabelle didn't notice the stone just large enough to shift her balance, turning her ankle as she caught herself with her right hand. "Ow," she muttered, wiping the dirt off her fingers, a chord of pain knotting her leg. Panic overtook the curiosity that had roused her in the first place. There was no sick policy. Performers were expected to show up no matter what. Earl had told her traveling days were for resting, so best to save the aches for then. She'd seen Emmaline dance all weekend with some kind of stomach rot, running off the stage four times to puke in a pot.

She breathed in against the pain and prayed she could muster the grit to come down on that ankle a thousand times. She knew it would swell, but if she wrapped it tightly, she might get by. She had no choice. She couldn't very well tell Earl she'd been out before dawn trailing the bearded lady.

As she hobbled back, each step sent fire shooting from her toe straight up the bone. Tears collected in the corners of her eyes, rolling off the ledge of eyelid onto her face. Her steps shortened, the pain biting at her heel. Ten paces from her door, she lowered herself onto her hands and knees, robe dragging in the dust, as she crawled, tears hatching, mucus gathering, pitiful as a drenched cat.

Emmaline demanded to know what had happened. The way she spoke hammered the maul of isolation even deeper into Lisabelle's chest. Her ankle throbbed silver as she rested it on her pillow at the far end of her bed.

"I was chasing after the bearded lady because I thought she dropped something on her way back from the privy."

"What were you doing up so early you'd lay eyes on her?"

"I couldn't sleep. I had to go. She didn't see me, but after she passed by, I saw something on the ground." She feared as soon as she said it, Emmaline would demand to see it.

"My heel came down on a stone. Twisted my ankle. I couldn't catch her, but if you could leave a note on her door, she'd know to come down."

"Honey, I won't be delivering no message to the freaks. Gives me the creeps to get near the sideshow."

"Couldn't you just leave it outside her trailer?"

"I'll tell Earl or one of the boys to tell her." Emmaline looked at her ankle, swelling already. "I'll fetch you some ice for it, and a shot of whiskey. That'll kill the pain. Just sip a little throughout the day."

"Don't get me drunk."

"Don't worry. Sip it slow and eat something so it don't mess with your head."

Emmaline returned with ice wrapped in a towel and an inch worth of liquor in a mason jar. Lisabelle didn't ask where she'd found it or what it was; she just pinched her nose and swallowed.

"That's enough," Emmaline chided, tugging at the jar. "Save the rest for later, before you go on. I'm going to go eat. You want anything?"

"No, I think I'll try to sleep."

"Stay put and I'll come back to get you."

"Thanks," she grimaced. As often as her father had hurt her, she'd forgotten the specific throb of a twisted ankle. She shut her eyes and imagined what she would say to the bearded woman if she appeared. *Hey there.* No, that sounded rude. *Hello. My name is Lisabelle. I saw you this morning on the path and after I come up behind you I found a locket and wondered if it was yours.* The lie gave her a way in. Lisabelle sat up, the pain gnawing at her shin bone as she lifted the leg off the pillow. She looked in her dresser drawer for writing paper but found none. Who would she correspond with? But beneath the blouse Earl Sr. had given her, she found a piece of tattered paper that lined the drawer. She tore off a corner the size of her palm and sat back down on the bed. Leg propped up, the paper spread on top of a Bible the youngest Beasley son had left with her, she printed each letter as if she were coaxing seedlings up from the forest floor.

After she wrote what she'd already thought of, she knotted her face, wondering what else to say. She had only an inch to conclude. *Stop by on the way to your show if you can. My trailer has a red door, three up from the split in the path.* As soon as she'd written the words, she realized by the time it got delivered, they'd both be in the midway working. If she scratched it out, the lady might wonder what was underneath, and Lisabelle didn't want to arouse suspicion. Still, it was foolish to tell her to come to the trailer if no one was there. She shut her eyes, the tears pushing at her eyelids as much from the loneliness streaking yellow as from the pain.

She wanted her mother's hand to graze her cheek, brush the hair off of her forehead, tuck her safely in. She could barely find her anymore, buried under too many years. Right after her mother died, she would lie in bed next to her sister, begging Jesus to send her back. She died before Lisabelle had outgrown "Mama," but whenever she uttered the word, the angry stump came screaming.

"She's gone," he'd boom. "You little wretches killed her." They didn't, but by the time Aunt Lou told them it was consumption, the sound of "Mama" burned on her tongue.

She opened her eyes and stared at the ceiling. A mosquito buzzed overhead. Her belly began to grumble. She closed her eyes and tried to conjure a vision of baked sweet potatoes and a wild turkey her father had shot and dressed and she'd cooked just right. The mosquito buzzed by her ear. She swatted, then opened her eyes to see if she'd killed it. She hadn't. It flew out of reach. She shut her eyes again. The pangs kneaded her gut and she decided not to think about food. She looked down at her ankle. Its size alarmed her, bloated like a satisfied tick.

She lay back down and drifted, the pain and hunger a dizzying mix. She did not feel sleep overtake her. Without knowing, she sank into it, her breath stirring the fine ends of her hair.

In the dream, she is back on the train, sweating, the car full of hogs, dirty, grunting, repulsive. The hogs are like the men who hoot, their fingers rooting as they slip a quarter in the slender swatch of cloth that covers her most private region, a region she does not dare to name. From it radiates a thirst for sensation, wilting in the arid heat. A touch she cannot visualize because there is no such image stored. Not even in sleep can she conjure a picture of the long, slow strokes up her thigh, a finger tracing the line of her neck, whispering into the hollow of collarbone, tiny, soft kisses meandering from cheekbone to ear—followed by an explosion that rocks her back and forth, her body rupturing, that long blue note beginning to whine as her muscles tighten. She, like pigs bound for slaughter, has neither images nor words to express longing.

The knock startled her awake.

"Who is it?" she called, unsure in that split second where she was.

"Name's Bettina."

"Come in," she said, still confused. None of the dancers used that name. She'd never heard it before.

She saw the beard before the face, and jerked upward in the bed.

"How'd you get here?"

"Walked."

"No, I mean, how'd you know to come?"

"Ewell told me."

"Who's Ewell?"

"Colored worker. Tends to ... folks like me." The woman glared. "What you want with me?"

"I, I found a locket on the path. I thought it might be yours."

"No, ma'am. Ain't mine. Thanks for asking." She nodded at Lisabelle's foot, still propped up. "What'd you do?"

"Twisted it this morning." It seemed so long ago, the hours distended. "I was coming after you."

"I seen you at the shower the other day."

"My name's Lisabelle."

The woman kept staring. "What d'you want from me?"

"Nothing. Like I said, I thought you might have dropped a locket."

"'Cause if all you wanted was a closer look, just ask."

"No," she bleated. "No, I, no."

"I best be going then." She turned before Lisabelle could think of what to say.

"You don't have to. Stay and talk for a while."

Bettina cocked her head. Lisabelle could see the dark opening of her mouth.

"What you want to talk for?"

"Lonely lying here all day."

"Where them other girls?"

"I don't know."

"Don't you talk to them?" Bettina tilted her head the other way. "Around here, folks seem to keep to their own."

"I don't think I have my own here. How about you?"

"There's others make their living on how they look."

"Like me?"

"I thought you got paid according to how you dance."

"How I look when I dance. It's not the dancing they come for."

"What is it then?"

"They come to see our titties shake and pretend we belong to them. To say nasty things and think we're listening."

"Why'd you come here?"

"Ran away. Big Earl was at the train when I hopped off. He came to fetch a two-headed heifer. That's what he said. Hired me on the spot, even though I didn't look a bit like the cow." She smiled for the first time in days.

"They love them two-headed heifers. Had one when he hired me."

"How long you been here?"

"Two years."

"How old were you when you started here?"

"Sixteen. And you?"

"I'm eighteen and a half. I've only been here five months and I hate it."

"Can't you go home?"

"No."

"What's a girl pretty as you got to run from?"

"Plenty."

The weight of Bettina's glare stiffened the air. "I got a sister pretty as you. Couldn't wait for me to leave. She'd probably like sashaying in front of all those men."

"Well, I don't." She wanted to tell Bettina to pull up a chair but she feared any suggestion of staying would scare her away. "I have a sister, too."

"No mother?"

"She died when I was thirteen."

"Sorry."

"You sing?"

"You ask funny questions."

"My mama sang, that's all."

"Mine, too. Hymns mostly. I don't recall all the words."

"You carry the tunes in your head?"

"Sometimes."

"If I gave you that locket, you think you could hum one?"

"It ain't mine."

"Could you sit, just for a moment?"

"Why?"

"You know that one about the Old Ship of Zion?"

"I gotta go." This time Bettina moved more quickly, her hand on the door before her feet had crossed the floor.

The latch thwacked shut, Bettina on the other side. Lisabelle lifted the jar off the windowsill. A quarter inch of whiskey remained. She brought it to her nose. It smelled enough like him to make her spit. Her saliva floated on the liquid until she hurled the jar at the door.

That night, Emmaline wrapped her ankle and Larry, the fellow who operated the spotlight, offered her his flask. The pain vibrated bright as the orangest jewelweed, the sweat glistening on her skin. The other dancers tried to cover, pushing her to the back of the stage so she could rest a beat while they high-stepped and shimmied before the howling men.

The ache in her ankle eventually dulled, but the one in her head roared. By the final number, eyeliner streaked her cheeks. She thought of Stony, lashed to his chair, wishing for his hand on her face. In the blur of pain, as the men moved forward, their hands groping, coins slipping from their fingers, she imagined Bettina, waiting at the edge of the tent, locket on her neck, a pale blue hymn poised on her lips.

THE CAROUSEL MAN

O rvis Leominster stood outside, the world white around him. The winter sky met the powdery ground cover of snow with only the stark line of blank trees interrupting the satiny, still horizon. He'd been up since five in his trailer, writing cards to his folks back home, the tiny scratches of print like whispers of an easier time. It wasn't until twenty of seven, when the first light breathed across the sky, that he opened the trailer door and stepped out, his boot soles sinking ever so slightly. The snow transported him to his grandmother's table, the scent of cinnamon rising, her fingernail scissors cocked in his right hand, the square of onion skin paper crimped in his left. As she turned out pies, he snipped divots of paper, creating a giant snowflake waiting to be unfolded.

He made more snowflakes at the kitchen table than he saw falling outside all those years in Pine Bluff, Arkansas, which accounted for the memory rising as he stared into the dull white field behind the Beasley homestead. Orvis had been fixing machinery and operating carousels since 1907. He joined Beasleys' Traveling Amusements in 1920, when he was thirty-five. On the morning the world turned white, he turned forty-five.

He had hoped he could make it home for his birthday, which fell six days before Christmas Eve, when his remaining family—two sisters, their husbands and children, his mother, her two brothers—congregated at his grandmother's house. She had died in 1909, but the family still gathered there same as always. His uncles, neither of them married, had moved into the house after she died. Much as he tried to get back there on December eighteenth, he missed the whole month altogether the last four years in a row. It wasn't that the Beasleys didn't give him the time off. The show shut down in the winter. But Orvis made extra money repairing rides in the off-season. He lived with the part of the entourage that wintered in Memphis, their trailers lined up behind the Beasley homestead, but he traveled wherever he could to fix machines. He was saving up his money to build his own carousel. Unlike the hand-painted horses that gracefully trotted around all the ones he'd ever seen, Orvis dreamed of dolphins he'd seen in the encyclopedia. People would some-day straddle great gray dolphins rising out of turquoise waves. He loved the line of their bodies, the way the arc followed the swells, suspending them for an instant in midair. Motion so graceful the image filled him, their movement pragmatic but whimsical, looking for all the world like their travel was play.

He'd never encountered them, having seen open water only once, but he carried the illustration he studied in childhood, when he stumbled across them in the volume marked D. He'd looked up dentistry to gath-er information for a school report on his father's profession, and there he found them, such glorious creatures lifting themselves about the salty foam. Their movement first attracted him. Caught frozen in a book, he freed them, imagining the full range of motion splashing across the page. For as long as he could remember, he noticed how things moved, the minutiae of gestures—the way a leaf separated itself from the tree, or a cricket launched itself across the grass. He watched his own foot-steps and the blur of passing trains. When he saw the great Ferris wheel at the International Exposition in 1904, he noted how it lurched slightly as the wheel entered the sky. At that moment, his preference for carou-sels emerged, their movement as smooth as the graceful dolphins leap-ing midair. That's when he knew, standing in St. Louis, holding a scoop of vanilla ice cream tucked into a flat pastry rolled into a cone, that one day he would build a carousel of dolphins. Since that day, he had drawn it a hundred times and built a miniature prototype that he carried in its own suitcase. He had shown it to no one for fear they would fail to see the grandeur of it in its small scale, but he knew once he built the actual carousel, people would travel—picnics in hampers, overnight on trains—to ride it.

෨

Because he spent winters in Memphis, Orvis had befriended the odd-ities, most of whom had nowhere else to go. The human attractions who traded on skill, not appearance, didn't stick around—they met up with lovers or family, or struck out to explore—which left the visual-ly bizarre oddities for Orvis to socialize with in the off-season. While he extended courtesy to them all, Stony drew him in with his limited movement. Watching him, Orvis revisited the sensation of watching a rosebud, waiting for the split second the petals opened. Even though Stony had some use of his arms, shoulders, neck and head, he had devel-oped an economy of movement from twenty years of sitting still in an effort to convince viewers he had miraculously turned to stone.

Because he spent most of his life stationary, thinking became Stony's preoccupation. He was the only man Orvis knew who pondered as much as he did. Other fellows thought about what to eat or how to spend their money, but Stony didn't laugh when Orvis wondered aloud whether dolphins played as they swam. Like Orvis, Stony traveled in his head. He began compiling riddles, making up his own. Not the kind children asked, more like strips of cured meat the listener would have to chew on to appreciate.

Since Orvis had offered his services as a scribe to the fossilized and blinded man, he missed spending his forty-fifth birthday at home, pass-ing up the offer of a ride with the Ferris wheel operator headed to Little Rock. Stony had decided to put all the riddles in a book, more as a way to distract himself than to provide a service to others, and since no one else offered to help, Orvis did. But the book, which Stony figured would take only a few days to write, sprawled across one week into an-other, the riddles turning into rambling sentences with no proper end. Stony strung them together like the lines of cranberries Orvis's sisters would be draping on the Christmas tree.

"You got to get it all done now? Can any of it wait?" Orvis asked Stony on December sixteenth.

"It could, but I can't. Every day's a bonus with me. Folks in my predicament don't generally last long. But you can go if you want to."

But he could not. Much as Orvis wanted to sit down with his family and exchange stories, have his uncles sing him "Happy Birthday" slightly off pitch, he couldn't leave. The more he ached to go, the more he realized how painful it would be for Stony, who hadn't seen his family in twenty years. On the forty-second page of the riddle collection, written in a lined composition book donated by Miss Emma, the matriarch of the Beasley clan, Orvis had paused as he heard the company truck rattling down the drive, Randy, the ride operator, at the wheel, headed west.

The snow resumed falling about ten minutes after Orvis stepped outside that first morning of his forty-sixth year. No one else moved about. The oddities slept deep into morning and the Beasleys stayed in the house. He shut his eyes and drew in the deepest breath he could, imagining himself inside one of the caves he had explored as a boy, the air cool, damp, the silence lush. He felt the snow catch on his eyelashes, in the stubble of beard raised overnight. The longer he took to inhale, the calmer he became, until it felt safe to open his eyes and gaze out at the white world again. The flakes scurried around him with a force peculiar to something so light. He wondered how a thing so fragile it melted on the tip of his nose could fall so rapidly. No appreciable weight. No real density to speak of. That's when Orvis realized the sheer power of gravity. It wasn't the snowflakes hurling themselves to the ground; it was the earth's surface pulling the tiny particles into itself.

Why else would everything on the ground appear more or less glued to a surface round as a ball even though it stretched out flat before the human eye? That's why Stony had the edge. He wasn't fooled by the straight line of horizon. No matter where Stony got placed, he stayed put, his body tugged more fiercely than most by a force reluctant to let him leave. Orvis could jump, even haul himself upward, but Stony clung to the earth's surface, the most faithful man to the force of gravity there ever was. What could be more fitting than Stony riding his carousel, rising on the back of a dolphin, laughing at gravity with each leap?

Orvis watched as his boot tops whitened, the sky lightening at the widest point of dawn. Seven fifteen, his watch read. His mother would be frying ham, cracking eggs into a skillet sizzling with just enough grease to ensure a speedy release. He could almost smell his mother's coffee, flavored with chicory, the cream to go with it thick as the snow accumulated on his shoulders. He loved breakfast at home most of all. His sisters made the best biscuits, lighter than anyone's since his grandmother passed, and the preserves they made—blackberry, peach, strawberry—melted as easily as snow on his tongue. The thought of returning for one breakfast so delectably sweet, now relinquished to help Stony, raised a lump of bitterness in his throat—almost enough to curse his godforsaken undertaking, but then he thought of Stony asking him why cats sleep in the sun.

"Because it's warm there," Orvis had answered.

"And dogs, why do bird dogs like to swim?"

"It's bred into them to retrieve."

"And why do urchins like the sea?"

That one puzzled Orvis. Stony had never been to the ocean, so Orvis asked, "How do you know they like it?"

"It takes 'em places. It's why they don't need legs."

How could he begrudge a man who thought like that, in strange, fragmented strands?

He had first befriended him a couple of years after Stony surrendered his eyes. There was something about the sight of a man, two gray glass eyes motionless as the rest of him, humming in his wheelchair at the edge of the midway.

"Eye trouble?" Orvis inquired that first day he spotted Stony sunning himself.

"Not anymore," he replied, slicker than a pool of oil.

"Why'd you do it?"

"Got tiresome. You ever been stared at for a living but never really seen?" Stony asked.

"No. I operate machines."

"Well, then, no point asking what you can't know."

That's when Orvis realized Stony talked in riddles, rarely expressing anything outright, like an intricate machine with all imported parts. The kind of rig he had to watch and listen to for a long time before he ever picked up a tool.

Orvis took to stopping by Stony's trailer when he had time. He brought him beef jerky and peppermint sticks from his trips into town. He began reading to him from the small stack of books on the floor next to his bed. Three Civil War histories, a biography of Stonewall Jackson, and a book of childhood poems. No photographs, no momentos. Not even an old baseball glove. No scars on his face from a fight, no travel souvenirs collecting dust on a shelf. No letters from women who missed him tucked in a drawer. The man carried everything inside, surrounded by people who paid to stare at his outsides. No wonder he'd let them take out his eyes.

He scooped a handful of snow by his feet and held it to his right cheek, the cold nipping the tender patch of skin above the line of his beard. Orvis drew in his breath as if he could breathe in the icy crystals and exhale them in some other form.

As a boy he had watched the sky, waiting for the appearance of stars, for the precise moment of darkness when the faraway dots emerged. It was those moments, indistinguishable in themselves, that fascinated him. He thought of the exact second when a bud burst forth, a leaf unfurled, the instant the moisture in a cloud let go. How was it, he wondered, that such moments went unnoticed most of the time? Did a thousand snowflakes fall simultaneously from a bank of clouds? Or was the departure staggered? It was not the moment of volcanic eruption or a tornado touching down, but the quiet moments, easy to miss, that called him.

He had taken up fishing as a boy to gain patience. To stand or sit for hours waiting for that flicker of tension on a line taught him to watch the darkness spread in the evening sky. Unlike the boys his age at school drawn to speed, Orvis relished the span of moments so protracted the wait became delicious.

The cold settling in his toes, he knew what to buy himself as a birthday present. A tankful of fish.

"You got to change your water every seven days. Just take a little off the top with a suction tube and replace it. Say twenty percent."

Orvis nodded at the store clerk, transaction completed. He carried the tank to the truck and tucked it under the dashboard on the passenger side. All the way back to the Beasley homestead, he kept one eye trained on the goldfish circling in a large lidded glass jar on the front seat. Did they know any better? Did they ever get dissatisfied? Were they always content to swim in circles inside by glass walls? He thought of the trout he had caught so often, and striped bass. He had wondered about them too. Did they ever see their own colors reflected back in water? He thought of them as go-getters, swimming here or there to find food, dodge predators, catch warm currents, but looking at such small fish, the questions bubbled up. Did they ever frolic like dolphins? Did they swim to stay active? Out of instinct? To satisfy some infinitesimal fish-sized soul? Removed from a natural environment, would their sense of purpose fade? With no risk of being eaten and meals provided, what would drive their days? Would they feel like Stony, purposeless but for being stared at? Would they, too, willingly relinquish their eyes?

Behind the main house, Orvis pumped water from the well into his tank. Too cold for goldfish. He went back to his trailer, put on a clean white shirt and his Sunday shoes, and knocked on the back door of the house. One of the colored workers, Martha, opened the door.

"What you want, Orvis?" She looked at the tank.

"I need to warm some water." He met the glare of her stare. "Just a little bit."

She stepped back so he could pass by. "What for?"

"For my fish. I got me some this morning."

"You fixing to boil 'em?"

"No, they're to look at. Not to eat."

"Why you want fish to look at? Go take a gander at Flipper Boy."

"You know's well as I do he doesn't resemble a fish." He looked at the enamel soup pot hanging from a wrought-iron rack. "I believe that size would do."

"You aim to use Miss Emma's good pot?"

"Just let me heat some water to add before..."

"You get my hide in trouble?"

He moved the tank to the counter nearest the stove. "How come you work in the off-season anyway? Don't you and Ernie ever rest?"

"We're saving our money. 'Nother year or two we might have enough to start us our own place. Not have to travel anymore." She pointed to the rear burner on the stove. "Set the pot there. How hot you want it?"

"Barely tepid. Just this side of warm."

"Ain't never heard of watching fish. You want some coffee?"

"If it won't trouble you."

She poured a cup from the percolator and offered him the open cookie tin. "Go on, take you a couple. Made 'em myself."

He lifted the disks, taking notice of the surface terrain. The splits on top looked like dry rivers met by ginger banks. His grandmother had favored gingerbread to ginger cookies shaped liked men, but she had indulged Orvis, decorating such cookies with white icing once or twice a year. Much as she baked, he figured she wanted to keep certain things special, like those cookies and her pumpkin chiffon pie, which appeared only at Thanksgiving.

"What you studying those cookies for? Ain't nothing in 'em to suspect." Her tone grated him.

"Just looking at how they bake. The miracle of heat, the way it turns dough into cookies, ore into steel."

"Cold water into warm. I think it's ready."

Cookies in hand, he dipped a finger into the pot. "Sure is. Thank you, Martha." He set the cookies down so he could pour the water in the tank.

"Can I ask you something, Orvis?"

"Sure," he replied, still pouring.

"What kind of upbringing you have?"

He turned just enough to glimpse her. "What made you ask that?"

"Strike me as peculiar, that's all. The way you study a cookie and how it's baked. Heating water for them fish. Staying here through the winter. Seem strange for a man runs a carousel."

He stirred the water in the tank with his right hand. "Raised by my granny mostly. My mother and father worked."

"What kind a work they do?"

"My father was the town dentist. Mother helped him."

"Your daddy a dentist! What you doing fixing machines?"

"No interest in teeth. Except to have them." He looked at her, skin the color of a cinnamon stick. "I best be going. I appreciate your help."

"Don't forget your cookies." She nodded toward the counter where they lay.

She must have caught the way he glanced down at the tank in his hands because she reached over and tucked the cookies in his jacket pocket. He wanted to invite her to come see his fish, but something about inviting her into his trailer seemed awkward. Maybe if her husband, Ernie, came, too.

"You and Ernie want to see the fish sometime, you're welcome." He smiled and nodded, the weight of the full tank nudging him on.

When he watched the fish, his eyes would tire from the rapid movement, but he liked the way staring emptied his head. He would set a spot in the tank he thought the fish would swim to next and then lay bets against himself in another direction. He found when he sat with his fish, all kinds of questions surfaced, so he started writing them down. He had three pages' worth, lettered in his tiny script, full of musings about water and motion, about light and whether fish had eyelids, and if not, did they ever get a break from having to see. That led him back to Stony's riddles, which were more like puzzles with a missing piece. Or one too many.

What do you call a horse with three legs? Dinner. What do you call a man with three legs? Star attraction. What's the difference? One's devoured, the other consumed. Horse makes you burp, man makes you blink. Put the two together, it'll make you think.

Orvis wondered what pleasure Stony found in delivering the riddle, dry as unbuttered toast, when he couldn't even see the face of the person guessing. The thought of Stony, sockets filled with glass, and those wide-eyed fish, set Orvis on edge. When he placed his face close to the tank, they didn't return the gaze, the way Stony had never let his focus clamp on anyone when he could see. What flashed through goldfish brains as Orvis peered at them?

He could ask Stony. No one else would understand the question.

The next morning, he found Stony in his trailer listening to the radio. Miss Emma had persuaded Earl to get him one. Poor fellow had nothing else to do all winter. Earl made Stony give him a year's wages, which didn't bother Stony since he had nothing else to spend his money on. He loved listening. Made the rest of the year worthwhile.

Orvis didn't bother to knock. "Can fish close their eyes?"

"That a riddle or a greeting? If you are aiming to talk, Orvis, turn the radio down."

Orvis obliged. "I've been watching my new goldfish but I never see their eyes close."

"Maybe they ain't got eyelids."

"What do you think is worse? Being blind or having to always see?"

"You already know my answer."

"But you could shut them at night, when you slept."

"Fat lot of good it did me then."

"You don't ever miss seeing pretty women, a full moon rising, the way carousel horses move up and down?"

"Last horse I rode ended me up in a chair for life. Only pretty woman I saw close up, I wasn't but twelve. I don't need eyes. I got the radio."

Suddenly the air felt bitter. Grateful to be invisible, he imagined the glare Stony would have given him. "Hey, you ever hear of that performer Prince Randian? Colored fellow, looks like a caterpillar?"

"Don't believe I have."

"He's married. Might even have children. Nothing but a head and a trunk."

"Did you say Prince?"

"Yeah."

"Damn, all those years I thought I was foolish for thinking I could be king."

"King of what?"

"Slitherers, folks just like him who had to wriggle like snakes, or crawl on their belly. I used to pretend folks like that looked up to me." He turned his head away, cocked it like a question mark. "I don't know why I told you that. Something I imagined as boy. Used to picture how they'd crown me king and send around a horse-drawn carriage for me."

Stony's vision hung in the air like a cloud of winter breath. Orvis waited for it to vanish before he spoke.

"Beasleys don't go in much for royalty. Not like some of the other shows I've seen."

"They turn 'em into something religious. Made the giant into some kind of saint."

Orvis gnawed at his thumbnail. "I think you would've made a great king." He wished Stony could have joined another act. Barnum and Bailey might have elevated him, except they had wonders far more unusual than Stony. Still, they might have come up with something better than being a fossilized man. If Stony had been billed as a prince, or even a general, for the last twenty years, instead of a stone, would he have kept his eyes?

"You miss anything, Stony? Anything at all?"

"I miss red. Straight up red, not leaning toward orange or bent toward purple."

"You miss red more than your family?"

"Not a question of more or less. Red's still out there. Something I could have. Red in a paintbox. Red on a platter. A new red flannel shirt."

"A cardinal or the crest of a pileated woodpecker."

"The stripes on the flag."

"Lipstick." The word loose before Orvis could catch it, dangling there. "It sure is a glorious color."

"Kissed one of 'em's titties once."

"Whose?"

"One of the dancing girls. She had red lips and coppery red hair."

"Really?"

"Her name was Lisabelle. I don't reckon she's still working for Beasleys. Is she?"

"I wouldn't know their names. You know they got that policy. Workers aren't allowed in the tent." He studied Stony, the whiskers rising on his gaunt cheeks. Small, straight nose. Sandy hair falling across his forehead. "How'd you manage that?"

"Mr. Earl himself. Wheeled me in there. Told her to show me a good time. I don't know why she did it. Pity, I reckon. Let me see her bubs and then gave me a taste."

"Shoot, you're a lucky man."

"I was twelve. I told you. More scared than staring down a cottonmouth. I didn't know what to do or how to touch something like that. Hell, I'd never seen one dead-on before."

"You seen any since?"

Stony shook his head.

"You feel anything down there?"

"Empty. Easier without the eyes. But I'll tell you something. If red had a sound, it'd be that long, loud whistle you hear from the train."

"Something about the color red always announcing itself."

January first, Orvis made a new sketch of his dolphin carousel. As he drew, Celeste Grimsby came to mind. How she smiled at him as he helped her onto a painted horse in 1908. The only day he saw her, she returned to the carousel three separate times. She told him she loved to read—everything from English ladies to H. G. Wells. She gave him her address and said he could send postcards from all the towns he traveled to; and for five years, they corresponded. She was the only person besides Stony who would have understood his questions, including the one that rode heavy on his chest all these years: what would life have been like had he settled down with her?

Had he courted her, he never would have asked her hand in marriage. Her physician father would have disapproved. An itinerant ride operator, even the son of a dentist, was no match for his daughter. He could have returned to college, but formulas and Latin names did not intrigue him. Peering into mouths, or wounds, diagnosing illnesses held no fascination. The laws of motion did. The opening of a flower, the darting of a fish. What spun a web of wonder could not be woven into a profession suitable for Celeste Grimsby's father or his own. After the first summer Orvis landed a job at the fairgrounds, his father pleaded with him to return to school to become an engineer. Why not learn to build bridges or steam engines? Anything would be grander than operating a carousel.

Maybe, but not much would surpass building it. Fitting the gears. Finding the right music. Making it travel at just the right speed. Adjusting the mechanisms so that the dolphins would rise and descend smooth as the water rolling off their shiny backs.

He studied the goldfish, tails flicking as they circled the tank. Back and forth. Such a limited range of motion, like Stony. Like his own heart. Much as he had fancied Celeste Grimsby, he couldn't stretch enough to turn into someone else.

On the sheet of paper before him, a charcoal dolphin leapt into the air.

He got up from the small desk and pulled out the suitcase he kept tucked under his bed. The latches open, he lifted the top half and pulled off the cotton batting and the velvet covering. A smile broke across his face as he set the tiny carousel on the desk to admire.

Orvis tucked the notebook under his mattress. Wiped his hands on his rumpled shirt, then held the carousel as if he were lifting a newborn infant into its first light. Gingerly, he set the carousel in its case, tucking it in, smoothing the velvet, securing the latch.

The snow had melted and the ground tightened beneath his feet.

Because it was early, he knocked on the door of Stony's trailer, but there was no sound. He knocked harder and then pushed the door open far enough to stick in his head.

"Stony, are you awake?"

"Am now."

"Happy New Year."

"That why you come over so early? Be the first one to wish me that?"

"Truth is, I got something to show you."

"All right. Well, come in."

Orvis stepped inside and found Stony adrift in his sea of pillows.

"You sure you're awake?"

"Getting there, but coffee and a biscuit would help."

"I could see if there's any biscuits in the kitchen. Martha may be in there."

"Well, go wish her a Happy New Year and rustle us up something to eat."

Orvis looked around the trailer for the best place to set the suitcase out of harm's way. He set it on the floor across from Stony's bed.

"What you got there?"

"A surprise. A riddle you can feel with your hands."

Orvis pulled the door behind him and headed up the path to the kitchen, where he found Miss Emma and Brother Stan.

"Morning, Orvis," Stan greeted him, stirring the cream into his coffee cup.

"Happy New Year, Stan. You, too, Miss Emma. Hope I'm not disturbing you. Stony asked for some coffee and a bite to eat."

"Well, we don't want the fossil going hungry. For something supposed to be petrified, that man sure likes to eat." Stan withdrew the spoon and set it on the table.

Orvis stifled the impulse to reply. Stony had told him how his mother had rationed his food after the accident, worried he'd grow too heavy to lift. Miss Emma filled two cups with coffee and set them on a tray.

"You fellows take it black?"

"A little sugar would do me just fine."

"Help yourself to cream, too. Don't let Stan get in your way. It came from the cow, not him."

"Lord, sister, you catering breakfast now? I thought Martha fed them."

"I gave her the morning off. It's New Year's, Stan. Don't start it being ugly." She handed the tray with the coffee and a plate of biscuits and ham to Orvis. "Tell Stony I'll be over to change him in a little while."

"Yes, ma'am. Thank you, Miss Emma. Nice to see you, Stan."

Orvis set the tray on Stony's table. "Miss Emma said she'd be over in a while."

"Hard to believe that woman's been changing my drawers since 1912. First night I come here, I'd messed myself in the car. About died having to lie there and let her wipe me like that."

"I reckon you're both used to it now."

"She's a damn sight better than Ewell and Cheever. Act like it'll kill 'em to get near a shriveled dick."

Orvis propped two pillows behind Stony's back and set a chair beside his bed. "Give me your hand."

Stony raised his right arm, his fingers closing loosely around the biscuit.

"You want me to hold your coffee?"

"No, pour it in my mug over there." He pointed to a large mug with a handle big enough to accommodate his entire hand.

"So what you got to show me?"

"Something I made. Something I've yet to make."

"Your fortune?"

"You could say that." Orvis poured Stony's coffee into the big mug and then took a sip of his own.

As soon as Stony finished the last bite, Orvis opened the case and removed the packing. "Ready?"

Stony nodded.

Orvis set the case next to Stony and lifted the carousel out. He set it on Stony's lap and then guided Stony's hand to it. He watched as Stony's fingers traced the object, first the base, then the poles attached to the top, across the canopy, and back down to the dolphins. Orvis's eyes followed the fingers as they rubbed each figure.

"Give me a hint."

"Sea creatures. No legs. Smooth. Long snout."

"Some kinda fish?"

"Close. Dolphins. You ever heard of them?"

"Not that I can think of. What color are they?"

"Confederate gray. They're mammals, like whales, but way smaller."

"This the carousel you're going to build?"

"Aiming to."

"You going to strap me on and let me ride?"

"Of course. You and me, we'll be the first ones to ride it, soon as it's built."

Orvis reached over to move it off of Stony's lap, but the weight of Stony's hands holding on to it stopped him.

"You built yourself a mighty fine dream, Orvis."

"You got any dreams left?"

"Maybe your dolphins will ride me to the sea."

"Wouldn't need legs there."

"Don't be a fool. I'd sink. But I could hear it roaring. And you'd tell me what it looks like. Bet there's good colors in the sea."

"Don't you want to finish your book?"

"I better or you'll never get home. I appreciate your help." Stony tried to raise the carousel. "Damn, this thing's heavy."

"Got a miniature motor inside."

"That sure is something, Orvis. Now let me rest for a while, dream about the sea."

Back in his trailer, Orvis scooted the suitcase under the bed. He pulled out his notebook and sat down at his desk. *Save money,* he wrote at the bottom of the page. He let his gaze wander over to the fish. Two circled the tank. One hovered near the side. *Ask Beasleys who they know who might want to get rid of a broken down carousel.*

He looked up from the page at the fish. The hovering one didn't move. *Find a woodcarver,* he wrote, his gaze still fixed on the fish. Slowly it began to float upward, an angel ascending, the tiny gills like a closed accordion, the last sound traveling out.

"Damn," Orvis muttered as he dipped his hand in the water to pull it out. A wave passed through him, not nausea but something close. He held the dead fish while he pulled a clean handkerchief out of his dresser drawer. He wrapped the fish in the cloth and took it outside, but found no place to bury it in the frozen ground, so he walked to the edge of the field where he crouched, unfolding the small creature from its shroud. Orvis hollowed out a well in the snow and set the fish in, covering it over. It was as close to a burial at sea as he could offer.

He trudged back up the field, the cold nipping his ears and nose, the air dry and unforgiving. The aromas of his grandmother's kitchen tickled his memory. He wanted to go home. Stopping at Stony's trailer, he pushed open the door to find Stony sitting in bed.

"Let's finish your book."

"Grab a pencil," Stony ordered.

Orvis barely caught sight of the sun as it lowered in the sky. Stony's riddles spilled across the trailer. Orvis heard his belly rumble, but didn't suggest a break. Miss Emma brought a supper tray over at six: hopping john, cornbread, and a pork chop each. "New Year's Dinner," she said, setting the tray down. Orvis stepped out while she attended to Stony, and watched as the first stars glinted in the evening sky.

They finished the book at eight thirty. Orvis handed it to Stony, who held it, admiring the bulk of it as if the words themselves held palpable weight. Then he pressed the book against his chest as if he were drawing the riddles back in. They sat quietly for a moment elongated into a comfortable silence.

"Here," said Stony, thrusting the book toward Orvis. "Set it on the table if you don't mind."

Orvis placed it carefully, studying Stony as he did.

"Thank you, Orvis."

"My pleasure."

"I never asked, is your handwriting good?"

Orvis chuckled. "Too late to be asking me now."

Outside, the night felt deep as the ocean, the snow underfoot quiet as sand. For a moment, he thought of going back in, dressing Stony and carrying him outside, but there would be no sound of waves breaking, no sound of the shore drinking in the surf. Only the quiet darkness, moonlight on snow.

That night Orvis dreamed of his carousel. He heard the music playing, its beat the rhythm of an open heart, and he knew in his sleep, before Stony died that next afternoon, the dolphins would carry him seaward under a canopy of cardinal red.

THE GEEK

The Geek rolled the toothpick in his mouth, then lifted it, delicate as a feather, and used it to pry out a piece of pork caught between his back teeth. Lucky for him, his teeth were hard as nails and the back ones never rotted. A couple on the side gave him problems every now and then, but his bite was still strong enough to take the head off a chicken in one jerk, the same way Muscle Man snatched the barbell, heaved it, and then hoisted it overhead. First he would bite down, and then with a twisting motion at the moment of the bite, he could tug hard, pull the head off, and spit it out. That's what they paid for, to see him spit it out. Lots of folks who lined up to see him wrung the necks of chickens and butchered their hogs. There was no mystery or challenge to that. What was special was to see a man put that squawking head next to his lips. For a dollar extra, he'd put the head in beak first and bite it off, but it was tougher to tear through that way with the outer neck muscles roofside up in his mouth. There was something about that moving beak that brought his jaws down twice as hard—the sensation of one creature fighting for its life, no matter how measly, triggered an equal response. No doubt that's how he'd managed to slit Joe Riggs's throat all those years ago. Once he had him in that head hold, Joe's legs twitching and his arms still landing punches, it became the simplest thing in the world to pull out a straight razor and slice down through the muscle, across the windpipe, right down to the spine. Nothing to it, really. Once the body feels the fight, it just does what it's supposed to do: fight back.

That natural reaction had landed him in prison for thirty years, but most of that time he just kept wondering what he'd done so wrong. A man had come after his wife, which riled him. Of course he had to admit he would have stolen a look, too, so that alone wasn't enough to kill him. It was stealing his whiskey and lying up there with her like it was his own house. There were just some things a man should never do, no matter how stupid or how rich. All it took was feeling Joe Riggs struggle, and the razor practically slid across his neck of its own accord.

Something that instinctual didn't seem worth punishing for all those years, but then the parole board kept telling him how lucky he was to get out early. They could have left him in there for life. He wanted to tell them he *had* spent his life in there. He'd gone in a day shy of twenty-two and come out thirty years and four months later, looking grisly as a fought-out rooster. He spent six months riding the rails and camping in hobo towns, rustling through other people's garbage like a hog rooting through swill. After all those years of being fed slop, he figured it wasn't too different, except he had to go looking instead of having it pushed through bars on a tray.

When he saw Stan Beasley dressed up in a suit tiptoeing through the puckerbrush growing along the tracks, he thought he'd died and gone to heaven. He couldn't imagine where else he'd see a fellow dressed like that, looking worried he'd slip on something nasty in his fancy wingtips. He could still picture those brown and white shoes. What man in his right mind would wear something like that? Probably the fellow who went after his wife. That alone should have been enough to keep him from trusting a slick-suited gentleman approaching a clump of hobos that day in the weeds, but as soon as Stan Beasley said he'd give a home-cooked chicken dinner, complete with all the potatoes, biscuits, and gravy a man could eat, to the first one who stepped forward and bit off the head of a chicken, he knew in his belly the fellow wasn't all bad. The others looked at each other like he was evil, out to torment hobos and ne'er-do-wells. But he knew the man was looking for something, although he didn't know what. Thirty-one years after the taste of his last home-cooked meal, which had been his wife's own stewed chicken and biscuits, it struck him as a fitting invitation to accept. The moment Stan Beasley opened the door of his car, letting him crawl out of that puckerbrush, Jimmy Williams knew if he hadn't found heaven, he'd surely stumbled out of the gates of hell.

The ride back to the fairgrounds pleased him, but not half as much as the meal cooked by a colored woman named Martha, who hummed as she worked and said, "Yes, Lord," when the roasted chicken came out of the oven golden brown. Normally, he had no use for conversation with the colored—they were like mules, meant to haul and dig and keep things clean—but the dinner pleased him enough to ask her where she learned to cook. He was so grateful to taste food prepared right, after thirty years of fearing he would die with the taste of prison chow lingering in his mouth.

He'd spent the first ten years picking rock behind the prison, three guards with their rifles trained on him the entire time. He and a dozen other fellows swinging a pickax, loading a wagon, hands so blistered the ooze turned green. But then they callused, and his back turned syrup brown. One of the men took to calling him "darkie," but he busted his ankle with the pickax for that.

Much as he loathed the endless hours picking rock, the worst came five years into his bid, cornered by three white men all bigger than him as he stood under the dribble of water overhead, eyes shut, lathering his hair. Hands so large they swallowed his wrists before he could turn around. He gagged against the sudden shove of washcloth jammed in his mouth, while the huge hands tightened around him. He tried pushing against the force, but there was nothing he could do. He lifted a foot to bring it down on his captor's instep but without being able to see, he splashed the draining water instead. The grind of a heel bit into his toes. He felt his own bladder give way as he yelped into the cotton cloth, which swallowed the sound and sucked his mouth dry. Not even spit left to call his own. He was sure he felt blood running warm between his legs. When the man pulled out, he could feel his ass tear. Before they left, just to make sure he didn't get a look at them, they tied a strip of sheet around his eyes and kneed him so hard he stayed buckled on the floor till the water ran out. The guard who found him put in solitary for wasting the water. Too sore to sit, he lay on the cement floor for the first week of his sixty days in the hole—a six-by-nine cell.

❧

He brought the razor across his cheek and under his nose. Stan Beasley insisted he shave so the customers could see the chicken head flying out of his mouth more clearly. He'd never liked shaving. All those years in prison he'd had to, for security reasons they said, and once he got out, he let his whiskers grow whichever way they wanted and however long. It wasn't till he got in front of a mirror in his trailer that he noticed the small black hairs growing like mold on his ears. He left his ears alone, since nobody was paying to see them. It was enough to have to shave every day and shower. Since prison, he preferred a bath, but on the road he'd rarely washed more than a few square inches at a time, using rainwater collected in cans.

Once he joined the Beasley brothers' operation, he had to wash regularly, but he got to live in a tiny trailer by himself, where he rinsed his face and armpits every day. He showered only once a week, at two in the morning, with his eyes open wide. When he first arrived, he strolled around the carnival, inspecting the painted banners strung across the midway, advertising the sideshow acts. All the human attractions had a sign. He studied the banner for Lizard Man, portrayed with a tail and a reptilian head. The fat lady's likeness depicted a porcine snout. Flipper Boy's picture showed a seal-like figure in bright blue water with a ball balanced on his nose. Inside the oddities' tent, he found the creatures more pathetic than those featured on the signs, marred by their deformities—ugly and undesirable, but not truly fascinating or beast-like.

The other human attractions traded on skills or unusual talents, like the contortionist, the strong man, and the snake handler. They considered themselves a different breed from the oddities; that he could tell by the way they socialized only with each other. So when Stan had the idea to make him monstrous, he tried to imagine the sign he would have: wild-eyed, fang-toothed, blood dripping from his mouth. Secretly, he breathed a sigh of relief when Earl Jr., who had pretty much taken over running the show, vetoed the idea. Earl preferred the image of an everyday guy who just happened to bite the head off a chicken, and while that may not have qualified as a talent, it certainly spared him from being cast as a freak.

Mornings, he stood beneath his sign, which showed him with the head of a chicken inserted in his mouth, blood dripping down his white shirt. Grisly as it seemed, no one else did what he could, and in his own mind, that elevated him beyond the man covered with tattoos or the skinny fellow who stuck pins in himself.

After a lifetime of feeling like he was nothing more than a greasy stew stain, the Geek had something to show for himself. He took to smiling at any ladies who ventured over to see him, and he chatted with the boys who tagged along with their fathers. One afternoon, a boy about nine pushed at the rope.

"Hey, mister," the boy called, "bet you can't swallow a frog."

"What you bet?" he called back, looking at the boy's fist wrapped around a little croaker.

"A dime."

"Make it quarter," someone else called and then another fellow shouted, "Half-dollar." Voices popped all over like kernels of corn until some fellow with a big old hat hollered, "A dollar bill to see you swallow that frog whole."

"You got yourself a bet, mister," he called, reaching over the rope to get the frog. He cupped his hands over the boy's fist so the frog wouldn't get away, and the man with the big hat stepped forward. The others opened a pathway for the big spender, but as soon as he was up front, the rest crowded in to see.

"Stand on a box so's we can see you," hollered a fellow way back.

The Geek stepped up onto his platform and held the frog by its hind leg above his mouth.

"Straight down, no chewing, and the dollar's yours," said the man with the bet.

Head upturned, throat open, the Geek dropped the frog in and swallowed fast, knowing it would try its damnedest to leap back out. The first gulp was enough to hold him, and the force of the second pushed him down. Triumphant, he opened his mouth and stuck out his tongue.

"Shoot, he did it," cried the boy, and a couple of the kids started to clap.

The man with the money stepped forward and handed him the bill. "You might want to keep that in the act," he whispered. "Have some child step up like this one. Extra cash for you, a little extra fun for the folks." The man patted him on the shoulder and walked away.

He thought about the man's advice. It wasn't so bad swallowing it, but he'd reserve judgment until the frog came out the other end. Course once Brother Earl caught wind of it, he told him to incorporate it into the show.

There was a limit to how many he'd do. They didn't digest well, so he agreed to swallow one once in each town. That way folks would never know when, which fueled the element of surprise. Within a month of the first frog-swallowing, word spread and the lines to see the Geek were second only to the dancing girls.

Outside of Montgomery, one Saturday when he was fighting off the nastiest cold, the Geek looked out into the crowd and spotted a man he swore had been his neighbor before he went to prison. The fellow had gray hair instead of brown, but the face was the same, with eyebrows that looked like a hoot owl's and a nose to match. Johnny Lang was his name. He thought about whether to holler over to him, but he wasn't sure he wanted to be recognized. Johnny knew he'd gone off to prison. Everybody did. But then there was Johnny lined up to see the show, and what was worse, biting off a chicken head or paying to see some fool do it?

He waited till the man moved closer, up near the front row. "Johnny Lang, is that you?"

The fellow squinched his eyes and the Geek knew. "I'll be damned, it is you."

Johnny Lang tilted his head, like he expected a genie to appear.

"You don't recognize me, do you?"

Lang didn't reply. He just kept studying the Geek. The show was due to start in a couple of minutes, so he leaned forward and told him. "Jimmy Williams. Archer Street."

"Good God, Jim, what are you doing here?"

"You're about to watch."

"Last I heard you were rotting in prison."

"Rotted so much the place started to stink, so they had to let me out." He chuckled for the first time since he could remember. He hadn't seen anyone he'd known in twenty years, since the last time his baby sister came to visit before she died.

The music began. "Got to start now," he said, pulling himself back up and moving toward the crate he stood on to perform. He was relieved it wasn't the day he had to swallow the frog. Somehow biting the head off a chicken seemed a little more dignified than swallowing an animal whole.

"How about we meet up after?" Johnny called.

"Yeah, stick around and we'll talk." He knew he had continuous shows till nine thirty, when the midway shut down, but he didn't want to risk Johnny slipping away.

They'd known each other briefly, before Jimmy got married, from the trolley they rode down Archer Street. Johnny Lang had clerked for the bank. Always worn a clean white shirt and necktie. They'd had a beer together the night before the wedding.

As he lifted the hen, her feathers ruffling, wings flapping, it occurred to him that Johnny might know what had happened to Evelyn. When he got out of prison, he knew not to track her down. Her brother had written him early on to say she'd gotten the marriage annulled and threatened to kill him if he ever spoke a word to her again.

She was the prettiest girl he'd ever seen, with hair the color of rain, so light it made her seem like an angel sent by God. He wasn't much of a believer until he saw her riding the trolley he stepped into on a Friday afternoon in June of 1895, sweaty from a day's work, wishing he smelled better, hair matted to his forehead, stubble on his cheeks. Embarrassed, he lowered his head but the sight of her tugged it up again. "My name's Jimmy Williams," he told her, "and you're the prettiest girl I've ever seen." He remembered how she blushed and dabbed her neck with her hanky. The heat burned through him hotter than the foundry where he worked.

"You'll have to excuse my appearance," he said, wondering where the words were coming from. He wasn't raised in a house of smooth talkers. That's when he knew God must have sent him the words to speak to an angel. And if God had her say something kind back to him, he'd take better care of her than God himself.

"I don't mind the looks of a workingman," she said, with a smile sweeter than his mother's blackberry pie. He begged God for more words and though he could barely hear them coming out of his own mouth, much less remember them later, he knew the Lord had come to his aid, because he would always recall the vision of her waving, the words rising like cream, "See you Saturday, then." He had done it. He had asked her out. They courted for thirty-one days. He counted, and then he asked her to marry him.

They were sitting on a bench near the town square. He'd taken her for a soda and they'd gone for a long walk. The air was warm, and a few stars shone overhead. He was sure they were God winking, telling him to go ahead. He got down on one knee because someone had told him women found it romantic, and he gazed into her eyes, biting down so hard on his lip it almost bled. She said it was fine by her, but he'd have to ask her father. The thought of that made the soda ride halfway back up his throat, but he figured God wouldn't let him down now.

Evelyn Mary Sommersworth's father stayed drunk more than he stayed sober, so he asked Jimmy Williams to meet him alone for a drink, man to man. Jimmy came on a Friday evening, and the father took him in a back room of a small apartment where Evelyn, her mother, younger brother, and father lived. He followed the older man's lead, sitting when he did, sipping after he had, wiping his mouth with the back of his hand like the father had. He studied the man, his eyes darting like frightened birds, leg jiggling even after he'd swallowed two shots. After a while, the man grew animated, telling him stories of his own youth and his escapades with Evelyn's mother. He never inquired into Jimmy's line of work or family background. Instead, he asked him about baseball and the best beer he'd ever had. The drunker her father got, the more he swatted Jimmy's shoulder and laughed like someone who'd been doing it so long he'd forgotten why. By the end of the evening, Jimmy had to prop him back up in his chair and wipe the snot running from his nose. No sooner did he step out of the room than the man slid down in his chair, so he went back and arranged him so it looked as though he had decided to take a nap instead of melting into the floor, passed out.

Jimmy never got her father's approval, but when he stopped by the next day, Evelyn's mother hugged him and whispered into his ear how thankful she was that he'd be taking Evelyn out of her father's house. Evelyn's mother worked as a nurse and if it weren't for her husband's rummy ways, they could have afforded a nicer place. The father once had a promising future, but he drank it away, changing directions more times than the wind. At the wedding, the man stumbled up the aisle, babbling so much the preacher cut the service short.

They moved into a tiny flat off of Fuller Street, in the back of a building owned by a widow and her invalid brother. In exchange for rent, Evelyn looked after the old man and Jimmy did repairs. He kept his job at the foundry and for a few sweet months he smiled at work, swapping stories, and bragging about the ruby blossoms on his wife's chest. He gloated at his good fortune, because it was the first he'd ever had. He told how she'd have his supper waiting when he walked through the door and how she never resisted his advances, until one day, one of the men at work wagged his finger in Jimmy's face and warned him not to boast.

"You brag so much about what you got, you best be careful or you'll lose it."

Jimmy cocked his arm, ready to swing, but a pal put his hand on Jimmy's shoulder.

"Jealous bastard," Jimmy spat, pleased by the fire in the other man's eyes. But those words came back to haunt him when he found traces of another man's presence in the apartment. He noticed his whiskey gone and told himself his father-in-law must have stopped by. He kept silent until he found the hair of another man's chest in his bed. His knew the dark curls on the sheet were not his own. He called Evelyn in, pointing at the evidence.

"Don't I love you good enough?" he bellowed. Then he threw her on the bed.

She told him a friend of the family had come to call. He'd forced her, she insisted. The warning he'd heard at work sizzled in his brain. He had to decide to either take her word or believe a cruel God had tricked him and sent a demon girl instead. Faced with that choice, Jimmy Williams did what any reasonable man would do. He hunted down her attacker and slit his throat. He figured any man would understand the instinct to protect his wife. It never occurred to him that slicing open the neck of a planter's son would lead to trouble, much less the loss of the wife whose honor he'd sought to uphold.

By the time he was sentenced, Evelyn was nowhere to be found. She had taken the train north to her sister's the week before. He told himself, lying on his bunk in jail, that the pain of seeing him shackled at the trial would have been more than she could bear. It wasn't until a year of sleeping in a damp, spider-infested prison cell, smelling the stink of other men, eating food that soured his stomach, breaking rocks ten hours a day, that he allowed himself to realize the Devil must have sent her after all.

The months without a letter turned to years, and then he knew she had tricked him, offering kindness like those tiny triangular sandwiches she'd set on a plate. Just when he'd learned to lift one daintily as the doily it sat upon, she poisoned him with betrayal, disappearing so as not to watch him choke. The rocks he smashed became her, the pain splintering in his head until he swore the throbbing would never go away. The chaplain promised it would pass if he asked God for forgiveness.

"No," he spat at the wrinkled man clutching the Bible, pointing at a verse, "God ought to ask me. Sent her down here and then let the Devil take her away." The chaplain buzzed on, until Jimmy raised his hand to swat him. "Go," he hollered, already stung, "get the hell out, old man, and take your lying God with you."

"Blasphemer," the chaplain muttered on his way out.

⚭

"I ain't seen her in thirty years. She never came back from her sister's." Johnny Lang drew a sip from a bottle of bootleg beer.

The Geek studied him, the way the veins on his hand rose like swollen rivers and ran toward the fourth finger encircled in gold.

"You married long?"

"Fourteen years, this time. Lost the first wife to yellow fever. This one's given me two daughters and a son."

"What brings you here, without 'em?"

"I've always loved the fairs, so I sneak a visit in whenever I can. Last place I figured I'd run into you."

Johnny showed him a picture. Pretty little daughters and a handsome son.

Bitterness collected like acid on Jimmy's tongue.

"I ain't got nobody." He tightened his hand around the bottle and lifted it to his mouth, draining the contents before he set it down.

"Didn't turn out as it seemed, did it?" Johnny asked, but the Geek knew he didn't want an answer so he let the question drop like peanut shells.

"It's getting late, Jim. I best be going. Glad I caught up with you." Johnny Lang stood, cupping his hand on Jimmy's arm. "Good to see you, buddy," he said, tightening his grip and then letting go.

After Lang left, the Geek knocked on the door of Tattoo Man's trailer and traded him three cigarettes for a half-inch of whiskey poured out of a flask. In his own trailer, he thought back to his conversation with Evelyn's father. Who the Christ wouldn't have wanted to get away from him? Pretty as she was, he couldn't have been the first to ask her. That's what puzzled him. Why did she even look at him, much less speak? It had to have been God. She wouldn't have wasted two words on a fellow like him, smelling of sweat, skin shadowed with grime. But God had consorted with Satan. What else could make a woman betray a man like that?

And what became of her? Had she found some rich fellow up north?

Maybe she lived alone, never having recovered from the loss of him. He belched right through the taste of liquor, until he burped up the truth. Sure as he was lying alone in that trailer, she was lying next to a man in a big brass bed.

The next day, head banging, guts churning, he stopped by the Snake Man's exhibit and snatched a baby snake. Stan was furious. As soon as word spread, the lines to see the Geek swelled clear past the rides. "Now you done it," Stan said, shaking his finger. "Who's going to be happy watching you bite the head off a chicken anymore?"

"I don't give a shit what makes 'em happy," he hissed.

"Well, I do, and I'm the one that pays you. Who the hell else you think would hire the likes of you?"

"I got two hands and a strong back."

"I reckon a bum comes awful cheap."

He narrowed his eyes, giving Stan Beasley the meanest look he could.

Stan just ran his index finger up and down his neck, scratching. "Who the hell knows what you'll do next?"

"That's where the thrill comes from, don't it?" He grinned wide.

"Just make sure you give them what they pay for."

"Yes, sir," he said, sending a glob of spit perilously close to Stan Beasley's shoe.

The problem with snakes was their amazing jaw. The could open their mouth almost wide enough to eat him. Once that jaw opened it could fill his throat and choke him, so he had to knock it out first. That was simple enough, but not too dramatic, so he devised a build-up where he pulled a snake from a pot and held it at the base of its head while he yanked its tail. The snake's mouth flew open and he inserted its tail. The trick was to get the tail in there so fast the snake had already begun to bite. When it caught its own tail on its fangs, it was madder than hell. That distracted the crowd so he could snap its neck, immobilizing it before he bit and spit.

Martha refused to cook snakes so he had to keep biting the heads off of chickens if he wanted a special meal. She roasted chicken every Sunday for the human attractions, but he got his own all to himself. He liked to bring it back to his trailer and eat it there, as if he'd come home to dinner.

Even with the sharp rise in popularity of his act, he knew the other attractions still looked down on him, thinking they'd developed natural abilities twisting like a pretzel or lifting weights. He was just a man desperate enough to swallow frogs and bite the heads off chickens and snakes. They reminded him of men in prison who'd acted hoity-toity because they'd pulled off some elaborately planned heist, ignoring the fact they'd ended up in the same place as him. He recognized the look of pity, edged with contempt.

It wasn't until after Johnny Lang came that Lizard Man sidled up to him, still wet from the shower, and asked what had possessed him to bite the head off a snake. At first, he considered ignoring the question. Why bother talking to a scale-covered man whose only claim to fame was his unsightly complexion? But as he looked at him, wrapped in his robe, water dripping from his hair down the parched riverbed of his face, the Geek realized as pathetic as Lizard Man was, he'd been spared—never tricked into thinking he'd been given something sweet, only to have it ripped away. Spared waking up in a stinking, cold cell 11,079 mornings in a row, without so much as a word from the one he'd done it for. Born a joke, but not made into one.

Seeing Johnny Lang had brought it all back, how excited he'd been the night before the wedding, how she used to peer out the window watching for him to come home. The day he found Joe Riggs was the last time he saw her.

He looked for her in the courtroom, but she never appeared. He asked his lawyer, even the sheriff, to find her. "Boy," said the sheriff, "she ain't got time for the likes of you."

"Well, tell her to send me a letter," he told the lawyer, who nodded, but then he always lied. At first, he figured she was too upset. That's why he sat in the basement of the county courthouse, locked in chains, pen held so tight it dented the tips of his fingers, ink seeping out, blotting the page. The lawyer stood over him, watching so he wouldn't steal the pen, or take the nib. Sweat beaded on his forehead and rose on his palms as he pressed out the letters, some short, some tall. "I TRied to SAve you. PLeAse AnSWeR Me. Love JIM." He folded the paper in thirds so the lawyer wouldn't read it. As soon as he twisted the cap back on the pen the lawyer unscrewed it, inspecting it before he slid it back inside his jacket. "I'll get it to her," he said, taking the letter, crushing the folds in his hand.

"To answer your question, snakes ain't half as nasty as some folks I met."

Lizard Man squinted against the midday sun. "I can't help thinking they belong to the Devil."

"All the more reason to bite off their head."

Lizard Man shrugged, then started to move up the path.

"Remember being a boy?" the Geek asked.

"What about it?"

"Stealing an apple from a cart? Running so fast you thought your neck would snap? Dreaming of touching some girl's hair?" As he looked toward the midway, he could see the lines forming for the afternoon show. He pulled a toothpick from his pocket and slipped it in his mouth.

"Back when I was stealing apples, I didn't want to be no geek."

As he walked to the exhibition tent, he gingerly pried a fleck of skin lodged between his teeth.

THE MIDWAY TABERNACLE
OF THE HOLY METAPHOR

H ad Earl Beasley Jr. encountered Greta in 1922 as he traveled the hollers and dusty roads in search of acts, he could not have imagined a figure so beguiling ever associating with the misfits and oddities he collected to put on display. Not that he would have been inclined, much less able, to board a steamer and cross the Atlantic, find his way to Berlin, and gain entrance into the home of Ernst and Esther Gottleib, whose beautiful only child would have appeared the epitome of perfection. Willowy, with hair the color of afternoon sunlight falling across a bare root black gum, opal eyes cast downward to perfectly manicured hands resting in her lap. At age twelve, she might have been persuaded by her parents to recite a poem by Hayim Bialik, possibly Rilke, both of whom would have been lost on Earl Beasley, who would not have recognized the poetry of Edna St. Vincent Millay or T. S. Eliot either. Though Earl thought he cut a suave figure in his charcoal serge suit and Florsheim shoes, literature, fine art, and what he called that *godawful hi-falutin' every bit as bad as Tommy's come to Jesus* music held no interest. "I'm a businessman," he was fond of saying, "with an eye for oddities worth paying to see."

Had the Gottleibs met Earl Beasley at any point in life, they surely would have seen him to the door or excused themselves from his company. He had the unsophistication of an uneducated man who confused money with refinement and misconstrued profiting off the misfortune of others as benevolence. Nothing like Ernst, whose life of letters made him erudite beyond the inherent curiosity that fueled a career in journalism. First a writer, then an editor, he relished every aspect of working for a large daily paper. Esther had known him to slip out in the wee hours or wait to come home until after the type had been set and the great rolls of newsprint breathed out the day's events and commentary. Ernst read widely and thought deeply, a man of cognition, not emotion, who sought to improve the world by revealing truths as long as they did not cut close to home.

Appearances mattered to Ernst Gottleib, who, true to his surname taken by his grandfather, considered himself a lover of God. He sought a practical piety that compelled *tikkun olam*, repair of the world, in the ways that aligned with one's natural talents. Unlike his brothers who became rabbis, he expressed his love of God through writing and reading the great works of others who crafted words as carefully as Elohim had wrought Creation. When he married Esther Sorensohn, he delighted in her beauty, elegant as the spray of white roses she carried out of the synagogue in London, where they'd met when he had first traveled there on assignment to cover the Olympics in 1908. She, the daughter of a solicitor and a suffragette, read as voraciously as Ernst and privately penned sonnets she never showed him despite his love of words.

Though Esther preferred London to Berlin, a job offer for Ernst, writing for a large daily paper, compelled her to leave. Once she gave birth to Greta in 1910, settling into the routine of motherhood and entertaining Ernst's literary associates, Berlin flowered for Esther, scenting her life with gardenia and Reisling. Raising Greta only added to the magnificence of the garden.

Greta grew to be a lovely child: well-mannered, poised, often eager to please. As she stood beside the family piano singing, her voice, the morning sun an hour after sunrise, drenched the day in light. Quick in school and perpetually curious, she gobbled the words her father printed, perhaps her only indelicate act. The poetry she imbibed, the art songs she sang, the revelations she heard from a source beyond the cantor or rabbi amalgamated into a core she came to rely on as the world came to play upon her its discordant chords.

At fourteen the first awareness comes. The girl two grades above her with long dark chocolate tresses only Greta recognizes are not black but the deepest of browns smiles at her as if passing a note Greta continually unfolds. Over the course of the school term, the language of visual exchanges expands; notes of mutual desire uttered without words. The moments spent with Elizabeth, innocuous enough: a girlish hug held too long, fingertips grazing an arm—the stroke of a cheek moving a wisp of hair—cast rays bright enough to illumine even the grayest of Berlin skies; yet the clouds gather, an impending storm in Greta's chest.

Ernst and Esther notice the quietude that befalls her. Initially they attribute her uncharacteristic taciturnity to adolescence, a time of such interiority that the inner murmurings fill a young person's head. Esther probes with occasional questions about school, and Ernst lures her with invitations to read antiphonally his treasured poems, but the drought continues in concert with the ever-darkening sky.

"Why," Elizabeth asks, "do your words shrivel in the presence of such joy?"

"No matter how fragrant the blossom, it grows in dung," Greta responds.

As a Jew, Greta knows of the sixth day of the Hebrew month of Sivan as Shavuos—the festival of weeks, a harvest celebration and the commemoration of God giving the Torah to His People assembled at Mount Sinai, a day she does not realize coincides with the Christian celebration of Pentecost, the descent of the Holy Spirit upon the apostles in Jerusalem as they celebrated Shavuos. Nor does she know about Trinity Sunday in the Lutheran church Elizabeth's family attends. What she learns on the warm June day Elizabeth invites her to come to church, promising there will be no repercussions for her tawny-haired Jewish friend, is that there in that unfamiliar sanctuary, God finds her nonetheless.

Between the Apostle Paul's exhortation in the epistle reading not to lust after evil things and the bass singing, *When I look into my conscience and see my accounts so full of defects… How can I escape from You, righteous God!*, Greta

205

hears an admonition so deafening she falls mute. God sees her misplaced yearning, unmoved by her prayers laced with shame.

As the lines of Bach's cantata unfurl, *And if your conscience convicts you, while you stand here mute, then look at the Guarantor who cancels all debts!... the blood of the Lamb, o great love! Has canceled your debt and reconciled you with God,* Greta, convinced the blood of the Lamb doesn't reach her, vows never to touch Elizabeth again. They must rely only on notes penned or glances passed, nothing more.

For Esther and Ernst, the silence becomes interminable, then terrifying. The experience of parenting a seemingly perfect child affords no preparation for a daughter suddenly mute. Greta refuses to speak to the rabbi or the handsome young psychoanalyst their physician recommends. In school she nods, forces the slenderest of smiles at her teachers as she hands in work, but no reprimand jars the words loose.

If the adults in her life fray the edges of their worry, Elizabeth bears hers as a yoke. Though their caresses had been nothing more than fingertips grazing the softness of an inner arm and would have raised no suspicion, Greta's resolve to forsake all physical contact does not weaken. Disconsolate, Elizabeth sings into the silence until finally Greta joins her, shame comingled with relief, tears welling as her voice surfaces only in song.

At home, Greta's parents rejoice at the first melodic sounds accompanying the piano. "Oh, darling," Esther gushes, yet the instant the music stops, the words vanish. Though she stitches a melody to the question, *My lovely daughter, why won't you speak?* inviting Greta to sing back a reply, Greta simply leaves the room. Much as she wishes to comfort her mother, to lay a palm on her arm, she fears the imprint of desire on her fingertips will befoul Esther's skin.

As her sixteenth birthday approaches, Ernst, bereft that the cable of connection wrought from words has collapsed in front of him, cries out to his God, *restore my daughter!* He implores his brothers to pray, certain their piety will evoke an efficacy far beyond his—and yet Greta remains mute, their lively exchanges and poetic recitations a blight of memory, a boil rising on his skin.

Realizing that their daughter will not gain entrance to university if she does not speak, nor will she marry, Esther and Ernst encourage her to sing. Greta, not given to burlesque, allows Elizabeth to introduce her to the music director at her church, who sees before him a budding Marlene Dietrich he can mold.

It is there at the great stone cathedral that the American heiress Constance Hunnewell settles into a middle pew to hear the young woman stirring music aficionados across Berlin. She delays her departure a fortnight so she can return to the church the next week. The second performance, even more glorious than the first, compels Constance Hunnewell to wait at the exit and invite Greta to return to Boston with her.

Daunted by nothing, Constance follows Greta home. Seated on the sofa in Ernst's extensive library, Constance recognizes the coup: her beautiful songbird is a Jew. Now her offer extends far beyond luxurious accommodation and the opportunity to sing for Boston Brahmins in well-appointed concert halls; her proposal provides an escape from the din of Nazis growing louder. Weeks before the first annual party conference in Nuremburg, Esther and Ernst consult the esteemed Leo Baeck, president of the Rabbi Association, to ask his guidance. Do they hand their only child over to a woman they have just met?

It is Greta writing feverishly on a notecard, reminding her parents of last summer's invitation to sing at an event of Hitler Youth, that seals her fate. Within three weeks she bids her family and Elizabeth farewell, boarding the SS *Admiral Nahkimov* in late September 1927 as Constance Hunnewell clutches her hand.

The grandeur of the foyer—the marble floors turning her footsteps into crisp percussion, the gilded mirror reflecting back exhaustion lit to perfection, and the enormous vase of rhododendrons stippled with roses, the petals white satin—elicits a sound. Constance turns to Greta.

"Darling, are you about to speak?"

Greta turns, her face glassine. The smile she offers, a whisper. But no words. By now, Greta finds the silence liberating. The chatter around her no longer magnifies her silence; it merely enrobes it. Great swaths of conversation fall about her shoulders, sometimes grazing her neck, occasionally resting in the hollow of her collarbone. There, the resonance of another's speech echoes a thought, a sensation welling within. In those instances, she slows herself enough to feel the vibration of sound permeating her throat, her vocal chords claiming external utterances as their own.

Though it was the yearning for Elizabeth's touch that swallowed the words, that made even thoughts dangerous, Greta receives Constance's hand alighting on her forearm, even her cheek, without alarm. Whether it is distance or resignation, Greta accepts her touch in lieu of words, knowing there must be some currency of communication exchanged. Here there are no zealous youth thrusting arms in the air to punctuate *Heil Hitler*, no menacing glares, no hushed conversations between her parents or rabbinical uncles fearing the worst.

Soon enough financial prognostications will reach a fever pitch, but for now the sound of Constance playing the flawless ivory and ebony keys of the Steinway in the grand living room with its brocade drapes and divan fill Greta's ears. Evenings she sings while Hollis Hunnewell pores over papers in his study, bemused by the girl his wife has brought home, alluring in her reticence. In time he will find her as enchanting as his wife—seeking to bed them both. But for now, he remains content to listen: to the music, to the singing, to the murmur of his wife's delight.

As the months pass, the snow sighing on city streets, Greta and Constance visit concert halls and even grander living rooms, arranging performances throughout the Northeast. Not content to consign her protégé to a classical repertoire, Constance introduces Greta to the music of Gershwin and Copeland, Ellington and Armstrong, Milhaud and Weill. Immersing herself in this new world of jazz, the scat Greta sings, so delicious in her mouth, sates any atavistic longing to vocalize— the senseless syllables a choreography of feeling actual words could never express.

Upstairs, in her room, decorated with floral hues to complement the hand-carved four-post mahogany bed, Greta succumbs to Constance's charm, closing her eyes and then opening them to watch the impeccably manicured hand stroking her leg, fingertips circling her taut midriff, and finally the ruby lips latching: the absence of words transformed into an onomatopoeia of desire. What she denied herself and Elizabeth, she yields to Constance, so removed from Greta's context, their entwinement bears the quality of a dream, not the ignominy of sin.

Accustomed to a feminine peck on the nape of her neck or the lightest squeeze of her hand, Greta finds ease in the day trips and overnights with Constance. Appreciative audiences sweeten the growing pleasure of singing, and occasional evenings spent in jazz clubs delight her. They travel to the Cotton Club in New York, Friar's Inn in Chicago, and finally to the mecca, New Orleans. The medley of humanity thrills her, the city as improvisational as the music it spawns. So removed from the climate and constraint of Berlin or Boston, she feels herself unbridled, her body an arabesque. Loathe to leave, she implores Constance in her elliptical script to extend their stay. Atop the Pythian Temple Roof Garden, Constance charms members of the black elite while one of the band members slips Greta his calling card. The wink he offers elicits a rare smile. For a moment, Greta imagines a life here, spending evenings at Economy Hall or more intimate venues in Storyville, singing scat and dancing among people as varied as the voices she hears: Creole, Spanish, French, English, even German—with accents languorous and staccato. Drawn to the multiplicity of hues, Greta suddenly cannot imagine returning to the monochromatic existence she left in Berlin and largely experiences in Boston.

By now Ernst and Esther have listened to jazz recordings at Greta's urging, phonograph records assiduously packaged and posted at great expense by Constance, glad to keep the Gottliebs informed of their daughter's flourishing life. Greta has become more than a fixture in the

Hunnewell household: she reigns as the orienting star Constance orbits and Hollis tracks. Their attention exhausts her, singular in direction; Greta begins to feel more like a showgirl than a songbird housed in a gilded cage.

September 1928: a year after she and Constance set sail for Boston, Greta knows she must leave. By now, she travels freely through Boston, though moments alone come rarely, and she seizes the first chance to slip out, ostensibly to return to the dressmaker for a fitting. She collects a few belongings, tucks them into a valise and scurries out the front door. The lack of a note feels impolite, but any expression of gratitude will signal her departure. She does not wish to be followed or found.

At South Station, she purchases a ticket for New Orleans, pressing a neatly printed card with her destination toward the clerk. Pacing as she waits for the train to depart, she hums "Ol' Man River," summoning Paul Robeson's baritone to sweep the heaviness gathered in her chest from the night before, when Hollis entered her bedroom, she in her nightgown, he in his robe, taking her face in his hands. Greta smiled as she shook her head *no*. It wasn't the kiss light on her lips, but his grin as he backs out of the room that determines her departure date.

The train whistle startles, the Pullman porter takes her bag, and before her body registers it, she hurtles south. In New York she changes trains, boarding the Crescent that runs through Washington, Atlanta, and Montgomery before reaching New Orleans the next day.

The engineer on the Crescent will swear later he never saw the cow. In the seven years he's worked the route, no bovines have interfered, though several times they've wandered within view. Shortly after crossing into Alabama, the train collides, the cowcatcher failing to divert the animal off the track. Part of the flank and leg bone jam the truck right as the track curves, derailing the engine and the first car. It will be hours before the track gets cleared and the passengers on the

Crescent resume travel. As the dusk purples the sky, Greta, rattled and restless, steps off the train, valise in hand, striding toward a crossing she somehow anticipates. Jelly Roll Morton's "Someday Sweetheart" in her head, she reaches the road and turns left, just as Sven Anders bears right in the 1925 Ford pickup touting Kimball's Traveling Emporium on both doors.

"Evening, ma'am," he offers out the window. "Can I offer you a ride?"

The blonde Swede looks familiar, a taller version of the sweet-faced Hitler youth she remembers from Berlin, benign in his overalls and dusty work cap, a smile blooming to reveal a slightly chipped tooth.

Greta nods to the lanky gent, who quickly hops out, helps her in, then removes his clean chambray shirt to wrap around her small case before setting it in the bed of the truck. She can't help but notice the broad chest, the muscled arms, the single tattoo on his right deltoid: *Tiny* unfolding in Edwardian script. She has never sat beside a man in his undershirt, nor one so obviously comfortable with himself in such an unassuming way. For a moment, she yearns to speak, to ask who he is, where he is going, and whether he likes jazz—but the words remain tucked inside, caught beneath the lack of longing for his perfect physique, a confirmation so clear it mutes her again.

Sven Anders is no more interested in the elegant creature before him than she is in him. He longs only to see Tiny Laveaux. That once in seven years, Kimball's Traveling Emporium arrives the evening before boil-up day for Beasleys' Traveling Amusements bestows a measure of good fortune the affable sword-swallower cannot fathom. Each show with its own turf and tenor follows a circuit dependent on the same rail lines and fairgrounds, careful not to overlap or saturate the market of weary farmers, curious tradesmen, housewives, and youngsters all eager for entertainment.

Recognizing that the beautifully bedraggled young woman next to him will need lodging for the night, he drives to the only safe place he knows of in Newsome, Alabama, with actual beds and clean sheets: a brothel run by Jean Delacroix out of an eight-room residence that once belonged to a minor tycoon embroiled in scandal and eager to offload his house.

"This here's not strictly for lodging," Anders offers as he pulls up in front of the row of crape myrtle Miss Jean planted to ensure discretion, "but it's the only place fit for a lady, even if it is Saturday night."

Anders doffs his cap as he enters the bordello behind Greta.

"Evening, Miss Jean."

"Why Sven, it's been a while."

"Yes'm, it has. I'm hoping to run into Tiny before Beasleys' hits the rails Monday, so I am not here on business. I found this young lady walking along the tracks and thought maybe…"

"I could use a girl pretty as that?"

"No, ma'am. Miss Greta here," he lowered his voice, "don't talk. This here's her card."

Greta Gottleib, vocalist par excellence

Hunnewell Estate, Four Beacon Hill

Boston, Massachusetts

"Why, honey, you're a long way from home. Do tell, what's a fancy girl like you doing in a place like this?"

Anders eyes the pen and pad on the hall table and hands it to Greta, who writes:

"Going to New Orleans."

"Well, soon as Sally finishes up in room six, we'll get you some fresh sheets and a place to sleep. Breakfast on Sundays is at eight, though some girls don't wander down till ten."

Anders wastes no time in leaving, anxious to get over to the far edge of the fairgrounds to catch Martha, one of the Beasleys' cooks, before she turns in for the night. She's his one chance to get word to Tiny to meet him Sunday at the only restaurant in Newsome, down the road from Grossman's Mercantile and the feed store. Maybe after they meet up and eat, Miss Jean will let them use one of her rooms.

Greta sleeps fitfully, alone with the stark truth her affections consistent-ly displease God. If it had been only Elizabeth—the passing fancy of schoolgirls, or acquiescing to the charms of Constance—but no, in that house full of women so willing to service men far courser than Hollis Hunnewell, she knew nature had forsaken her, setting her irredeem-ably apart. The derailed train a sign that she, like Cain, would be left to wander, her muteness the mark she set upon herself, the songs a feeble attempt not to lose the last remaining filament of connection to God.

Obadiah MacEnroe had been sitting in the fourth car of the Crescent when the train collided with the cow. Initially aggravated by the delay, he soon realized the Lord's mysterious ways. Already a day behind his travel-ing schedule, in order to get to New Orleans for the big revival Tuesday night, Obadiah would have to skip the stop in Newsome, a godforsak-en place filled with carnival freaks so full of the Devil the Almighty had marked them with fins and fur, scales and blubber. A revival preacher with his gifts had no reason to waste even a single Sunday at such a sorry outpost, even if the patrons of the fairgrounds were ripe for salvation.

It hadn't been all that far from Newsome that he'd encountered the first of God's hellish minions, a small boy scaled like a serpent wearing angel wings, prophesying on a street corner in Montgomery just two blocks from where he stood on a soapbox testifying to the powers of the Lord. Obadiah, with his six-foot frame and pearly skin, clearly a physical specimen meant to display God's favor, devoted his life from the age of sixteen to bringing souls to Jesus. Why anyone flocked to that unholy child with his wretched skin, worse than any leper Jesus might heal, befuddled him. Blaspheming the Lord by spouting Bible verses he clearly knew nothing about, offering assurances to broad-faced womenfolk beset with grief or misgivings only a real preacher could tame. That's when Obadiah understood freaks as nothing but evil—and now he could see that God in His infinite mercy sacrificed that cow in the grate of a fast-moving train to spare him a stop where the taint of Satan would surely throw his revival off-track.

Little matter that the local fellows charged with setting up the tent and sign had no idea the preacher would skip town. Let the oddities congregate without him, left to face the deformities God levied to forever match their sin-sick souls.

Word spreads faster than lice about a tented temple less than a mile beyond the fairgrounds. Half-sheet fliers appear announcing a 10 a.m. service on that boiling day. The Geek hands Lizard Man the fractured paper creased and oiled by many hands. Pops a peppermint into his mouth. Lizard crumples the flier, tossing the ball back. "Why don't you eat this crap while you're at it? Nothing so desperate as people peddling lies to people more desperate than they are. *Tchewh.*"

"Seen enough of that, have you?"

Lizard repeats the sound. If he had the mighty tail pictured over the midway he would flick it—the horsefly of memory landing hard: the angel-winged little boy on the edge of Main Street doling out dollops of hope to stout women tucked into corsets bending over to receive God's message from the smooth lips of an otherwise puckered, fake emissary of the Lord.

"If there's any kinda God at all why the hell would He make a man to be so lonely?"

The Geek knows the answer, though he says nothing.

It is the lonely who in their turning toward God stave off God's loneliness.

It appears a mirage at first, the clay dust rising in a holy wind around the open-sided tent, folding chairs arranged in a circle as if the ark of the covenant hides in the center. Anders peers down the alley across the previously empty lot, where the tent stands twenty feet beyond a painted wooden sign that reads "Midway Tabernacle," where someone has written beneath "of the Holy Metaphor."

"What the hell is that, Tiny?"

She cranes her neck up at the six-foot Swede.

"A tent, Anders. It's just a sideless tent."

"No, babe. The hand-wrote part."

Tiny loves him for his looks but more for the way he lifts her, half his height, so she can gaze into his glacial blue eyes, nose to nose.

"A metaphor is a fancy word for a fancy word that means something you can't know straight on, so you compare it to something solid. Love is a full moon rising orange in an indigo sky."

"How the hell you learn to talk like that, Tiny?"

"Same way you learned to swallow swords. Practice. I read. What else would I do? What else could I reach besides a stack of books next to my pallet on the floor?"

"I would have built you a set of teeny shelves."

"That's why I love you, darlin'."

He slips her onto his shoulders, holding her ankles steady so she can admire the sign.

"What makes a metaphor holy?"

"Nobody but Moses got a glimpse of God and that was only the backside. Christians never really see Jesus except for in their illustrated Bibles and made-up pictures. I hear tell the Hindus got elephant gods—so if everyone's got their version of what God looks like, sounds like, acts like, they got to find a way to make it all plain, so I reckon a holy metaphor is just a way to fingerpaint God."

In Miss Jean's house, at a treacly scented table, women cast as Jezebels bellow full-throated laughs, mouths agape, heads tipped back as if gulping delight. How, Greta longs to know, can they summon pleasure at breakfast when by noon their licentiousness will defile them in the eyes of their Maker?

Perhaps they are not religious or worship some other god. Could the blood of the Lamb cancel *their* debt? Could there be enough blood to cleanse them daily, reconciling them no matter how often they sully themselves?

She has never seen women so free, able to leave a house defined by the passage of men, who choose instead to remain in an edifice devoid of books or art, an ode to carnality without pretense or regret.

Unsettled, she steps out in her blue satin shoes dyed to match her dress, one of two she packed to catch the eye of a bandleader in Economy Hall. The canopy of the tent at the end of the road draws her—reminiscent of the tabernacle her forebears assembled in millennia ago. The notes of a Bach aria fill her until she must give them voice. Eyes closed, sound magnified by the lack of visual distraction, each word forms a prayer of contrition, a yearning to return to Elohim's embrace.

The Geek notices her immediately at the back of the tabernacle, her dress an oceanic hue he glimpsed on a picture postcard, her legs long, arms slender. She returns no gaze, appearing transfixed, eyelids fluttering, her short bobbed hair the color of red oak split and polished to a sheen.

The sound begins as a purring deep in the throat, becoming silver strewn across a cerulean sky. Syllables indistinguishable in their unfamiliarity penetrate his chest. His inhalation slow, her song filling his lungs, he savors its presence, reluctant to exhale. The notes fill him in a way both reassuring and terrifying, for he has never felt this way before—known.

Though the Geek never cottoned to Lizard—nobody does—he must get him to come. The Geek has never met a more tortured fellow, not even in prison, not even old Sam Kennedy who hovered like a haint on death row. Lizard's own internal cage binds him tighter than Isaac lashed to the rock, and though the Geek has seen Lizard moving among the sheep in the agricultural exhibit, he can tell no ram of God has come to save him.

The Geek bangs Lizard's trailer, insistent.

"Why the hell should I go?"

"Because her voice will split you down the center sure as lightning cleaves a tree."

"Why would I want to be split down the middle? Scorched even?"

The Geek knows better than to tell him her voice might just have the power to break the cage Lizard spends his days and nights thrashing in. "She's prettier than daybreak over a new mown field, and I am telling you, man, how she sings is right as rain."

"I told you the first time we met I got no use for Jesus."

"She don't sing them kind of songs. Ain't nothing about the blood of the Lamb or the burden of the cross."

"I got no use for God's salvation. How all we got to do is forsake our sins and give our cares to Jesus and he'll wipe 'em all away. That's horse-shit and I am living proof. Folks like my mother believe so hard they break a sweat, then swear they got holy water coming out their pores when it ain't nothing but the brine we stew in."

"No wonder you ain't never been laid, Lizard. You ain't got spit in the corner of your mouth; it's bile."

"That's rich coming from a man bites the head off a live chicken."

"Hell, I slit a man's throat. I can be one nasty critter, worse than a pack of raccoons under the porch. I spent thirty years in a cell the size of your display booth, but I ain't blaming Jesus or Big Daddy God or even that poor sot Joseph who didn't get to lay with his girl—had to step aside for the Lord to have her instead."

"Nothing in the Scriptures about God fornicating with Mary."

"Don't that make *you* godly then, Lizard? You and the Lord, no men-tion of fornicating."

"Shut your ugly-ass mouth, Arnold."

"My name ain't Arnold."

"No, but it's the name of another sorry-ass pecker reminds me of you. Now leave me be. I got to get rested today before I go back on display."

"I'm telling you, man, you need to escape this place. Dammit, Liz-ard, get you a few minutes' sweet relief from the sorry confines of that tortured soul you haul around. Just come now. If you don't like it, leave. And if you do, buy me a beer to thank me."

"I'm not promising."

"I ain't asking you for my sake, Lizard. I'm just telling you, you'll be a changed man."

"Arnold, don't start with that crap. If Jesus were going to drop these scales he would have done so a long time ago."

"I don't know that holy book backwards and sideways like you do, but I could swear the only scales he made fall were on some fellow's eyes."

Because he isn't up thirty cents in a Sunday morning card game, Lizard grabs his hat, a felt fedora—gray as a rain-soaked sky, with a black band—smooth against his forehead, and follows the Geek out of the fairgrounds without saying a word.

The space where the flaps don't hang slow his breathing. Geek didn't lie. Doesn't look like a church at all. Just a tent top without the rubes. No acrid smell of anticipation, no titters or chortling. Quiet for a moment: the hush before the wind picks up and dust coats a man's shoes like cornmeal.

His left eye twitches. Deep in his trouser pockets he clenches his fists, bracing for the onslaught of agony: stout women clucking over him on the street corner. The willowy man with the dark brown hat pleading to save his child and returning later to ask if she were with Jesus now.

He turns to go, slinking out the way he slunk in. And then he hears her as she begins to sing again: the first several notes the silk of Jesse's fur against his fingertips, the palms of his hands, the soles of his feet, landing so provocatively he has to close his eyes. The pale yellow of the ewe's wool fills his balled hands. His panting commences as drizzle, progressing to rain. Mouth open, lips dry, he breathes the sound deeper into his body—chest, belly, loins—tightening and releasing in a way so unnerving he checks his fly, thankfully flat and dry. But if it isn't that, what is it causing the shudder that mesmerizes him?

The air changes in the tent. Electrifies. The notes are no longer hers alone—now taken in and given back. This she knows, she feels as she sings, yet she cannot yet open her eyes.

Elohim, Elohim, have you come for me? The words rising, cresting in her body.

From deep within, Jimmy Williams responds.

Tis the old ship of Zion
Tis the old ship of Zion
Tis the old ship of Zion
Get on board, get on board,

Next, Bettina in her rough-hewn alto, lets the verse rising in her ribcage out.

I was standing on the banks of the river
Looking out over life's troubled sea
when I saw the old ship that was sailing,
is that the old ship of Zion I see?

Cheever's voice, richer than the darkest loam, rolls in.

Its hull was bent and battered
from the storms of life I could see.
Waves were rough but that old ship kept sailing.
Is that the old ship of Zion I see?

From a place she feared she had lost, Lisabelle trills the words.

At the stern of the ship was the captain
I could hear as he called out my name
Get on board the old ship of Zion
It will never pass this way again.

Finally, Tiny Laveaux reaches the top of the tabernacle.

As I step on board I'll be leaving
all my sorrows and heartache behind
I'll be safe with Jesus the captain
Sailing out on the old ship of Zion.

Though she had never heard it before, the hymn fills Greta as she has never been filled—not by Bach, nor scat, nor the Hebrew melodies of home. The wave of voices breaks her open.

Elohim, Elohim, you have come.

She turns to face the choir behind her, moving into the middle of the space, beckoning—each one forming the circle except for the man standing alone at the edge of the tent, watching as she approaches, trembling as she takes his hand.

Skin smooth against skin, his palm pressed into hers, body awakened, Julian Henry weeps. Greta places her arm around him, guiding him to the center as the congregation reprises the hymn.

AFTERWORD

The precursor of this collection emerged during graduate school when I wrote a story called "Ida and Oden" about a ten-year-old boy enamored with Miss Beulah Divine, the fat lady in a carnival sideshow. Her plentitude, so unlike his mother's stingy flesh, captivates him—more than the two-headed heifer or body parts preserved in jars. There's something about her he recognizes, more than the pointy-toed black oxfords that resemble his own Sunday school shoes: he perceives a connection expressed in the coin he gives her embossed with each of their full names. When he asks her real name, breaking not just the prohibition of speaking to a performer, but the fourth wall of the performance space, she answers—so taken by the experience of being seen. Not gawked at. Not voyeuristically consumed like freak candy scooped from a jar. For the first time in a long time, perhaps ever, another human being wants to know who she really is. When Oden Fenton Parks presents her the coin, she cherishes it, tucking it safely away as soon as she returns to her trailer that night. It is her only tangible reminder that for an instant she—in her wholeness, not her enormity—was truly seen.

The writing professor who read "Ida and Oden" noted that I "had the beat on freaks," though I recall him showing little interest in the story beyond its verisimilitude. At the time I wrote it, in my mid-twenties, I had experienced my own sense of freakishness sufficient to feel confident in my writing. As I heard a few years later, writers can only give our characters the feelings we've felt. I could do the requisite historical research on people displayed in carnivals and circuses, faithfully reproducing details of appearance and circumstance; but, as with God breathing life into *Adamah*, earthly creatures, I could only animate my characters through the exhalation of my emotions.

Born in an unambiguously female body, I felt unequivocally male. A Reform Jew growing up in what Flannery O'Connor so aptly called "the Christ-haunted South," in proximity to my Conservative Jewish cousins, I felt implacably odd with my love of ham sandwiches, Christmas, and my longing to preach like Martin Luther King. As a child, the injustices of a segregated South riled me, likely instigating what I would identify in adulthood as a call to prophetic ministry.

When I began writing the subsequent stories about characters from the midway, I was interested in exploring the veracity of inner and outer lives: anchoring them in historicity and emotional authenticity. The characters I created sought empathy, not sympathy; they sought to matter, not entertain. The dozen stories I completed by the mid-1990s remained related but not seamlessly linked—and largely ignored after a few submissions to literary magazines proved fruitless. Still, the characters lurked in abeyance, not waiting so much as abiding. They understood what I did not—that we were not done with each other. Nomadic though they were, they stayed the course, planting themselves in my consciousness, occasionally surfacing as I would pull one or another story out, each time grateful for the encounter.

Finally, in 2015, I resurrected the collection, placing the stories into a single document I printed and shared with one person, an epistolary friend I sensed would understand the imaginary world I had created. Her favorable response ignited sufficient faith in the stories that the printed manuscript she returned moved to a bookshelf in my bedroom instead of a box: a visible reminder that my relationship with what I called Beasley World wasn't finished.

I came to realize what I thought I had written—an exploration of Otherness primarily based on appearance—actually articulated a much more explicit yearning for redemption. The characters created a funhouse mirror of sorts, with just enough distortion and distance to reveal a clear reflection of the desire to belong.

Ultimately, as the final story, written in 2019, suggests, all words are metaphors for what the body experiences—and whether the experience hollows us, hallows us, or both, we reach for ways to convey what is happening. The title of this book contains the word *unfolding* for the simple reason our stories continue to unfurl and entwine.

FURTHER ENGAGEMENT

This fictional world offers a rich resource for reflection for book groups, schools, correctional facilities, workplaces, congregations, and community centers. Prompts for further engagement are available electronically at no cost if you request them via my website. If you are interested in working together, I am available for customized on-site artist residencies, theological programs, and empathy education workshops.

You can reach me through my website: www.leafseligman.com

ACKNOWLEDGMENTS

M ost books take a village. This one, a hamlet. Deep appreciation to early readers, Lisa Parsons and Mary Jo Marvin; to the team at Bauhan Publishing: Henry James, Jane Eklund and Sarah Bauhan, for giving life to these words; and Robin Lunn, who first saw the tabernacle and helped raise it.